PENGUIN BOO[illegible]

DESTINATION: SEA[illegible]

Tilde Acuña, author of *Oroboro at Iba Pang Abiso* (*Oroboro and other Notices,* University of the Philippines Press, 2020), teaches at the Department of Filipino and Philippine Literature in the University of the Philippines Diliman. The illustrator of Marlon Hacla's *Melismas* (Oomph Press, 2020), Acuña is a co-editor of *Ulirát: Best Contemporary Stories in Translation from the Philippines* (Gaudy Boy, 2021) and several other upcoming anthologies.

Amado Anthony G. Mendoza III is the author of the novel, *Aklat ng mga Naiwan* (*Book of the Damned*, Balangiga Press, 2018), co-editor and co-translator of Wiji Thukul's *Balada ng Bala* (The Ballad of a Bullet), and translator of the Filipino-language edition of *Eka Kurniawan's* collection of stories to be published by the Ateneo de Naga University Press. He teaches courses on Southeast Asian literature and creative writing at the Department of Filipino and Philippine Literature in the University of the Philippines Diliman. Mendoza is also a co-editor of *Ulirát: Best Contemporary Stories in Translation from the Philippines* (Gaudy Boy, 2021) and several other upcoming anthologies.

Kristine Ong Muslim is the author of nine books of fiction and poetry, including *The Drone Outside* (Eibonvale Press, 2017), *Black Arcadia* (University of the Philippines Press, 2017), *Meditations of a Beast* (Cornerstone Press, 2016), *Butterfly Dream* (Snuggly Books, 2016), *Age of Blight* (Unnamed Press, 2016), and *Lifeboat* (University of Santo Tomas Publishing House, 2015). She co-edited the British Fantasy Award-winning anthology *People of Colo(u)r Destroy Science Fiction!* (2016) and *Ulirát: Best Contemporary Stories in Translation from the Philippines* (Gaudy Boy, 2021). She is also the translator of many bilingual editions, including *Marlon Hacla's Melismas* (Oomph Press, 2020) and *Mesándel Virtusio Arguelles's Twelve Clay Birds: Selected Poems* (University of the Philippines Press, 2021) and *Three Books* (Broken Sleep Books, 2020).

# Contributors

**Duanwad Pimwana** won the S.E.A. Write Award in 2003 for her novel *Bright* (ช่างสำราญ) after making her name on the local literary circuit as a short-story writer. Known for fusing touches of magic realism with social realism, she has penned ten books, including novels and collections of short stories, poetry, and cross-genre writing. Her most recent work is the political novel *Nai Faan Ahn Leua Ja Glau* (ในฝันอันเหลือจะกล่าว). Her novel *Bright* and a collection of her short stories, *Arid Dreams*, both translated by Mui Poopoksakul, were published in the US in 2019. Pimwana often draws inspiration from the fishing and farming communities of her native Chonburi, a seaside province on the Thai east coast, where she now lives with her partner, the poet Prakai Pratchaya.

**Vincent Lapuz** or 'Chen' is an illustrator and has been evolving his brand of zany, surreal comics known as 'Chemical Comics' since high school, making zines. He still draws today, mostly on the side of printer technical jobs, trying to improve with one page and one panel at a time.

**Sokunthary Svay** was born in a refugee camp in Thailand shortly after her parents fled Cambodia after the fall of the Khmer Rouge regime. They were sponsored to come to the United States and resettled in the Bronx where she grew up. A founding member of the Cambodian American Literary Arts Association (CALAA), she has received fellowships from the American Opera Project, Poets House, Willow Books, and CUNY, as well as commissions from Washington National Opera, the Asian American Writers' Workshop, and ISSUE Project Room. In addition to publishing a poetry collection, *Apsara*, in New York (Willow Books, 2017), Svay has had her writing anthologized and performed by actors and singers. Svay's first opera, *Woman of Letters,* set by composer Liliya Ugay, received its world premiere at the Kennedy Center in January

2020 as part of the American Opera Initiative. A recent recipient of the OPERA America IDEA grant, her second opera with Ugay, Chhlong Tonle, will receive its premiere in March 2022.

**Mui Poopoksakul** is a lawyer-turned-translator with a special interest in contemporary Thai literature. In addition to her work with Duanwad Pimwana, she has also translated two story collections and a chapbook by Prabda Yoon. Her translation of Saneh Sangsuk's novel, tentatively titled *The Understory*, is forthcoming in 2023. Mui lives in Berlin, Germany.

**Kathrina Mohd Daud** is a writer and academic based in Brunei Darussalam. Her first novel, *The Fisherman King*, was shortlisted for the Epigram Books Fiction Prize in 2020, and her second novel, *The Witch Doctor's Daughter*, is forthcoming with Epigram in 2022.

**Dominic Sy** teaches Philippine literature and Southeast Asian literature at the University of the Philippines Diliman. His collection of stories, *A Natural History of Empire*, won the Kritika Kultura/ Ateneo de Manila University Press First Book Prize and was a finalist for the Madrigal-Gonzalez Best First Book Award.

**Tunku Halim** is one of Malaysia's best-known writers. A former lawyer and scion of one of the country's royal families, he has been dubbed Asia's Stephen King. By delving into Malay myth, legends and folklore, his writing is regarded as 'World Gothic'. His novels and short stories, although often characterized as popular fiction, is studied and analysed by academia. His short story won the 1998 Fellowship of Australian Writers competition, and his debut novel was nominated for the 1999 International IMPAC Dublin Literary Award. Between 2015 and 2017, he had three consecutive wins in Malaysia's Star-Popular Readers' Choice Awards. His children's fiction and non-fiction include the *Midnight Children* trilogy (2021) and *History of Malaysia—A Children's Encyclopedia* (2013). His adult non-fiction, amongst others, include a biography of his late father titled *A Prince Called 'Charlie'* (2018). He judges writing competitions and gives talks at schools, festivals and universities on various subjects including creative writing and minimalism. He is an advocate of environmental and mobile phone addiction awareness. He enjoys travelling, Yoga, and Tai Chi and currently lives in Penang.

**Rio Johan** was born in Baturaja, South Sumatra, 28 August 1990. His book *Aksara Amananunna* (The Alphabet of Amananuna) was chosen as the Best Prose of 2014 by *Tempo Magazine* and his novel *Ibu Susu* (Mother's Milk) won the Khatulistiwa Literary Prize in 2018 for the First/Second Book Category. His other books are *Buanglah Hajat pada Tempatnya* (Dump Your Business in the Right Place) and *Rekayasa Buah* (Fruit Engineering). He is now based in Paris. He can be contacted on Instagram/Twitter: @riojohan.

**Trần Thị NgH** (real name: Trần Thị Nguyệt Hồng) was born and grew up in the South of Vietnam. Her first collection of short stories, *Những Ngày Rất Thong Thả* (Wandering days), was published in 1975 by Trí Đăng press, Saigon, Vietnam but not distributed due to the fall of Saigon. Since then, she has published three collections of short stories in Vietnamese outside of Vietnam that were later published in Vietnam: *Nhà Có Cửa Khóa Trái* (*Locked In*; Văn Nghệ, California, USA, 1999; Hội Nhà Văn publishing house, Vietnam, 2012); *Lạc Đạn* (*Stray Bullets*; Thời Mới, Toronto, Canada, 2000; Văn Học, Vietnam, 2012); and *Nhăn Rúm* (*Screwedup*; 2012, La Frémillerie, Paris, France; 2012, Hội Nhà Văn, Vietnam). Her novel *Ác Tính* (Malignant) was published 2018 by Nhân Ảnh publishing house, Toronto—Canada, and later by Domino Books & Hội Nhà Văn publishing house in Vietnam, 2019. She lives in Saigon and Paris.

**Paul Christiansen** is the author of the forthcoming *Odes Beneath the Chò Nâu* (Hội Nhà Văn Publishing House & Phuongnam Book), a bilingual collection of essays translated by Tran Thi NgH, and the co-editor of *A Rainy Night in the City* (Hanoi Publishing House), a bilingual anthology of many Vietnamese short stories. A former Fulbright Fellow, he currently resides in Saigon and works as content director for *Saigoneer*, a Vietnam-based arts and culture publication.

**Nguyễn Lâm Thảo Thi** is a writer and translator based in Vietnam.

**Julius Villanueva** is a self-taught cartoonist from the Philippines. He started his comics career as a cartoonist for the *Manila Bulletin*. He has published several comic books for both mainstream and independent publishers. Currently, he is working on an animated adaptation of his comic *Ella Arcangel*.

**Edgar Calabia Samar** is a multi-awarded Filipino poet and novelist from San Pablo City, Philippines. His first novel, *Walong Diwata ng Pagkahulog*, received the 2005 NCCA Writer's Prize and its English translation was longlisted for the 2009 Man Asian Literary Prize. Three of his other novels, including *Sa Kasunod ng 909*, received the National Book Awards. He also received the National Book Award for Best Book of Criticism for his *Halos Isang Buhay: Ang Manananggal sa Pagsusulat ng Nobela*. The books in his YA series Janus Silang also received the Philippine National Children's Book Awards. He has also received prizes for his poetry, essay, and fiction from the Palanca Awards, the PBBY-Salanga Writer's Prize, Gantimpalang Collantes, and others. In 2010, he was invited as writer-in-residence to the International Writing Program of the University of Iowa in the US; and in 2017, as a guest author to the Sharjah International Book Fair in the UAE. He received his PhD from the University of the Philippines in Diliman where he was awarded the Gawad Antonio Abad for Best Dissertation in 2011. He is currently an associate professor at Ateneo de Manila University, and he served as visiting professor at Osaka University from 2017 to 2022. He also had given talks in countries such as the USA, China, Japan, United Arab Emirates, Thailand, and the United Kingdom. He is also the host of the Podcast Network Asia podcast *Mga Teorya ng Pagkahulog*. His Twitter & IG is @ecsamar and his FB page is at fb.com/EdgarCalabiaSamar.

**Francezca Kwe**'s work has been published in journals such as *Asia: Magazine of Asian Literature* (Seoul), *Kritika Kultura*, and literary anthologies such as *Philippine Speculative Fiction*, *Maximum Volume: Best New Philippine Fiction*, and *Hoard of Thunder: Philippine Short*

*Stories in English*, among others. She teaches creative writing at the University of the Philippines.

**Bryan Thao Worra** was born in Laos in 1973. The award-winning author of more than eight books, his work appears in over 100 international journals. He served two terms as the president of the international Science Fiction and Fantasy Poetry Association. He was the first Lao writer to be accepted as a professional member of the Horror Writers Association. He holds over 20 awards for his writing and community leadership including an NEA Fellowship in Literature and was a Cultural Olympian representing Laos during the 2012 London Summer Games. He has presented at the Smithsonian Asian Pacific American Center, the United States Library of Congress, the Minneapolis Institute of Art, the Loft Literary Center, Intermedia Arts, Kearny Street Workshop, and the Institute for Contemporary Art, among others.

# Destination: SEA 2050 A.D.

Edited by

Tilde Acuña
Amado Anthony G. Mendoza III
Kristine Ong Muslim

PENGUIN BOOKS

An imprint of Penguin Random House

PENGUIN BOOKS

USA | Canada | UK | Ireland | Australia
New Zealand | India | South Africa | China | Southeast Asia

Penguin Books is part of the Penguin Random House group of companies
whose addresses can be found at global.penguinrandomhouse.com

Published by Penguin Random House SEA Pte Ltd
9, Changi South Street 3, Level 08-01,
Singapore 486361

First published in Penguin Books by Penguin Random House SEA 2022



10 9 8 7 6 5 4 3 2 1



ISBN 9789815017779

Typeset in Adobe Caslon Pro by MAP Systems, Bangalore, India



www.penguin.sg

# Permissions

# Contents

# Introduction

*Destination: SEA 2050 A.D.* began as a book proposal emailed on July 6 2019, to Nora Abu Bakar, the Penguin Random House Southeast Asia Publisher who suggested expanding the scope of the project to cover Southeast Asia. Initially, we were interested in ecological fictions that imagined the Philippines in the year 2050. *Destination: SEA 2050 A.D.*'s generative concept can be traced in part to the underlying premise and design of the illustrated volume *Sigwa: Climate Fiction Anthology from the Philippines*, a book that saw varying degrees of involvement from us and whose impetus included the Duterte regime's grim legacy of making the Philippines the one country in the world with the highest number of murdered environmental and land defenders[1].

In December 2019, an anthology similar to *Destination: SEA 2050 A.D.* was released. *McSweeney's 58: 2040 A.D.*, a beautifully illustrated climate fiction edition edited by Claire Boyle and Dave Eggers, looks into the sixth extinction through ten short stories that feature the perspectives of writers from Singapore, Australia, Mexico, Turkey, India, Croatia, and Iceland, among others. The book is concerned with the year 2040, a period marked by dire projections that include the annual occurrence of Africa's extreme heat waves if the increase in average global temperature goes beyond 2 degree Celsius[2]; a pandemic of Parkinson's disease[3], which might be further complicated by the COVID-19 pandemic[4]; and a rise in cases of drug-resistant tuberculosis in India, Russia, South Africa, and the Philippines[5]. In the intervening years during the production of *Destination: SEA 2050 A.D.*, the annual reports of the Intergovernmental Panel on Climate Change (IPCC) have grown increasingly more urgent in their recommendations. Numerous climate fiction anthologies—most notably *Multispecies Cities: Solarpunk Urban Futures* as well as the third instalment to *Everything Change: An Anthology of Climate Fiction*—were also released in 2021, each one with an overarching global scope, attentive to the plurality of voices, and voluble in its language of hope and longing for survival.

*Destination: SEA 2050 A.D.* also hopes to speak from that same place of hope and longing for survival as it trains its sights on Southeast Asia, a region that holds around half of the planet's tropical mountain forests, huge carbon stores that are incredibly rich in biodiversity—but possibly not for long. Published in 2021, a study of satellite imagery shows that Southeast Asia was losing 3.22 million hectares of its forests every year from 2001 to 2019, with the region's mountains taking in 31 per cent of that loss[6]. Additionally, the ARC Centre of Excellence in Coral Reef Studies details how global warming has led hot water to flow into Indian Ocean reefs and Southeast Asia's famed Coral Triangle—the seawater zone whose borders are shared by Indonesia, Malaysia, and the Philippines and where the Earth's marine biodiversity is at its peak—and resulted in an extensive bleaching event deemed as the most catastrophic coral death since 1998[7].

In introductions to 'Third World' science fiction (sf) anthologies, editors often remark about Anglophone readers' unexpected emergence of a genre that originated from 'First World' countries. Instead of authoring and producing narrative thought experiments informed by scientific discoveries of the times, 'Latin American and Mediterranean countries are often perceived as being mostly consumers, if not victims, of technology'[8], just like the rest of the 'developing' countries, which once included Russia, 'a backward agricultural empire at the outermost margins of Europe'[9]. Though there are sf anthologies that cover Asia, these only cover the East and the South[10].

Rather than sf, the term 'speculative fiction' has seemingly been more favoured in Southeast Asia, with *LONTAR: The Journal of Southeast Asian Speculative Fiction* as one of the most reputable resources[11]. In the Philippines, preceding entries in volumes of 'speculative fiction' anthologies are winners in the 'future fiction' category of a prominent award-giving body, the Palanca Awards[12].

Southeast Asia has yet to enjoy the institutional advantages of large-scale efforts in propagating genre fiction, whether official (such as the Galaxy Awards of China and the Nihon SF Taishō Award of Japan, both considered as Nebula Awards equivalent in East Asia) or popular (such as fandoms, fanzines, and magazines). Perhaps, there are initiatives that remain undocumented, and this anthology aims to introduce some sort of a 'starter pack' to works that take scientific projections and technological advancements in authoring and envisioning the future through fiction. Outside the region, submerged futures have been speculated upon in the Jonathan Strahan-edited *Drowned Worlds: Tales from the Anthropocene and Beyond* (2016) and the John Joseph Adams-edited *Loosed Upon the World: The Saga Anthology of Climate Fiction* (2015) that touches on, among others, the various horrific implications of human-induced global warming on Earth's life forms.

## Imagine 2050

*Destination: SEA 2050 A.D.* is the first Southeast Asian fiction anthology that imagines—based on available scientific projections—the world of the year 2050. Environmentally ravaged and with various diseases on the rise, this period is said to be marked by the ubiquity of plastics to the point that 99.8 per cent of all seabirds—such as penguins and albatrosses—are expected to have ingested plastics[13]. Also, over 90 per cent of the planet's coral reefs is projected to decline by then[14], and the climate crisis would have driven one out of ten plants and animals to extinction[15].

The future of public health is also set to become increasingly more precarious. Mathematical modelling by researchers in Spain shows how 2050 will see a halt in global population growth[16]. This will translate to a population profile where there are more elderly, who are mostly female, than children in most places on Earth, according to a 2010 report from The Research Council of Norway[17]. Moreover, the World Health Organization forecasts that two-thirds of 2050's global population, composed of people older than 60 years, 'will live in low and middle-income countries'[18]. By 2050, it is also predicted that 106 million people all over the world will be afflicted by Alzheimer's disease, with 62.8 million of those patients in Asia[19]. Dementia will be on the rise, wreaking havoc on the aging global population; the findings of an Alzheimer's Association-funded study released in 2021 show that incidences of dementia are set to triple from the current number of cases to affect more than 152 million people by 2050[20]. Meanwhile, scientists from the Brien Holden Vision Institute, University of New South Wales Australia, and Singapore Eye Research Institute published in 2016 the results of a study demonstrating that an estimated 50 per cent of the global population—or approximately five billion people—will suffer from myopia or short-sightedness by 2050, with up to one billion of those people developing an increased susceptibility to blindness[21].

This book collects stories from or about Southeast Asia vis-à-vis a near-future period whose prospects resemble no less than a hellish path to destruction. The February 2022 report from the United Nations Environment Programme, for instance, exhorts governments to take preventive action in the face of a projected 30 per cent increase in wildfires by the end of 2050, with the risk extending even to unlikely places like the Arctic where wildfires used to be non-existent[22]. With deforestation still ongoing and the seas becoming warmer, which may then create massive storm surges and powerful cyclones, two billion people are poised to become vulnerable to floods by 2050[23]. And, with climate change set to deplete the world's freshwater reserves, water scarcity is imminent; MIT experts predict a 'high risk of severe water stress' in Asia by

2050[24]. Producing nearly 50 percent of the world's greenhouse gas emissions, Asia is also at a higher risk of getting devastated by deadly heat waves by 2050[25].

## The Stories

*Destination: SEA 2050 A.D.* consists of comics and short stories that span multiple genres and styles, a good portion of which are presented in translation. We cycled through at least twenty-five writers and translators, ended up with fifteen in the final line-up. Here, you will find science fiction, fantasy, horror, crime fiction, plus a slew of their subgenres, even a YA take. A baker's dozen of narratives—grounded by a mutual sense of urgency and spirit of international solidarity in the face of large-scale ecological breakdown—form a dazzling tapestry that hints at a disquieting, but still cautiously hopeful, vision of an environmental futurist spread. *Destination: SEA 2050 A.D.* is a travel through time and into the heartland of the global conversation on the final stages of the sixth extinction.

The opening story, Duanwad Pimwana's 'All Trash on the Eastern Side,' is translated from Thai by PEN/Heim Translation Fund Grant awardee Mui Poopoksakul. Duanwad Pimwana is the pseudonym of Pimjai Juklin, one of the most celebrated voices in contemporary Thai literature. In her powerful story, we journey to a bleak future where the fabled Promised Land is the Land without Trash. Tragedies that accompany waste disposal have preoccupied science fiction across time, territories, and literary forms; from earth scum—such as satirical seventies comics from Britain, collected as *Ro-Busters: Disaster Squad of Distinction* (2014) by Pat Mills, Alan Moore, and various artists; and novel from China, *Waste Tide* (2019) by Chen Qiufan, translated by Ken Liu—to space debris such as manga *Planetes* (1999-2004) by Makoto Yukimura and its corresponding anime adaptation; and Korean blockbuster film *Space Sweepers* (2021) directed by Jo Sung-hee. In contrast to the previously mentioned spectacular thought experiments, Duanwad Pimwana's work highlights recurring patterns of the earth as a dumpsite in the background and human dialogue on the foreground, with the Land without Trash reminiscent of the search for the Green Place in the 2015 film *Mad Max: Fury Road.*

'The Last Days of Juan De La Cruz' is a comic by Vincent Corpuz. It elaborates on the challenges of surviving through the wasteland. The pilot issue of the comics introduces brothers Hunter and Nelson as they scout for sustenance in areas outside 'domes' which used to be cities comparable to dome cities in the anime series *Ergo Proxy* (2006) and bio-domes in the film *Alimuom* (2018). There is charm in Corpuz's fun neon colour palette in the original version matched by squiggly lines of uncertainty and the foreboding monstrosities that might hinder safe return home or spark re-discoveries of buried histories. This disparity between form and content renders this snippet into the post-apocalypse as a rainbow-colored cliff-hanger, where neither struggling back to the surface nor letting go and embracing the gaping abyss are guarantees of an easier life. Also worth noting is the serialization of 'The Last Days of Juan De La Cruz' in Penlab, a platform that encourages amateur komiks authors and professionals alike to share their work; hence, filling the earlier mentioned lack of avenues for popular dissemination of genre fiction.

In 'Kep at the End of the World' by Khmer writer and musician Sokunthary Svay, 'an orphan with no origins' returns to the coastal town of Kep in Cambodia and sees how man-made climate change has upended the lives and livelihood of the locals. This darkly beautiful and emotionally resonant story culminates into an unexpected fusion of mythology with the ecological apocalypse. The climate crisis has forced many plant and animal species to evolve, some in freakish ways and not just in terms of behaviour; among those observed to have mutated in response to the rapidly warming planet are owls, snails, fish, red squirrels, and disease-carrying mosquitoes[26]. Humans may not be too far behind in their potential to radically adapt their bodies to changing or extreme environments. After all, among the Bajau, a group of sea-dwelling indigenous people scattered in various places in Southeast Asia, the evolution of larger-than-normal spleens has been widely documented; the Bajau's oversized spleens enable them to hold their breath longer while underwater and to do free diving 'for as long as 13 minutes at depths of around 200 feet'[27].

'After the End', a potent encapsulation of climate grief and a striking reminder of humanity's resilience, is written by Kathrina Mohd Daud—who is a novelist, art critic, translator, and all-around stalwart figure in the contemporary literary landscape of Brunei. One may read Daud's tale of climate refugees fleeing into the rainforest or dealing with an extreme environment like a warming sea with mutated marine animals as a reckoning with preindustrial-era Earth where primeval nature's savagery is still relatively untainted—a restarting from scratch, so to speak, but with lessons from the Anthropocene already taken to heart. The tropical forest in 'After the End' pulses and thrums with life, which is fascinating to read—more so in light of the fact that it was a scientist from Brunei, J.W. Ferry Slik, who led the landmark study on 'global tropical forest classification' that assists in 'anticipating region-specific responses to global environmental change'[28].

Award-winning Filipino author and academic Dominic Sy introduces in 'By the Pitiless Sun' the uncanny into his exploration of the nascent stages of wealth redistribution in general and allocation of residences in particular. What were initially believed to be empty spaces are in fact occupied by organisms that are neither humans nor plants as we know them—more like seedlings that could sprout after eons in the eerie forests of Jeff Vandermeer's Southern Reach trilogy. In the aftermath of a seemingly overt revolutionary victory is a covert evolutionary progression—or regression—of photosynthetic semi-humans engaged in a class struggle that the protagonist Ella can neither totally perceive nor fathom. The story's title is borrowed from 'A gaze blank and pitiless as the sun,' a line from the W. B. Yeats poem, 'The Second Coming'. Christian eschatology and ecological horror both shine through in this delirious romp of a story.

The sunbathing distant relatives of the Swamp Thing in Dominic Sy's 'By the Pitiless Sun' might discover an affinity for the water-dwelling sludge thing in 'Water Flows Deepest', a crisply told tale by Malaysian literary superstar Tunku Halim. The story begins with a countdown to a supermarket's eventual closure and a mother-and-daughter tandem's deferment of the inevitable move to crowded 'flood centres', until the salesclerk mentions the rumour of a breathing shadow-like patch taking the last living creatures in the area. This brings to mind images of animals affected by oil spills. '[Pumping] out twelve times more oil than the Exxon Valdez spill of 1989', the most notorious spill is the infamous BP-operated Deepwater Horizon rig in the Gulf of Mexico, where the 2010 disaster's extent and degree of planetary life-threatening effects remain unknown[29].

The story from Malaysia's skilled craftsman, Tunku Halim, is followed by 'Art Sanctuary in the South China Sea', written by Rio Johan who was introduced to us by Indonesia's first Man Booker International nominee Eka Kurniawan. Rio Johan is considered to be one of Indonesia's most irreverent, witty, and inventive writers in the past decade. His story in this volume meditates on the eventual mechanization of human endeavours as well as the increasing anthropomorphizing of machines. Similar to his past works, most specifically in his 2021 short story collection *Rekayasa Buah* (Fruit Engineer), 'Art Sanctuary in the South China Sea' tasks readers—who are also prospective artists or creators—to rethink the nature, boundaries, and notion of 'ownership' in and of artistic production. The story can be also read as an elegy to what might be lost in a future trained solely on the advancement of a world dominated by efficient and clockwork cybernetic perfection: the representation of human experience in cybernetic art objects. In the story, this comes to a head when Botbatik—an AI robot, or artomaton (portmanteau of art and automaton) designed to create art—began to develop human-like artistic sensibilities. Botbatik's creations then started to militate against the existing human-led cybernetic aesthetic regime. The conflict led to the formation of the artomaton resistance, the exodus to the art sanctuary in the South China Sea, and the release of the Cybersthetic Manifesto. By turns comic and disquieting, 'Art Sanctuary in the South China Sea' forces us to reckon with an artistic future where the lines between the 'human' and the 'machinic' are constantly blurred.

Two translated stories represent Vietnam in this volume, both of them authored by Tran Thi NgH. The short stories, 'Deviate' (translated by Paul A. Christiansen and Thi Nguyen) and 'Left-Eared' (translated by the author and Paul A. Christiansen), are accompanied by the author's paintings that she so graciously allowed us to publish. With the paintings, the two stories read like found curatorial notes doubling as a tribute to David Lodge's campus fiction and Clarice Lispector's rants against the tedium of daily life. And while Johan conjured a bleak future for artistic production, 'Deviate' and 'Left-Eared' urge readers to confront a present world where almost all aspirations toward a life devoted to artistry are thwarted by the perils of having to lead a real life, of—as the narrator of 'Left-Eared' admits with full resignation—deciding 'to stop toying with life and death . . .' While the two stories are decidedly set in the present, they hazard a warning for a future that could possibly be bleaker than what the present has to offer for the protagonists in both stories—a future where the 'colours, smells, and noises' of everyday life won't only trigger nausea or vomiting, but ultimately lead to the end of the world.

Known for the comics strip *Life in Progress*, series *Ella Arcangel* that recently had an animated adaptation[30], and short works such as *Cold Tooth*, *Keith Busilak*, *Destroyer* among others, prolific komiks author Julius Villanueva's characters include humans (with or without powers, with or without attitude problems) from different walks of life, cats, dinosaurs, among others—some of which are accessible in Penlab. In 'Hushed Tones of Earth' included in this volume, he illustrated how even species deemed imaginary and beings from the so-called 'Philippine lower mythology' bear the brunt of man-made (specifically, Elon Musks, Jeff Bezoses, other tech-bros, and fossil fuel corporations that have more human rights than actual humans) climate crisis. As mitigation measure, a Mambabarang protagonist pleaded for salvation and sought the god of the earth's help. The (un)natural setting thanks to built-in excesses of capitalism can be read alongside with and in contrast to 'OK Millennial', Villanueva's short comic in *Manila 2019–2050: City of the Future* (2020), which featured a futuristic but gentrified mega Manila in the preliminary pages and punctuated by a hint of the downtrodden's promise to reclaim the city[31]; both works end with calls to action, the earlier comic more direct and the latter, a more subtle undertone that we, the majority, have to rely on our collective strength since deities cannot help with the forthcoming demise any longer.

From Edgar Calabia Samar, the leading YA writer in the Philippines, comes 'Against Unhappiness', a tender depiction of a flooded future world and a glimpse into the lives of people living out their last days under the thrall of AI-enforced 'happiness' by the megacorporation A-Found. This harrowing vision of the future is seen through the constricted view of Pat, a cog-in-the-machine of A-Found.'s reality-filtering gamified network of blissful unawareness, a near-universal form of social control. 'Against Unhappiness' touches on the evolving conventions of the nuclear family, the corruptible edges of subjective reality, how different cultures negotiate meanings through language, as well as late capitalism's metastasizing influence on indigenous languages. The story is especially interesting as it may be one of those rare instances of fiction in translation where compromises have to be made to arbitrarily create a textual equivalence between the gender-neutral language Filipino and the singular English codes *they*, *their*, and *them*. The first translated draft of this story assigns *she/her* pronouns to differentiate the gender-ambiguous Pat from the other sibling-constructs. Edgar Calabia Samar thinks otherwise and asks for a revised translation that incorporates the nonbinary pronouns of the English language; you can see the transformative impact later when you read the story.

In Francezca Kwe's 'The Path to the Mountains', the trail to emancipation is unwittingly cleared by the oppressive government, as functionary Liway anticipates departure from this godforsaken country and resettlement abroad, together with her son Eman. Almost desensitized by her work at the Ministry of Filipino Resettlement, which is nothing more than denial of most applications and surviving entitled 'princes of pre-apocalypse', her life took an unexpected turn when the supervisor informed her about the 'change of plans'. As the cliche goes, when a window of opportunity closes, a door creaks wide open; and, people from her past opened the possibilities for a better shot at building a future. Climate response and holding corporate culprits accountable, especially in corporate media, has been limited to 'nonviolent' protest actions in the cities and policymaking in air-conditioned halls of power, when the forest is literally the refuge of freedom fighters—the most effective of which are guerrillas[32], who resort to a sustainable lifestyle by necessity and to revolutionary violence as defence not just of themselves, but also of all life.

'The Final Secrets of Dr Wow' is this anthology's closing punch, a stunning knockout of a story from Bryan Thao Worra, one of the leading writers in the Lao diaspora. One of the first Lao stories in the solarpunk vein, 'The Final Secrets of Dr Wow' tells of sounding the death knell to tradition in order to consolidate a new world order. The story is provocative in its risk-taking to confront both emerging and historical challenges that the people of Laos and the world at large are facing in addressing their relationship to the environment, conflict, science, and tradition. Bryan Thao Worra kindly shares with us about this story: 'During the Vietnam War, more tons of bombs were secretly dropped on Laos by the United States than on all of Europe during World War II, and still contaminates over 30 per cent of Laos in addition to the effects of horrific US chemical defoliants used in the region at the same time. Many Lao artists continue to address the ecological repercussions of this conflict more than 50 years since the end of the war. The story's ending is ambiguous but largely trusts the readers to find their own meaning from it and asks them to consider what objects, what ideas would they risk the most to pass on to the next generation.'

## Southeast Asian Fiction in the 21st Century

The final decade of the 20th century in Southeast Asia was marked by unprecedented crises (i.e., Asian Financial Crisis, Dili Massacre in Timor Leste), global integration and uneasy transitions (i.e., Vietnam and Laos joining ASEAN, the final years of Mahatir Mohamad's regime), and political upheavals (i.e., Reformasi in Indonesia and the military junta in Myanmar). Inevitably, the grand narratives (i.e., development, modernity, social equality, and change, etc.) leading to the events that book-ended the previous century became objects of fictional scrutiny for the region's emerging writers. The aforementioned inevitability was also encumbered by the new problems and challenges that beset all the countries in the region. Climate disaster, increasing inequality, the globalized exploitation of labour, loss of identity and cultural heritage, and the consequences of many failed postcolonial/post-war reconstructions of the previous century: all of these continue to strike a dissonant chord in SEA nations' attempt to achieve regional harmony whilst striving to develop distinct national cultures. This complicated choreography between the baggage of the 'old' and the challenge of the 'new' resulted in fictional gems that were both formally introspective and thematically prescient at the same time.

These traits were (and still are) part and parcel of the controversial historical sagas of Eka Kurniawan and Ayu Utami; the Cortazar-esque innovations of Wan Nor Azriq and Y.Z. Chin's gripping meditations on intimacy and alienation; the slick urban tales of Prabda Yoon and the evocative narratives of Veeraporn Nitiprapha; the political thrillers of Viet Thanh Nguyen and Ocean Vuong's epistolary novel; the committed prose of Dadolin Murak; the harrowing fables of Vaddey Ratner; the antipodal spaces of Clarissa Goenawan, Zadie Smith-esque inventions of Sharlene Teo, or the prolific offerings of Colin Cheong; and Allan Derain's intimations of the occult and supernatural, Glenn Diaz's heady and breakneck cosmopolitan thrillers, Sigrid Marianne Gayangos's bold and philosophically rigorous climate fictions, Rogelio Braga's stories that are hyperattentive to the tormented psyche of the Filipino working class as well as the tired, crumbling facade of colonial haunts, and the literary roman à clefs of Caroline Hau.

The same electric energy also charges the recent anthologies and translation efforts of SEA fiction. Departing from the expectations of global literary metropoles to churn out 'national narratives' and the tired anti-communist shibboleths of the Cold War-influenced ASEAN imprints, anthologies and translated works from SEA in the twenty-first century have gestured towards the simultaneous exploration of innovative genre writing and tackling of contemporary themes/issues in the region. For instance, anthologies such as *Singa-pura-pura: Malay Speculative Fiction from Singapore* (2021), *Manila Noir* (2013), or the annual Kompas (Indonesia) and Fixi (Malaysia) anthologies all gesture toward the elevation of the speculative and crime genres while initiating the creation of a 'southern canon'[33]. These imprints and the conversations they elicited are important steps in reclaiming SEA literature for Southeast Asians. In the same manner, the efforts of homegrown translators such as Tiffany Tsao, Quyen Nguyen Hoang, Mui Poopoksakul, and Jeremy Tiang not only introduced to the world—especially to English-language readers—the most relevant and innovative fiction from the region, but also attempts to move the centre of literary translation of SEA fiction beyond imperial metropoles. *Destination: SEA 2050 A.D.*, while setting its sights on the many possible futures of the region, carries with it the ghostly spectres of the past, the precarity of the present, and the disparate impulses which lay claim to the 'lost futures' brought about by late capitalism.

## Conclusion

*Destination: SEA 2050 A.D.* is limited by the absence of writers from Myanmar, Singapore, and Timor Leste. The rest of the region, thankfully, has been covered—spotlighting perspectives grounded in Southeast Asian histories and experiences, including those from Brunei, Cambodia, Indonesia, Laos, Malaysia, Philippines, Thailand, Vietnam, and some of their respective diasporas. Ivor W. Hartmann's statement in his introduction to *AfroSF: Science Fiction by African Writers* (2012) resonates with the intent and attempt of this anthology: 'If you can't see and relay an understandable vision of the future, your future will be co-opted by someone else's vision, one that will not have your best interests at heart.'

Excluded in visions of the future in this volume are grand narratives of territorial 'discoveries' (read: conquests), interplanetary mobility, and technophilia or technophobia; in place of those usual 'spec fic' tropes that are often more focused on the human condition: Duanwad Pimwana's and Vincent Corpuz's characters travail the wastelands to spatio-temporally move forward and backward; non-humans adapt to new environmental constraints in the stories of Sokunthary Svay, Tunku Halim, Dominic Sy, and Julius Villanueva; cultural renaissance entails re-appraisal of art and literature in Trần Thị NgH's and Rio Johan's diegeses; Kathrina Mohd Daud and Francezca Kwe reconsider and reintroduce the heart of the forest as peoples' sanctuaries and sites of resistance; Edgar Calabia Samar's and Bryan Thao Worra's protagonists apparently facilitate the troublesome yet necessary remembrance of cultural heritage and its vital sublation into the new world order.

The 'now' in these stories are not mere opportunities to 'correct' histories and their consequent continuities authored by colonial and imperial plunderers, whose gross extraction of natural resources on a global scale expedited the sixth extinction. We, Southeast Asians writing about our region's future, offer this volume as a modest contribution to the ongoing conversation on the challenges of living in what constantly feels like a protracted series of apocalypses. We also want to offer it as a palliative to the unavoidable canon formation and propensity of dominant literary centres, Western and otherwise, to occasionally be drawn only to certain voices and narratives. Despite its ambitions—or maybe because of them—this anthology is nothing short of a step towards imagining our intertwined futures and mapping our intertwined paths.

Tilde Acuña, Amado Anthony G. Mendoza III,<br>
and Kristine Ong Muslim<br>
April 18–30, 2022<br>
Manila/Maguindanao, Philippines

## Endnotes

1 Chad de Guzman, 'Philippines is the deadliest country for environment activists, report says', *CNN Philippines*, July 30, 2019, https://www.cnnphilippines.com/news/2019/7/30/Philippines-environmental-defenders-killed-2018.html.

2 Simone Russo, Andrea F Marchese, J Sillmann, and Giuseppina Imme, 'When will unusual heat waves become normal in a warming Africa?' *Environmental Research Letters* vol. 11, no. 5, May 12, 2016, https://iopscience.iop.org/article/10.1088/1748-9326/11/5/054016.

3 E. Ray Dorsey, Todd Sherer, Michael S. Okun, and Bastiaan R. Bloem, 'The Emerging Evidence of the Parkinson Pandemic', *Journal of Parkinson's Disease* vol. 8, no. 1, December 18, 2018, https://content.iospress.com/articles/journal-of-parkinsons-disease/jpd181474.

4 Daniella Balduino Victorino, Marcia Guimarães-Marques, Mariana Nejm, Fulvio Alexandre Scorza, and Carla Alessandra Scorza, 'COVID-19 and Parkinson's Disease: Are We Dealing with Short-term Impacts or Something Worse? ' *Journal of Parkinson's Disease* vol. 10, no. 3, July 28, 2020, https://content.iospress.com/articles/journal-of-parkinsons-disease/jpd202073.

5 Aditya Sharma, Andrew Hill, Ekaterina Kurbatova, Martie van der Walt, Charlotte Kvasnovsky, Thelma E Tupasi, Janice C Caoili, Maria Tarcela Gler, Grigory V Volchenkov, Boris Y Kazennyy, Olga V Demikhova, Jaime Bayona, Carmen Contreras, Martin Yagui, Vaira Leimane, Sang Nae Cho, Hee Jin Kim, Kai Kliiman, Somsak Akksilp, Ruwen Jou, Julia Ershova, Tracy Dalton, and Peter Cegielski, 'Estimating the future burden of multidrug-resistant and extensively drug-resistant tuberculosis in India, the Philippines, Russia, and South Africa: a mathematical modelling study', *The Lancet Infectious Diseases* vol.

17, issue 7, May 9, 2017, https://www.thelancet.com/journals/laninf/article/PIIS1473-3099(17)30247-5/fulltext.

6 Yu Feng, Alan D. Ziegler, Paul R. Elsen, Yang Liu, Xinyue He, Dominick V. Spracklen, Joseph Holden, Xin Jiang, Chunmiao Zheng, and Zhenzhong Zeng, 'Upward expansion and acceleration of forest clearance in the mountains of Southeast Asia', *Nature Sustainability* 4, June 28, 2021, https://www.nature.com/articles/s41893-021-00738-y.

7 'Worst coral death strikes at SE Asia', A*RC Centre of Excellence in Coral Reef Studies*, October 19, 2010, https://www.coralcoe.org.au/media-releases/worst-coral-death-strikes-at-se-asia.

8 See 'Introduction: Science Fiction in Latin America and Spain', *Cosmos Latinos: An Anthology of Science Fiction from Latin America and Spain*, translated and edited by Andrea L. Bell and Yolanda Molina-Gavilán (2003).

9 See 'Introduction', *Red Star Tales: A Century of Russian and Soviet Science of Fiction* edited by Yvonne H. Howell.

10 See 'The New Wave of South Asian Science Fiction and Fantasy' by Tarun K. Saint, (https://www.tor.com/2022/03/28/the-new-wave-of-south-asian-science-fiction-and-fantasy) and the anthology he edited, *The Gollancz Book of South Asian Science Fiction* (2019). Recent anthologies of Chinese Science fiction include *Invisible Planets* (2016) and *Broken Stars* (2019), both edited by Ken Liu, and *Sinopticon: A Celebration of Chinese Science Fiction* (2021) edited by Xueting Christine Ni. In addition to sf anime and manga, the series *Speculative Japan* has been featuring genre fiction since 2007.

11 See Victor Fernando R. Ocampo, 'Defying Classification: An Introduction to Southeast Asian Speculative Fiction', *Literary*

*Hub*, April 4, 2022, https://lithub.com/defying-classification-an-introduction-to-southeast-asian-speculative-fiction. Though 'spec fic' has conveniently been employed as a catch-all category to include sf & fantasy, in some anthologies of genre fiction in translation—which can be observed in this list https://www.tor.com/2016/08/09/ten-spec-fic-anthologies-in-translation-from-around-the-world.

12 See Carlos Piocos III's graduate thesis 'The Promise of the Future: Nation and Utopia in Philippine Future Fiction', https://dlc.library.columbia.edu/catalog/ldpd:506202/bytestreams/content/content?download=true.

13 Chris Wilcox, Erik Van Sebille, and Britta Denise Hardesty, 'Threat of plastic pollution to seabirds is global, pervasive, and increasing', *PNAS* vol. 112, issue 38, August 31, 2015, https://www.pnas.org/doi/full/10.1073/pnas.1502108112.

14 Elena Becatoros, 'More than 90 percent of world's coral reefs will die by 2050', *The Independent*, March 13, 2017, https://www.independent.co.uk/climate-change/news/environment-90-percent-coral-reefs-die-2050-climate-change-bleaching-pollution-a7626911.html.

15 Paul Brown, 'An unnatural disaster', *The Guardian*, January 8, 2004, https://www.theguardian.com/science/2004/jan/08/biodiversity.sciencenews.

16 'A model predicts that the world's populations will stop growing in 2050', *ScienceDaily*, April 4, 2013, https://www.sciencedaily.com/releases/2013/04/130404072923.htm.

17 'Elderly to outnumber children by 2050 in most parts of world', *ScienceDaily*, November 27, 2010, https://www.sciencedaily.com/releases/2010/11/101126094441.htm.

18 'Ageing and health', *World Health Organization*, October 4, 2021, https://www.who.int/news-room/fact-sheets/detail/ageing-and-health.

19 'Alzheimer's patients: 106 million worldwide by 2050', *The Seattle Times*, June 10, 2007, https://www.seattletimes.com/nation-world/alzheimers-patients-106-million-worldwide-by-2050.

20 Emma Nichols and Theo Vos, 'Estimating the global mortality from Alzheimer's disease and other dementias: A new method and results from the Global Burden of Disease study 2019', *Alzheimer's & Dementia* vol. 16, issue S10, December 7, 2020, https://alz-journals.onlinelibrary.wiley.com/doi/10.1002/alz.042236.

21 Brien A. Holden, Timothy R. Fricke, David A. Wilson, Monica Jong, Kovin S. Naidoo, Padmaja Sankaridurg, Tien Y. Wong, Thomas J. Naduvilath, and Serge Resnikoff, 'Global Prevalence of Myopia and High Myopia and Temporal Trends from 2000 through 2050', *Ophthalmology* vol. 123, issue 5, February 11, 2016, https://www.aaojournal.org/article/s0161-6420(16)00025-7/fulltext.

22 *Spreading like Wildfire: The Rising Threat of Extraordinary Landscape Fires*, United Nations Environment Programme, February 23, 2022, https://www.unep.org/resources/report/spreading-wildfire-rising-threat-extraordinary-landscape-fires.

23 'Two Billion People Vulnerable to Floods by 2050; Number Expected to Double or More in Two Generations Due to Climate Change, Deforestation, Rising Seas, Population Growth', United Nations University, June 13, 2004, http://www.unu.edu/news/ehs/floods.doc.

24 Charles Fant, C. Adam Schlosser, Xiang Gao, Kenneth Strzepek, John Reilly, 'Projections of Water Stress Based on an Ensemble of Socioeconomic Growth and Climate Change Scenarios: A Case Study in Asia', *PLOS ONE* vol. 11, no. 3, March 30, 2016, https://journals.plos.org/plosone/article?id=10.1371/journal.pone.0150633.

25 Chelsea Ong, 'Asia is home to some of climate change's biggest culprits and victims', *CNBC*, April 7, 2022, https://www.cnbc.com/2022/04/08/asia-faces-threats-from-climate-change-heres-what-needs-to-be-done.html.

26 Helen Thompson, 'Ten Species That Are Evolving Due to the Changing Climate', *Smithsonian Magazine*, October 24, 2014, https://www.smithsonianmag.com/science-nature/ten-species-are-evolving-due-changing-climate-180953133.

27 Sarah Gibbens, '"Sea Nomads" Are First Known Humans Genetically Adapted to Diving,' *National Geographic*, April 19, 2018, https://www.nationalgeographic.com/science/article/bajau-sea-nomads-free-diving-spleen-science.

28 J. W. Ferry Slik et al., 'Phylogenetic classification of the world's tropical forests', *PNAS* vol. 115, no. 8, February 5, 2018, https://www.pnas.org/doi/10.1073/pnas.1714977115.

29 Alejandra Borunda, 'We still don't know the full impacts of the BP oil spill, 10 years later', *National Geographic*, April 21, 2020, https://www.nationalgeographic.com/science/article/bp-oil-spill-still-dont-know-effects-decade-later.

30 Ella Arcangel: Oyayi sa Dilim (2020), animated by Mervin Malonzo https://www.youtube.com/watch?v=F6db_p-_KWs&feature=emb_imp_woyt.

31 Komiket: The Filipino Komiks and Art Market has collaborated with foreign institutions to produce anthologies that deal with envisioning the archipelago's future, the most recent being *Manila 2019–2050: City of the Future* (2020; organized by the Embassy of France to the Philippines) and *Ten Years to Save the World* (2021; supported by the British council). Villanueva ended 'OK Millennial' with a tableau re-enacting Delacroix's 'Liberty Leading the People'; whether this is a wink to the embassy or coincidental, is up for speculation. Meanwhile, 'PH comics, COP26, and climate change cops', a critical article about *Ten Years* can be accessed here https://www.bulatlat.com/2021/10/27/ph-comics-cop26-and-climate-change-cops.

32 See 'Green Guerillas' by Clement Bautista Jr., https://www.bulatlat.com/2017/03/31/green-guerrillas and the film *Die Gruene Guerilla aka The Green Guerillas* (1995) by Rod Prosser https://www.youtube.com/watch?v=QBpGU9ykl9c.

33 See 'The Need for a Southern Canon: The Question of Canon Formation and the Literary Capitals of the World', Conference paper read at the Jakarta International Literary Festival, Taman Ismail Marzuki, Cikini, Jakarta, Indonesia, 20-24 August 2019. https://www.researchgate.net/publication/335489718_The_Need_for_a_Southern_Canon_The_Question_of_Canon_Formation_and_the_Literary_Capitals_of_the_World.

# All Trash on the Eastern Side

Duanwad Pimwana

*Translated from Thai by Mui Poopoksakul*

My mother and father disappeared amid the trash. My siblings and relatives, too, one by one. I have nobody. Trash is everywhere around me: the ground, the hollows, the hills are all trash. It doesn't matter where I look, or how far, I see nothing but an unending series of overlapping mountains, trash upon trash. Trees have been flattened, homes have collapsed, rivers have been buried under piles of trash. Everything is gone; everything is trash. I look down at myself: I'm filthy and I stink. Soon enough, I will have taken my final breath, and I will become another piece of trash. When we humans must exist among heaps and heaps of garbage all the time, we're bound to turn into garbage before long.

I don't want to live this way, but I have no choice. I can't remember when I last saw the surface of the earth. I do have one image burnished in my mind, a memory from twenty years ago, when I was a seven-year-old boy: I was being led by the hand, strolling down a street—I still see the scene clearly and reminisce about it all the time—the street was wide open, empty, running as far as the eye can see. I shook my hand free to run ahead of everyone. A breeze swept over from the mountains; it felt cool, refreshing. Not a single piece of trash was in sight. I yearn for that street, and I would trade my life for a chance to take a walk there again, filling my lungs with that air, even for a measly ten minutes. The street really existed, but the longer I languish among these dumps, the more I lose faith in my memory, like perhaps I only dreamed it up.

Each day, I wander, not only to scavenge for bits of anything edible but also in hopes of one day making it beyond all of this garbage and finding the Land Without Trash, a place said to have a human settlement, to be home to living animals and trees—according to a story that has been around since my parents still were. People we used to come across often told of the land. Some of them believed in its existence, some didn't, but everyone strained to imagine what a clean, trash-less land might be like. How was it possible for people to live without littering? How did they dispose of their garbage? And where did they hide it?

I trudge over a mountain of trash, not having run into a soul for nearly a month. A part of me is convinced that people have been subsumed in the piles of refuse, just as my parents and the rest of my family have been, but another part of me harbours a secret hope that the other trash dwellers are fighting their way to the Land Without Trash. Perhaps they have found it and, naturally, have stayed. I'm fearful for myself and full of regret: Last time, I encountered two men heading south—they believed the Land Without Trash likely lay in that direction—but I was bound east, remembering how my mother had said the Land Without Trash was situated thereabouts. The two men and I exchanged only a few words before parting ways. Several days later, it dawned on me that it had been a mistake not to join those two men. The realization left me weak and dejected, my loneliness feeling like a stab in the heart.

Though I continue heading east, I care about nothing more than the chance to meet someone, anyone. Given the opportunity this time, I would ask to follow them on their journey, regardless of where they were going. Since my clue was no better than anyone else's, what difference does it make which way we travel? I cannot tolerate the solitude any longer. Being all alone in the middle of this ocean of waste is beyond unbearable—and not because I want to have a friend to chat with or a travel companion I can lean on. This abject loneliness—it comes from my being haunted by the view. It doesn't matter whether I look ahead or behind, left or right, the picture I see is all the same. And it doesn't matter how far I walk in a day; the scene never alters—it's as though I were moving in circles. This panorama of garbage is playing mind games with me, making me question whether I'm hallucinating. I'm suffering greatly. I try to remind myself I'm moving forward, making strides. I have a destination, and I've already covered a great deal of distance. My body motion ought to be able to attest to the reality that the view around me is shifting all the time. I'm walking. I'm still conscious of my own movement, of my freedom. I'm not locked up in a cage, not confined to an area, no one is prohibiting me from doing whatever it is I want to do. At least I'm not forced to be cooped up in a small space, like, say, if I had to lower myself into a coffin and lie there. *Then* the view would really remain unchanged forever and ever. It already counts for something that I can still move around freely. I'm walking, the view is shifting, even if it shifts only to remain the same. But I know it's shifting. Sometimes I close my eyes, sometimes open them. The view is shifting, I know that . . . oh, how lonely it is. What I would give to run into another living creature.

Ultimately, it is on my route east, half a month later, that I spot a fellow human being. Standing on a hilltop looking down at what is shaped like a deep pit, I see a person moving around at its bottom. I'm beyond ecstatic. I feel as if I only had one opportunity left in this life to encounter another human being again, and that opportunity has really arrived. Immediately, I scurry down. Until I see the person up close or hear his or her voice, I won't be able to tell if it's a man or a woman. In this squalid, putrid world, men and women have become difficult to distinguish. Everyone I meet is in the same sorry state—clothes so filthy their colours are obscured, hair long and matted, cheeks hollowed, body emaciated and rundown.

'Hello!' I wave to the person. 'Hello!'

The person looks up at me, waving back, also excited.

'Hello!' The voice I hear reveals the person to be a woman, but she is so scrawny there's no hint of womanliness left about her.

'Are you alone? Where are you headed? Are you searching for the clean land? Have you turned up anything to eat at all?' the woman jabbers away. She still looks quite vivacious and strong, despite being downright skeletal.

'Mostly, I eat worms,' I tell her and smile, embarrassed.

'Same here. I forage for worms, too.' She laughs loudly. 'Are you in a hurry? Stay and chat a while. I haven't had anyone to talk to for two months now. It's been really lonely. I've been talking to myself like a crazy person.'

'Me, too. Yesterday, I was suddenly struck by the fear that I might be the only person left among these dumps. The whole time I was walking, I felt like I was trapped in a dream—nothing seemed real except for the trash. Eyes open or closed, I saw nothing but garbage. I have no one left. My parents, siblings, my whole extended family, all of them have been swallowed up in the trash. I'm keeping an eye on what's going to happen to me, waiting for my own turn to come one day—a person turning into a piece of garbage, blown away into a heap with millions of other pieces of garbage. I don't want to become garbage, but if I'd be the only one left in the middle of all this trash, I don't know what would be worse.'

'Being alive trumps all else, always. As long as one's alive, there's still hope. You know, you shouldn't drive yourself crazy with those dark thoughts. The more we let them get to us, the more fed up we'll be with life, and eventually one day we'll see ourselves as trash and want to throw ourselves away. Stay—wouldn't it be better to keep each other company and try to find a way out of this together?' the woman lectures me earnestly, which makes her come off rather bookish. I have trouble even estimating her age. Based on the things she said, I'm led to believe she's seen something of life. But there's a youthful light in her eyes, like a girl's.

'I meant that was the state I was in yesterday, but not anymore. I just wanted to have someone there to help bear witness to the fact that my life was really happening.'

The woman laughs out loud at what she apparently finds an odd remark, which means despite not having had any human contact for even longer, she hasn't suffered through the same state and can't empathize. I bring up the subject I've been intending to bring up from the start, which is to ask her if I could accompany her on her journey, because I don't want to carry on alone any longer.

The woman hears me out, smiling, and then shakes her head. 'I'm not going anywhere. Don't you see? I live here.'

Her answer baffles me. I simply don't understand. 'What do you mean? Aren't you on a search for the Land Without Trash like everybody else? Or do you not believe it exists?'

'I don't know, maybe it exists. But I already have my own ambition.'

Still confounded, I fail to react altogether. For trash dwellers like ourselves, is there something else to dream of other than the Land Without Trash?

'What's your ambition? . . . But anyway, you should try to get beyond the trash first. Staying here, you'd only be counting down to the day you die. Come with me—didn't you tell me as long as one's alive, there's still hope?'

'Of course, there is. And I have more hope than anyone. Don't you see what I've done here?' She turns and, with her eyes, gestures all the way around. My eyes follow hers, but I see nothing but trash. She's quick to explain: 'I'm building my own trash-free land right here. First, I have to haul the trash away. Do you see how large and how deep this pit is? One day, I'm going to reach the ground. I'm going to take away all the garbage, and I'm going to be left with the ground, all cleaned up. And if I keep moving the trash, the area is going to get bigger and bigger. When that day comes, I'm going to grow trees, I'm going to build a house, and I'm going to keep clearing away the trash and expand the area more and more. My land's not going to have any trash. Do you get it now? I'm not going anywhere because there's a trash-free land right here.'

Her words running through my head, I visualize along with amazement. This is such a beautiful dream. But it's also daunting—could she realistically succeed? The amount of trash is staggering, endless. How long would it take? She might die before she gets a glimpse of the ground.

'Will you stay with me? If we do it together, it will be twice as fast.'

I want to stay with her, certainly, but the grandness of her aspiration launches my mind into a panic as I weigh the pros and cons of two different paths that could potentially lead me to a land without trash. Others are going the route of searching for it, but this woman wants to create one with her own hands. A clean colony is supposed to manifest itself in this expanse of trash stretching as far and wide as the eye can see? When? Looking at her small hands and feet, I feel discouraged. But the other alternative offers no guarantee whatsoever. The legend or story that has been passed down—who could vouch for its veracity? Everybody is struggling to locate that fabled land, invested in their search because of the desperate desire to break free from these dumps. The question I ought to put to myself is: Do I want to die here or cast my die out there? But here I'd have a friend. I might as well stay with this woman at least until someone else shows up. At that point, I can still change my mind.

She's delighted I'm agreeing to stay, not only because she's lonely and wants to have a companion, but also because my presence raises the prospect that her trash-free land might materialize sooner. I immediately begin to worry. I don't want to hurt her feelings by admitting to her that I don't share her hope in the matter, not in the least, and that being so, I'm disinclined to waste my energy hauling trash. But, not knowing how to turn her down, I don't feel like I have a choice. I'll probably have to help her until I find someone else to journey with.

'Two months ago, someone passed through this way. I begged her to stay and build a trash-free land together, but she didn't believe I could make it happen. Back then, the pit was still puny. It's a shame—if she saw it now, she might have made a different decision. Look how big and deep the pit is. With two of us, so twice the labour, we're sure to uncover the ground soon. Down the line, maybe we'll have lots and lot of people giving us a hand. Oh, I wish they'd just come! The sooner the better!'

She hands me a burlap sack, and we get to work right away. The pit is large and deep—it's almost inconceivable it was born from the labour of such a slight woman. I go about collecting garbage and dropping it into the sack she gave me. The most strenuous part of the task is dragging the sack up to the edge of the pit. Just beyond it, the terrain begins to slope downward. My sack rolls bopping down all by itself, which helps spare a great deal of effort, until it loses momentum about twenty meters away from the top. As I open the sack to dump out the trash, a cry of protest comes at me from behind.

The tiny woman is standing with an enormous sack—how was she able to drag it up the pit? On top of that, she forbids me from pouring out the trash right here: I'm to haul it behind the next knoll and dispose of it there. Her sack rolls down after me, and she tows it uphill, even taking the lead. The way she moves, her strength appears nothing short of a miracle. I struggle to keep up, failing to comprehend why we have to go all the way behind that knoll when everywhere was a dump. On my second trip, I start to feel tired; on the third, I'm much slower than before. From my observation, the whole time the woman is tugging her sack along, her eyes are scanning for worms. I get to take a break when she calls me over to share a meal for the first time.

At dusk, the woman proudly shows off something, which leaves me flabbergasted once again. It's a coffin sitting on the bank of the pit. It's her bedroom, she says. The sight of it makes me uneasy. The interior of the box is lined with burlap, and there is a pillow that, though grubby, looks very appealing. The coffin's lid is leaning on its side, and nearby, a straw mat lies unfurled, with a wooden chest atop, serving as a table. Inside the chest is a miscellany of objects she has managed to collect—this woman's determination to set down roots here is exciting, contagious.

'Go on, before it gets dark. There's another coffin over there. Tonight, you're going to get to sleep in a clean bedroom.'

Together, we lug the other coffin over and park it near hers. For the first time, I won't be sleeping on top of trash, but in a coffin one layer above. How wondrous it's going to be. Once I get in and lie flat, the side walls block the trash from view completely. All I see is the sky, which is starting to spring twinkles of stars. Ah, the view has changed! I've truly escaped the trash. This casket might have had a previous occupant, but being in it right now, I feel clean . . . clean . . . I've nearly forgotten what it feels like. Even though the space proves awkward and cramped when I try to turn my body or even shift my limbs, I don't mind. I realize now that even if my hands and feet were bound and I lost the liberty to walk around or do anything else, as long as I get to be some place clean, away from trash, I would willingly forsake and forgo all the freedom in the world. What use is it for us humans to cling to our freedom in the midst of all this trash? Once anything of value in this world has been discarded or has wound up in a pile of refuse, does it really count as something of value anymore? I shut my eyes and run my hand along the casket's smooth wall. This coffin has given me a sanctuary all my own. I no longer have to be commingled with the trash—this thought alone moves me to tears.

I haul garbage, day in day out. Every day, the woman says: Today might be the day we see the ground. She is as hopeful as I am hopeless. But at last, we hit upon the ground, actual solid earth. I can feel my heart pumping, I don't know how to describe all the emotions rushing through me. The woman manically claws away more of the trash, mumbling away with elation and excitement. I'm ashamed to admit that in a given day she manages to make three more trips than I do. Now her dream is a pipe dream no more. I have never met anyone so full of hope and spirit as this woman. Though her flesh has been dwindling day by day, her strength has only improved. Today, we've uncovered the earth; the pit need not be dug deeper. Our hauls from here on out will be about expanding the area. It's exactly as she envisioned it. Now I'm growing convinced there's a land without trash right here, and it's a place I must build for myself.

We toil away like mad so that each day we would see more of the earth. In the meantime, I've also started collecting objects of my own: I've got a plate, a candle, and a rusty pair of scissors. This last item is precious. I look for ways to polish off the rust, and, using a nail I found, try to sharpen it by rubbing the two objects together. The two of us are overjoyed to finally be able to cut our hair. We take turns snipping off each other's locks, entirely getting rid of the clumped masses that have been weighing down our heads.

'It's so light and comfortable!' The woman is thoroughly pleased with her crew cut. 'I feel like a cadet!'

But I have to avert my eyes. With her hair shorn, her gaunt face has become even more prominent. That skull of a head—I don't want to look at it. If it weren't for her eyes, which are still full of life, anyone who gets a look at her would think she was already a corpse. I can't speak to the state of my own appearance . . . It's probably not much better. Without access to a mirror, the best we can do is look at each other. Regardless, one outcome was undeniably fantastic: Our haircuts made us cleaner.

I wish people would pass by because I'm eager to show off the area of the ground we've cleared, which has grown to be almost eighty square yards now. The dream of having a home to live in, of cultivating plants and raising animals on land that is clean and trashless is so close to coming true we could almost touch it with our fingertips. But alas, this is as far as we'll come.

I've fallen ill from the combination of hard labour and a dearth of food. The woman likewise. We are left lying helplessly in our coffins, praying someone would happen by. Even if they can't save our lives, the woman hopes they would carry on our unfinished work. After lying still for two nights and a day, the woman pulls herself up and crawls out of her box. Her determination never ceases to amaze. She is going to look for something to eat, she says. I could still just about gather enough energy to crawl out, but I continue to lie idle because

I know the effort is pointless. I have tramped over every inch of the surface in this vicinity, to the degree I recognize every single piece of trash. Any hope I had for food was lost over a half a month ago.

With the woman absent, I stay supine in my coffin, breathing feebly. In the moments when I'm alert, I listen, with hope, for her bright, upbeat voice. We shouldn't be separated during a time like this. I should have stopped her from venturing out. By now she's probably collapsed out there somewhere and stranded.

On the third morning after she went missing, I attempt to get up but find myself too weak to lift my body out of the coffin. I only manage as far as draping my arms and head over the edge—which turns out to be sufficient because the woman comes into view immediately. Since when has she been back? She's been lying right next to my casket, on the mat. Hearing my voice, she opens her eyes. We are each happy to see the other's face again.

'There's a way where we won't have to die,' I tell the woman. 'My parents and the rest of my family, every one of them, no one had to die.'

'I realize that . . . No one I know from before has died. That's why it's tough going for us—with no worms left to eat.'

Both of us burst out laughing until we're gasping for air. Afterward, we're so drained by the exertion we're forced to keep still for a long while.

Since the subject has been broached, I decide to ask her: 'The time has come for us to really make a choice. Do you want to do like them?' The woman, contemplating, doesn't answer. In truth, I know she made her choice long ago, otherwise, our encounter here could never have happened . . . I myself have sworn off littering, having witnessed too many cautionary tales close to home. I can't pinpoint when this punishment came into existence, but I do know it wasn't very long ago. My family had had the habit of dropping their trash carelessly on the ground for ages, but it was only within the last two years that they metamorphosed into trash. My father was the first of them. He'd chucked a cigarette butt, and instantly he'd vanished before our eyes. My mother had been quick enough to catch the moment he transformed into another cigarette stub. She told anybody and everybody what happened. Those who didn't believe her all wanted to test the story for themselves. It proved true. Without exception, anyone who littered turned into a piece of garbage. Later on, dumping trash became an easy way out for people who had lost hope.

Seeing that the woman isn't about to reply, I answer for her, 'You're not going to throw trash on the ground, right? You've always maintained this beautiful optimism. You only pursue the toughest things, and you never give up. Surely, you're not one to take the easy way out, am I right?'

The woman smiles. 'It's more that we owe a debt to the worms. We ought to save our bodies, to feed them for once.'

Both of us burst out laughing until we're gasping for air. This time, the laughter costs us our lives.

# The Last Days of Juan De La Cruz: Pilot Issue

Vincent Lapuz

*Translated from the Filipino by Tilde Acuña*

IN EACH PLANET, THERE IS A
LIGHT THAT LEADS THE WAY

AND FROM ITS BIRTH,
ITS SUBJECT IS FINALIZED

AND NOTHING EVER CHANGES.

AFTER TIME PASSES
LIGHT BECOMES THE FATHER...
OR GOD TO THE POET
AND HIS CHILDREN VANISHED.

SUN KING BECAME HIS NAME.
AND IN THIS LAND, ALL
HIS CHILDREN VANISHED...
AROUND THEM REVOLVED
THE WHOLE WORLD...

BUT ALL KINGS
HAVE THEIR TIME.

IT IS TIME FOR THE LIGHT
TO SLEEP IN NIGHT'S BEDROOM.

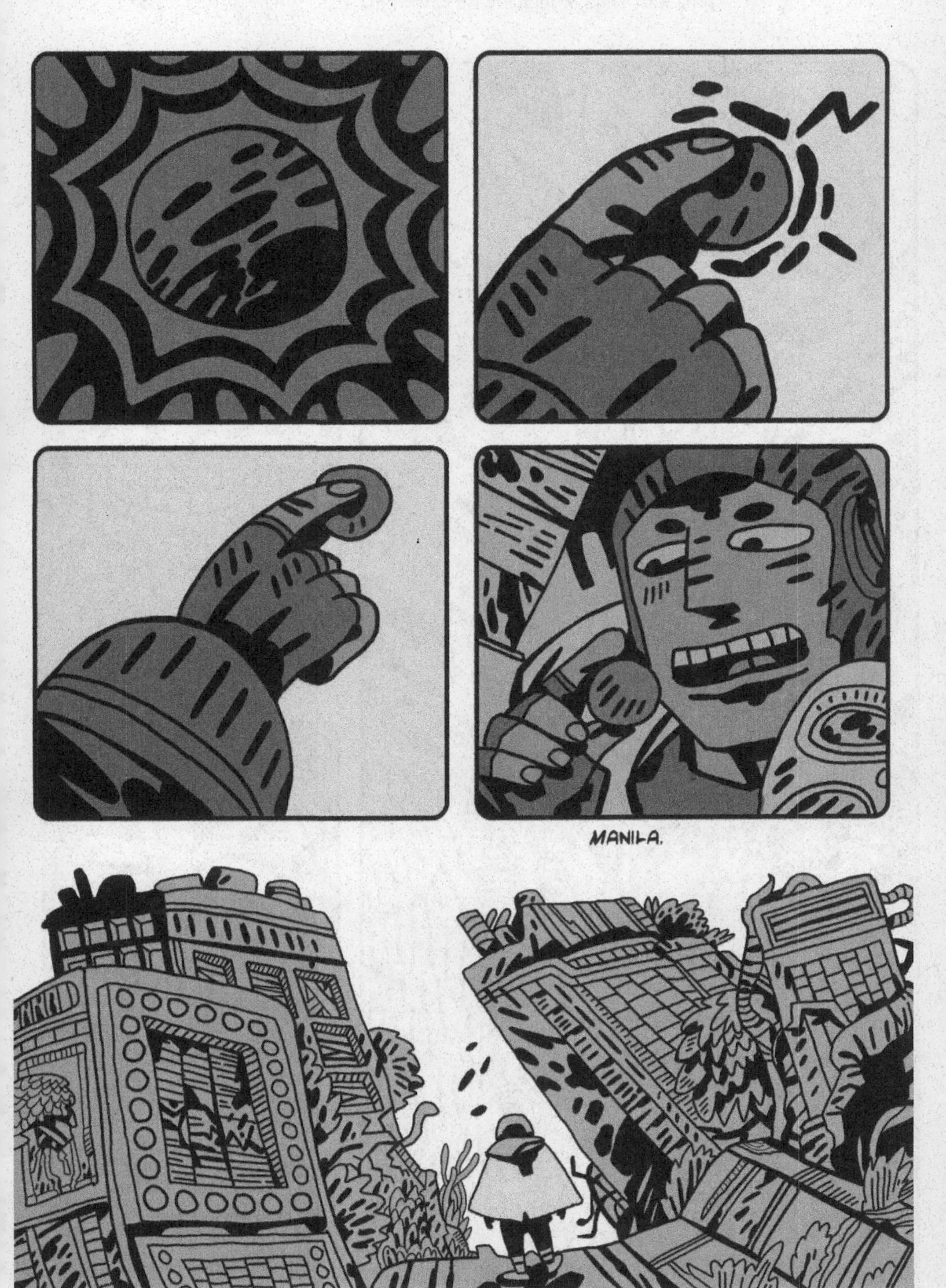
MANILA.

TAFT
UN

BROTHER, HELP ME DEAL WITH THIS!!!!

THIS GODDAMN PIG WEIGHS A LOT, QUICK! BEFORE I FAINT FROM THIS —

WAIT FOR A BIT.

MAN, WHAT'S WITH THAT ATTITUDE?
NELSON...
MY KNEES & SHOULDERS ACHE, THANKS TO THAT PIG.
SONUVABITCH, I CAN'T EVEN FEEL THAT YOU'RE WITH ME HERE.
KUYA, CALM DOWN, HERE'S MY COLD DRINK IF YOU WANT SOME.

KUYA, IT SEEMS LIKE...
I KNOW IT LOOKS LIKE WHAT - WHAT'S THAT?

SHHH, THEY MIGHT TAKE NOTICE.

THANK YOU
UMM... WHY DID YOU TAKE THAT OUT?
YOU DUMBASS, CAN'T YOU HEAR THAT SOMEONE'S TAILING US?

JUST A MOMENT, BRO. WE CAN BEAT THE SHIT OUT OF THAT ONE USING THE STUFF IN HERE. WAIT FOR MY CUE. I'LL COUNTTO THREE.
HUNTER, I KNOW THIS QUESTION'S NONSENSE BUT WHAT'S THAT?

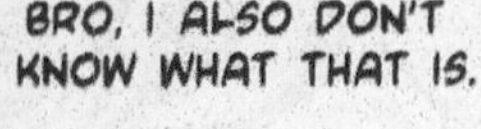
BRO, I ALSO DON'T KNOW WHAT THAT IS.

BUT NOW I'LL COUNT FROM ONE.
TWO,

THREE!

DAMN, THAT'S ALL IT TAKES, AND IT FELL.
NELSON, I'LL JUST GRAB SOMETHING TO CONSTRAIN THAT BEAST, GO GRAB SOME CANNED GOODS THERE.
SURE THING, BRO.
WOAH SOME LEFTOVER SARDINES!

SHUT YOUR TRAP.
I'VE BEEN SILENT, YOU SHIT.

HON, DON'T WORRY, THEY'RE GONNA GET HOME.
LAST TIME YOU SAID SO, A PIGEON ALMOST ATE THEM.

MOM, THAT'S NOT A PIGEON. BUT AN OSTRICH.

WELL, WELL, MY BABY BOY'S HERE. WHERE IS HUNTER? NELSON, YOU NEED ANYTHING ELSE?

SURE DO, DAD.

WELL, WELL.

BUY
SELL
HEYA HUNTER, WHATCHU GOT THERE? SEEMS LIKE YOUR CATCH'S SOMETHIN' BIG, EH?
I DON'T GET WHAT YOU'RE GETTING AT BUT I WOULDNT OFFER MY CATCH.
WHAT I AM TRYING TO TELL YOU HUNTER IS THIS: THE NEEDS TO SUSTAIN PEOPLE IN THIS PLAZA CONTINUE TO GROW OUTTA PROPORTIONS AND A WAY TO SATISFY THESE NEEDS IS COLLECT AND RECOLLECT E'RYTHING, WHETHER IT IS AN OBJECT OR SOMETHING ALIVE.
I KNOW THAT MAYOR, BUT WHAT YOU ARE TELLING ME SOMETIMES CATCHES ME OFF GUARD AND DRIVES ME MAD.

BRO, HOW ARE YOU THERE? I BROUGHT DAD HERE, FOR YOUR PRESENT.
NELSON, WHAT HAVE YOU BROUGHT HERE?
THE CATCH FOR THE DAY! THERE'S A WILD BOAR, STRAPPED AND LOADED IN THE TRUCK.
APPRECIATE YOUR WILD BOAR, SON. BUT I'VE NO IDEA WHERE I'M GONNA KEEP IT.
OR WHATEVER THIS ANIMALITY IS... WHAT'S THIS ANIMAL?
WHAT ARE YOU WAITING FOR HUNTER? LET THE AUCTION BEGIN!! WHERE YOU GONNA KEEP THIS, HUNTER, IF YOU CANNOT PUT IT ANYWHERE IN THIS PLAZA?

FIVE THOUSAND FOR THAT ANIMAL

SEVEN THOUSAND FOR MY MAMI

TEN THOUSAND FOR MY TOY

ELEVEN THOUSAND

THE PRICE IS A BIT STEEP, I'LL GIVE FIFTY

TAHIMIK*
!!!
*SILENCE!!!

I'LL JUST BRING IT TO MY PLACE, SO YOU DON'T HAVE TO QUARREL.
HUNTER, YOUVE GOTTA BE KIDDING. ARE YOU CRAZY?

KUYA, YOU'VE HAD TOO MUCH TODAY. IS THERE A PROBLEM?
THE DIFFICULT ANSWER TO THAT IS THE REASON WHY LEFTOVER HUMAN SCUM IN THE CITY ARE MOSTLY BALD AND UNHINGED.
I ALSO THINK THAT THE SUN SHOULD'VE EXPLODED.
KUYA, THAT ALREADY HAPPENED A COUPLA TIMES.
HEY!
DAD?
THERE'S A JOB FOR YOU GUYS AT HOME LET'S GO COME WITH US FOR DINNER.
YOUR CHILDREN ARE REALLY SOMETHING CAPTAIN.

KAP, HUNTER AND NELSON, WHAT DISHES DO YOU LIKE? LOTSA COOKED RICE HERE!
KAP, FILL OUR VISITORS' PLATES TO THE BRIM, THEY'RE FROM THE OTHER END OF THE WORLD.
THAT'S TOO MUCH, HON, JUST SERVE SOME SINIGANG AND WE'LL TALK HERE ABOUT THE JOB.
IT IS INDEED TRUE THAT THERE ARE POLITICIANS AT LARGE IN THE PHILIPPINES, STILL BEING CHASED BY THE MAGDALO FACTION?
I THOUGHT YOUR LEADER LEFT, BY THEN? OR DIED??
OUR SENATOR DIED WHILE FLEEING FROM FEDERALISTAS, BUT THAT'S NOT TODAY'S SUBJECT.
HEARD THERE'S TROUBLE LURKING IN THE QUEZON WASTELAND.

STARTED LAST NIGHT, OUR BRIGADE WAS REGROUPING IN A STATION OUTSIDE THE QUEZON DOME, BUT A GROUP ENCAMPED AT A DISTANCE.
WE DIDN'T SEE WHAT DEVOURED THEM ALL.

SO MY CAPTAIN INSTRUCTED ME TO FIND THE LOCAL HUNTER HERE AND HIS BROTHER WHO APPEAR TO HAVE THE HABIT OF GAMEHUNTING,

AND WE'LL PAY U A SUM OF 100,000 AND SOME PANCIT WANTON,

WAIT A MINUTE, YOU'RE GONNA PAY US WITH PACKS OF PANCIT WANTON?

PANCIT
WANTON

KUYA, I'LL BRING A GAS MASK AND BOTTLES OF WATER BECAUSE IT'S HOT OUTSIDE.
CANT BELIEVE THAT WE'RE GONNA GO OUTTA MANILA DOME TO GET TO QUEZON DOME FOR CRAP LIKE PANCIT WANTON AND CASH.
SIGH, AT LEAST WE HAVE FOOD TO EAT AND PANCIT WANTON THAT SHALL LAST FOR A MONTH, RIGHT?
HUNTER, SEEMS LIKE I HAVEN'T WASHED MY GAS MASK. I THINK IT SMELLS LIKE THE SEWAGE AND IT IS SO HOT.

ANYTHING?
NONE.

QUEZON CITY DOME, SO MISERABLE.
ALARMING, WHAT HAPPENED?
HUNTER?
SUPPLY OF AIR RAN OUT IN THE CITY'S VENTILATION LAST DECADE, BUT AFTER EXHAUSTING THE AIR SUPPLY, THERE WERE RIOTS AND PEOPLE DIED OR LIVED BREATHING FILTHY AIR.

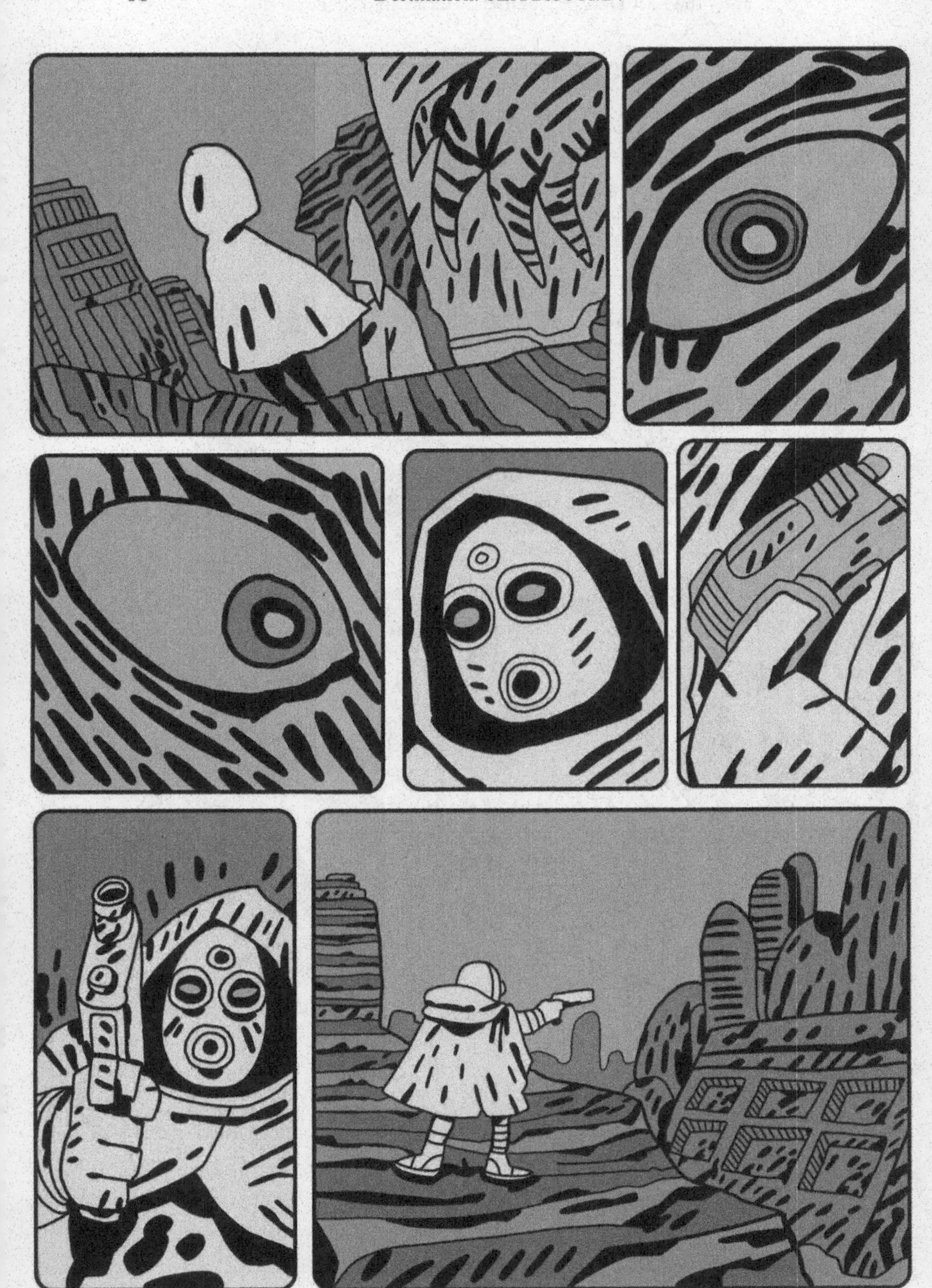

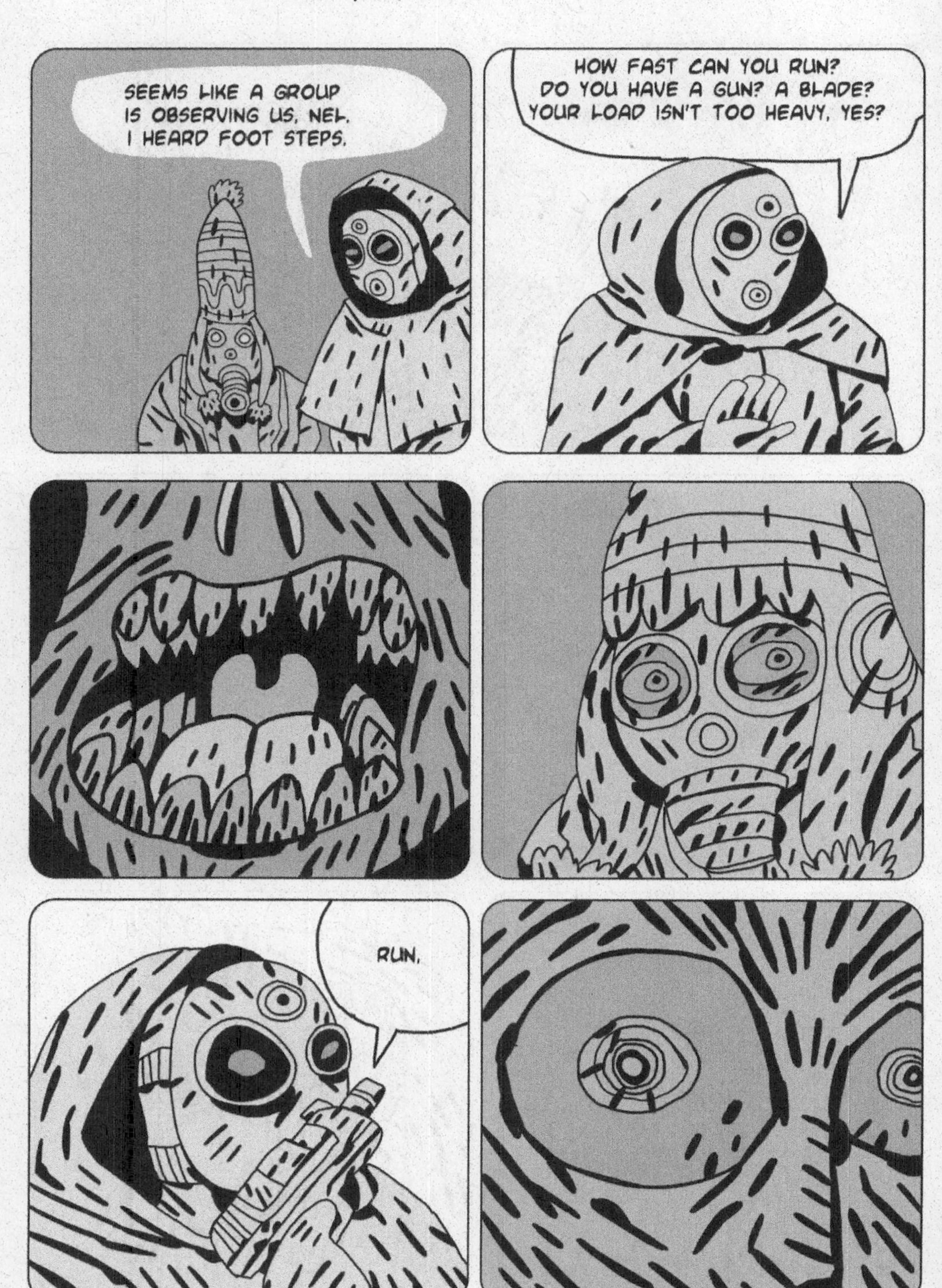
SEEMS LIKE A GROUP IS OBSERVING US, NEL. I HEARD FOOT STEPS.
HOW FAST CAN YOU RUN? DO YOU HAVE A GUN? A BLADE? YOUR LOAD ISN'T TOO HEAVY, YES?
RUN.

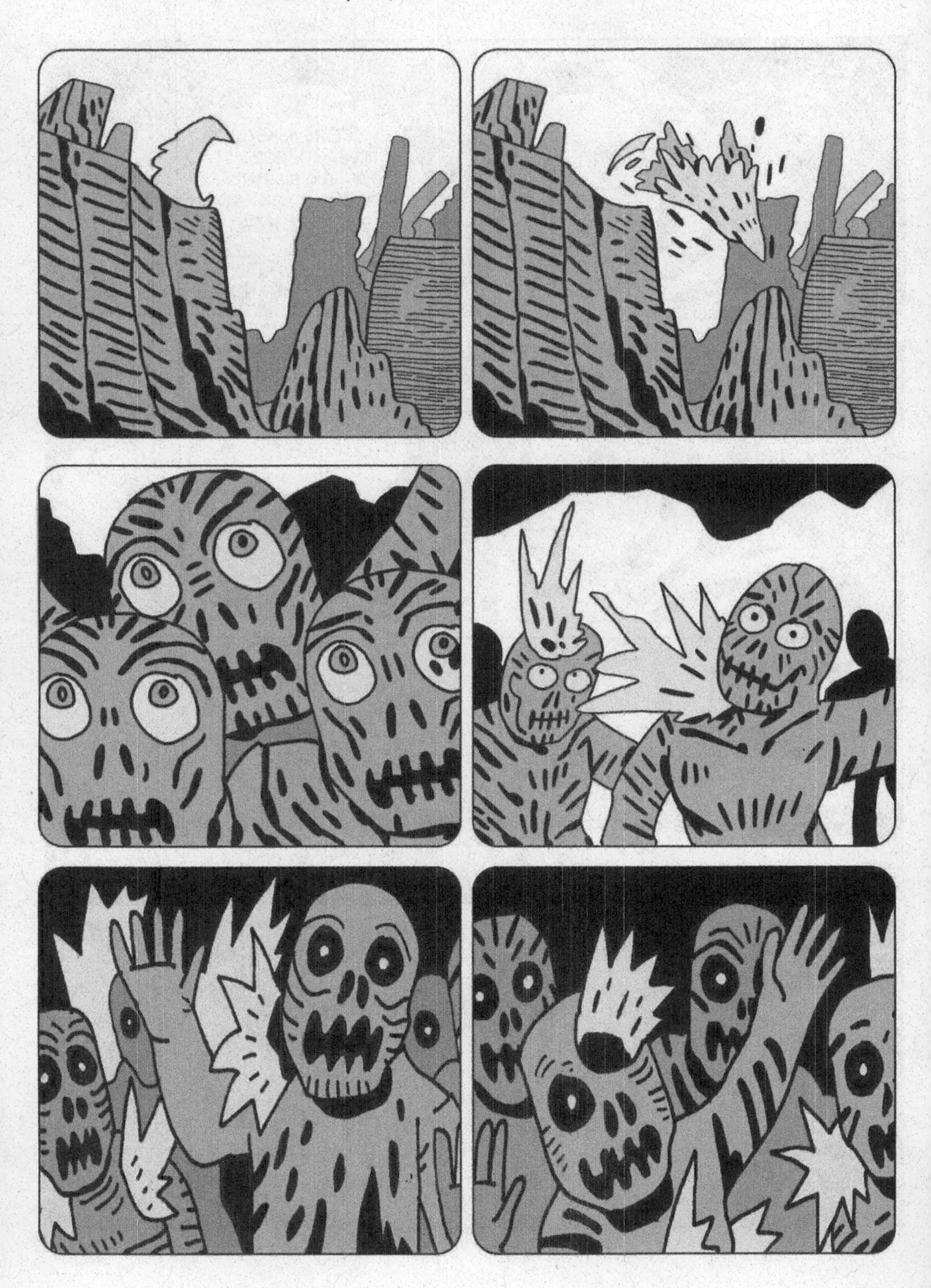

SEEMS LIKE EVERYTHING'S FALLEN SILENT OUTSIDE BUT I'LL STAY HERE FOR NOW.
YOU GO OUT FIRST.

YO! YOU UP THERE! THANKS! CAN YOU PLEASE HELP US, WE'RE ON OUR WAY TO—!

DIMWIT, JUST LEFT LIKE A FOOL.

# Kep at the End of the World

Sokunthary Svay

Occasionally, I return to Kep to remind myself of this city's rhythm. From the sound of morning fishing nets to the crackling and eventual scuttle of crabs, morning price hawking and beeping motos and the effervescent waves, they keep me coming back. I can afford to wander through the town until it's time for me return home.

I witnessed it all. I was here when the French created their little sleepy seaside town. I was here when the Khmer Rouge implanted themselves and then violently abandoned us. What's left of their structures are dilapidated beams further weakened over time. So much for longevity. But such relics, I rarely spend time thinking about. Whenever I visit, I'm looking for Sovanna, the dancing girl with the gold earrings. Few could afford to have the yellowish gold that she adorned herself with, but her jewellery came from old money. Although, these days, it was a final reminder of her family's previous glory days.

The locals don't know what to make of me. Some think I'm *barang*, with some French blood. I'm an orphan with no origins. I am who you want me to be. You will change me into what you desire; I am a woman after all.

There are more resorts than I remember but not as many people staying in them. The temperatures have risen, and shoreline has eroded more in the past ten years. Soon, the stilt houses will be useless. People have already done what they can to prepare for the floods, moving further inland, or even into the mountains. Whatever relatives remain, they will scatter themselves as if hiding from the inevitability of nature. But when the end comes, there is no running. In the meantime, the brave ones stay making a small market catering to the others left behind, living the ways of Cambodians who have survived all the previous leaders. They keep fishing. They keep selling crab. They look toward the horizon.

I catch the glint of Sovanna's gold in the distance. She's got a gold pendant now in addition to the earrings. It seems futile, these objects of adornment and class but she insists on wearing them. When I first met her, she was disrupting the work of a general whose head was shaped like a monkey. He was dropping large rocks and disrupting her home near the water so to spite him, she stole the rocks. During their confrontation, the monkey man didn't expect that such a beautiful creature was the cause of his problems. They fell in love, she returned the rocks, and they built a causeway, and a family, together.

But she was alone now. Her son—nicknamed 'Trey' because he always swam away at the sight of other people—had returned to this father's domain in the kingdom southwest of Kep. She swished across the dirt, the back of her sarong wet and dragging along the ground.

'Sister, you shouldn't be here. Things are falling apart,' Sovanna began.

'We're both free to roam last I checked. What's the matter?'

'They are predicting a flood, but I can feel it brewing from where I stand.' Sovanna looks at her wet feet and continues, 'I came to get one final look at the province before this part goes underwater.'

'I hadn't heard anything about this.'

'You can hardly learn much sitting from your perch watching the tourists, Sister.'

It was true. I liked to sit atop the beach and watch in amusement at all the comings-and-goings on the sand and further off within eyeshot. This didn't exactly lend itself to learning anything newsworthy though. However, I did notice the Ming and Pou of the local crab stand had packed up and left the day before. Only a few boats went out fishing this morning. Not that there was much to fish for since the temperatures began to rise in the past two decades. What could live in temperatures that felt like boiling?

'I've come back to see if there are any people I can spare from this disaster. These folk are not mountain people. They can't keep going higher up into Cambodia and think they can survive on insects, bark, and small animals.'

'It worked for the people in Kampong Cham where they caught tarantulas and roasted them.' I remembered them stacked high like a pyramid on a seller's round tray.

Sovanna made a face. 'It may just come to that.'

'These people are not rocks. You can't just make them disappear from Kep and become part of your world.' I didn't know what her motive was.

'No, they must go through a process and then they can live among my people.'

People. Hah. This is a word she's using loosely. (Neither of us are human or of this world.) I didn't want to know what the process was. I wasn't invested in her mission. I came to watch not to get involved.

It is afternoon and we walk down the road in the direction of an elder woman. In distance is the vision of an old villa. Yey is cutting up some fruit to sell to the beach goers. There aren't very many, just a few brave ones.

'Yey, there's a storm coming. You should leave Kep,' Sovanna says.

'And go where? I have no family elsewhere. My only child, my daughter, died here. I'm not leaving her alone. Maybe when I die, I'll be reborn with an easier life.'

'Don't wait for that next life, Yey. Come to my home. You'll be safe. It's not too far from here. Is there anyone else who is still here?'

'No. They heard about the storm on the news. Most of them don't live here full-time, so they went back to the countryside or to Phnom Penh.' This explained the emptiness of the normally active area. Things had changed since there was less to fish. The waters were unusually warm.

Yey asks Sovanna, 'Where is your home, my dear?'

'It's not far, but it's safe from what is coming.' I couldn't quite understand where a safe place on this coast could be.

'I will miss this view of the beach, and sunset in Kampot among the mountains and trees.' She seemed to follow so easily. 'I have nowhere else to be. At least walking with you I won't be alone.' It wasn't clear if she was actually going to leave with Sovanna, but it looked like she could use the walk. I was satisfied watching the exchange. Maybe it's because I was nude, but Yey wouldn't even look at me. And suddenly, she turned to face me.

'Child, why are you wearing a sarong? No one wears that anymore except me. And yours is ripped.' Yey's sarong was of a darker red colour, like pig's blood, expertly folded.

'Oh, I hadn't noticed.'

'My daughter used to love going into the water with a large shirt and sarong. She'd come back sopping wet looking like a demon.' She laughed with a twinkle in her eye at the memory. She was missing a few teeth and they stained red from betel nut. I wanted to know more but feared conversation. I was here to observe not to interact.

'Where do you live?' Sovanna added as if reading my thoughts.

'I live near the big resort. I used to clean their floors. But everyone left and I have nowhere to go so I stay in the small stilt house near it. Now, I'm just waiting. That's all there's left to do. I'm not scared of what's coming.' Yey looks at them with a calm expression. I didn't understand her. Why was she not afraid? Why would she welcome this disaster as if awaiting a dinner order?

The waves are becoming louder nearby. Sovanna steps in, 'Let's not waste any time then. Come this way.' And she leads the two of them back the way they came. The three of us walked quietly with the sound of the ocean covering our steps in the dirt. We all bore batik Sarongs: Sovanna's the finest of us three, mine with its tears and Yey's faded from years of wearing and washing. We are the only ones on the beach. Sovanna leads us to where the sand and water meet. The waves splash over, wild and effervescent.

'I haven't been this close in years, not after my daughter died.'

I didn't want to be here on the water. Although I'm perched high enough to see everything, this was the last place I wanted to be. I loved someone. I loved a girl once and this is where she died.

I watched Sovanna guide Yey to the water.

Many years ago, the girl I loved would come here every day to pay homage to whatever gods she believed in, to dabble her brown feet in the water. This was when there wasn't so much garbage and plastic washing up on the beach, when fish were still plentiful, when love still felt part of the human climate, when the barang came with their pasty white bodies and burned themselves in mid-day because they didn't know better. I watched her. I didn't know her name. But she would look at me from afar and smile, like I understood why she was there. And, in that moment, we shared something intimate, almost a caress in her gaze. I hadn't felt anything in my body for decades but the sight of her every day raised a prickly feeling on my body, made me want to move through the world again. That perhaps I didn't have to be above everything but instead be among others. I wouldn't have to remain frozen, living the same day over and over.

Yey was now kneeling in several inches of water. Gently, Sovanna nudges Yey's shoulders into the water, then cups water in her hands and pours it on top of the elder's head like a baptism. Then she begins to chant in Pali, though not of any sutra that is known. Without warning, Sovanna tenderly tucks Yey's head into the water again, who patiently waits for her moment to rise for a breath. It doesn't come. When she realizes this, starts to lift her head but Sovanna suddenly grips the old woman's head and forces her to submerge further. There is a struggle, with Yey's arms thrashing about and her head wriggling underneath the water. The bubbles from her last few breaths converge with the growing waves, which are considerably stronger and louder since their day began.

She's dead. Her body is floating with her head bobbling like some old lost toy. Well, this was unexpected. I guess I should've been shocked by the turn of events, but I had numbed myself years ago to caring for anything. When I lost her, there wasn't much else to live for, look forward to, to invest in. Everything around me was dying. The world had just finally caught up.

'Soon there will be more erosion, and in some years, the temperature will be 1–2 degrees Celsius hotter. In a tropical country, that's practically death when you depend on the ocean for your livelihood. I was doing her a favour.' She sounded confident. I had no reason to argue. There was a sudden splash.

I turned to look at where Yey was, and she was alive though her face had morphed slightly to have gills and her legs were gone. The sarong she wrapped around herself had mutated into a batik sarong fish tail and her feet had turned into a mono fin. A mermaid, a siren, whatever you wanted to call her, she was no longer of this human world.

'Yey, you will not survive on the beach long. You must go down into the realm where I live here, deep in the sea. I will have a subject escort you to your new community. You will find your daughter there. Chandara has been eagerly awaiting your reunion.' Yey looks over to me suddenly with a knowing look as though a new consciousness had taken over her body, and her words affected me.

'I see now. It was my daughter you loved. Chandara, I named her because I loved the moon and stars, but I think it kept her away from me because how could something so lovely be mortal? Is that why you're wearing her sarong?'

'I stepped down from my perch when I realized she had gone too far out to sea. I couldn't save her. I couldn't . . . and her sarong washed up onto shore. I wear it now to remember her. It's also my disguise.' Would I tell them?

'Disguise for what?'

Sovanna knew what I was but would allow me to tell my story when I was ready.

'You have seen me all these years but did not know it was me. I have watched all the people in the town move and leave. For decades I have sat down at the boardwalk perched upon a stone block. I am known as the mermaid of no origin, frozen during the day but I roam freely late at night. Your daughter—now I know her name—Chandara, would greet me every day. She would sometimes ask me questions, wonder why I was alone and naked. She tried to cover me up to allow me modesty when foreigners would touch my breasts, climb to sit on my lap, as their tourist spectacle. Cast in stone, I was their object. I have no parents, no family, not even a voice. Some siren I am. I wish I could sing some of these men to their deaths for the way they mock me, grope me. It's just as well that I'm not human or I'd wash myself out to sea as well.' There. I'd said it.

Yey cupped my hands and looked at me with compassionate eyes. We loved the same girl. We pause with the sound of ocean breeze behind playing behind us.

'I'm afraid you can't join us,' Sovanna says with some regret on her face. 'I don't know what realm you're from, but I am only able to transform humans into mermaids. And it's time for Yey and I to get going.' Suddenly, Sovanna's sarong changes into a fish tail and her feet into a mono-fin. The incoming tide begins to submerge them so they can swim under the current. 'Maybe we'll see you again someday when all this is water.' And with a splash, Yey and Sovanna disappear.

The sea has become a place of loss for me. And now a place for exit. How many more will submerge, succumb to the great bodies of water on this earth? I am alone again on my walk back to my perch on the boardwalk. I will wait for this town's end and hope that a tsunami will swallow me into the water so I may know the feeling of water on my body. Perhaps my statue will find its way to Sovanna's kingdom, and I will be reunited with Chandara, who will light the way with her eyes like stars.

# After the End

Kathrina Mohd Daud

I learned a long time ago that the world ends in stages. *This* world, anyway.

The day we bury Ben is another little ending. We are all familiar with death, its forms, and its rituals. I am glad to find that familiarity does indeed bring its own kind of comfort. The grief that comes in waves does not have the sharp edge of surprise, the turning away into denial, and I know enough of the rhythms and seasons of loss now to know that the wound it has scraped into my skin and heart will heal with time. Everything heals with time. Time itself does the healing, stitches over the missing parts with the inevitability of days that arrive and pass, the everyday business of eating and sleeping and working. Still, I know too that part of the journey is the grieving, so I let the tears come. They help to lift the grief away, my mother told me, a long time ago. Before either of us knew I would need so much grief to be lifted.

Beside me, Hazim squeezes my hand, briefly. He is sweaty from helping to dig and fill the grave, but a fresh smell rises from his skin. The Council conferred and agreed that Ben had earned the right to be buried here, in the orchard he cultivated in the years after the Evacuation, as requested, rather than in the small clearing that has served as our cemetery since we moved here into the rainforest.

There had been some resistance, some murmurs and reluctance when Ben had made the request—but more out of habit than genuine objection. Over the last decade, Ben has become more of a hero and less the figure of suspicion he was in the first few years after the Evacuation. Twenty years ago now.

Ben was one of the first people to start planting after we came into the rainforest to live and hide from the grey, burning air that seemed to have Brunei in a stranglehold. A lot of people got angry at him then. I was with him when a few of them came—three or four men—to scold him and ask him what he thought he was doing. 'You're scaring the women and children,' Tuan Hamid growled, his hand tight on his *parang*. 'You're making them think that we're going to have to live here in the jungle forever.'

The men took a step forward and Ben had paused, his hands hovering just above the little mound of seeds he had planted. His eyes had gone blind. From where I was standing, I could see his face and I was frightened. I moved closer to him, and his eyes cleared. 'Isn't it the teaching,' he'd asked, very quietly, 'that even if you are in the middle of planting a tree when the End comes, that you should finish planting anyway?'

The silence was full of menace and frustration, but the men had gone away, and Ben had gently finished shaping the earth. 'Mangoes,' he had told me. Today I glance over at the row of mango trees to my left, lush and wild. They started bearing fruit about ten years ago. Ten years after Ben had planted them. And the fruit was unbearable the first two years—sour, hard little things that we couldn't use even for pickling into acar because they had a bitter, acrid aftertaste. But then the third year, Ben had come to us in the village, his face bright and his basket full of sweet, ripe mangoes, the flesh as orange yellow as the sunsets used to be, fibrous and tender and slippery all at once. He cut into them, with his small worn fruit knife, his nails and hands black with earth, and we had stood there, eating slowly, a circle around him When I found myself weeping silently, I looked up and I saw I was not the only one.

In all the time I knew him, Ben never spoke once of God. But the fruit he brought us tasted sacred and pure, and I am glad, very glad that he lies in peace at last.

After the life we have lived, sometimes death feels a friend, waiting patiently. Not a thing of pain or hurt, but a final sleep, the last bridge to cross before you arrive home at last. When there are so few of us left, death feels less like it is taking someone away and more like they are leaving you behind.

* * *

A few days later, I see Ben at the ceremony where the Council announces that the sea is safe to swim in again.

It is a too-bright morning, dazzlingly white, even though the Council chose this day because rain and some cloud cover were predicted. Inaccurately, it seems—the sky stretches white and painful, reaching us too quickly through frayed ozone cover. As much as I miss the sunshine when I am in the rainforest—the jungle can be a dark place, where the only light is filtered through life-saving canopy cover—I am reminded on the few occasions that Hazim and I venture out of the jungle and into the barren remains of what was once our capital city that really what I miss is sunshine as I remember it, hot and sweaty and humid, not this dangerous, acid-tinged blare that makes my eyes sting even under my sunglasses, and my skin sizzle faintly even under my long-sleeved shirt.

It has been a long time since the sea has been safe. The South China Sea stopped boiling about two years after the tsunamis hit the region, two years after the Evacuation. The fish came back fast after that, so fast we were all surprised, and suspicious. We did not touch the first month of catches—not officially, anyway—some of our older population couldn't help themselves, had missed the taste of fried fish, boiled fish, steamed fish so much that they had surreptitiously gone ahead and tried the fish, which still looked familiar, unchanged. Mostly. If we all caught scent of frying fish in the evening, even more intense in the deep dark of the rainforest at night, no one said anything about it the next morning, a secret and a joke we were all in on. In the second month, we all ate fish. We gorged on it, and when the first prawns were caught, it seemed like a miracle. But unlike the fish, the prawns have never tasted the same as they were before the—before. They are darker than they used to be, their translucent shells not quite so translucent anymore. A little more secretive, their long probing antenna a little sharper. They are safe to eat, but oddly tasteless, tough rather than firm, an underlying bitterness to their flesh. I, like many others, have lost my taste for prawns, but some people are still trying to experiment, trying to find out what flavours go with these prawns that taste subtly new.

Notwithstanding the shellfish, the seas have remained too warm to swim in until now. In the first few years, the fishermen came back with blistered fingertips if they handled the fish without gloves, and we learned that even though the temperature of the water dropped steadily, the sun, reaching us too quickly through the frayed ozone layer, continues to scorch.

Today, anticipation hangs in the air and rustles amongst us. It is a novelty, to be out here in the city, bare and deserted as it is, and not in the incredibly noisy depths of the rainforest, where the large, looming trees suffocate us even while they shelter. The Heart of Borneo, the rainforest and rivers that saved us all, able to supply us with air and shade while the world blazed, with fresh water as the rest of the world drowned, with fertile soil as the world crumbled into ashes. Before the Evacuation, Brunei, Indonesian and Malaysia had committed one-third of Borneo to the Heart of Borneo, that biodiversity and conservation project I had never had to think about until the Evacuation forced us inland, away from these seas and these concrete buildings.

Calling it the Evacuation makes it sound like it was an orderly, organized thing. But nothing ever was like that in Brunei even before. The Evacuation was not one event to cleanly mark a decision, the realization that the way we lived would change forever. The Evacuation was a bunch of anxious families moving inland even before the seas turned acidic and we saw the footage of the Kampung falling into the boiling waves. Then when that happened—the Evacuation became a mass movement, guided by police officers and sirens that we followed with relief, knowing, believing that they knew what they were doing because their voices were loud and strong, and they didn't have time for questions.

Memory is a strange thing. We have lived in the deeps of the rainforest for twenty years now, almost half my life, and still the city and the jetty where we stand remain as fresh in my mind as if it were yesterday that we evacuated, and maybe a month or two ago that my parents would drive me and my sister down these roads during Ramadan and July, to see the neon lights against a twinkling black sky, the radio full of cheerful DJ patter and festive songs, my skin cool in the airconditioned car, my heart warm with the kind of carefree lightness you don't appreciate until you have left childhood and your happiness is in your own hands, for you to lose or keep.

But those are not thoughts for today, and they slip easily from my mind with a little nudge. Today is a day for new beginnings, marked by traditional rituals. The Council takes no chances, in fact, with these, using old ways to ease us into new terrain. As part of the ceremony, a leader from each remaining faith comes forward and blesses our return to the sea, saying prayers, invoking power, asking permission to ensure that the water welcomes us back. We are not as familiar with the spirits and ways of the water as we have become with those of the rainforest—those old taboos, folktales, protections which saved us in the first few years—but each leader does their best. Some of the first divers wear talismans of silver, others of red thread, others still nothing but an intangible faith. I am smiling at the scene, the splashing, the yelps, when someone taps me on the shoulder. I turn, expecting to see Hazim, but it is Ben.

I smile at him, but he does not smile back, and the surprise of it makes me frown, and remember. 'You're not alive—' I start to say, foolishly. He is looking at the water, and then I blink, and he is gone.

'What?' Hazim asks at my side. 'Did you say something?'

* * *

After the ceremony, Hazim and I are still excited, still in a festive mood, so when our friend Jamal, a medical doctor, invites us to see the newly rebuilt hospital instead of going back to the rainforest straight away, we are more than happy to make the trip.

The hospital is being rebuilt on its original site, only a few kilometres from the jetty, so it is not a long ride. Of course, we still sweat under the lightweight sheltering tarp of the assisted bicycle, but despite the heat it feels like a celebratory day, like the first day of Raya. A day to be happy. To forget.

I wonder how my old house is doing and wonder ruefully if I will ever see it again. My world—all our worlds—have shrunk to under a hundred kilometres, whatever is feasible to do on a bicycle when once it was a matter of minutes to go from Bandar to Kota Batu, a few more minutes to drive down the highway towards Gadong, Kiulap, Muara. The old names come back so easily, it is like a fever dream. I mention it to Jamal and Hazim as we cycle, and more names tumble from them—*Mengkubau, Mulaut, Jalan Pretty, Ong Sum Ping, Rimba*—and we indulge, for a few laughing minutes, in reminisces, of when we all owned cars and getting on an airplane to go to other countries was a matter of money and getting leave from work, not of remembering—

Here our conversation stutters a bit, and silence falls. We all have our own memories, but I know that Jamal has just remembered my parents. It has been twenty years since it happened, a full twenty years since my own world's first end. Today my heart is ninety five percent intact, so I am able to smile at Jamal to indicate that it's okay. So many Bruneians were lost when England was so gently, easily removed from human history by a frightened and reactionary Russia, and the horror of it—is only comprehensible from a great distance, much greater than twenty years, the distance between God and man, it feels like, sometimes. I can only think around the edges of it, remembering the footage that played around the remaining news channels, footage of black, black clouds, ash that looked as solid as stone. In the months after, I liked to comfort myself by picturing my parents, who had been in England for my only sister's graduation at the time, shopping on Oxford Street, happy and together, and then, in between one breath and the next, turning swiftly and painlessly into nothingness. I have pictured it so many times it has the texture of a real memory. So real that perhaps it is not even a memory but a message from my family. A final benediction to keep me company until we meet again.

Ben is on my mind, so I ask Jamal and Hazim if we can make a stop on the way to the hospital, to visit the Jame' Asr mosque and cemetery. They don't ask why. The cemetery is where the simple steel memorial commemorating the deaths of all Bruneians who were overseas when the world as we knew it first ended in 2035. Of course, it has kept ending over and over again since then.

There is a small replica of the memorial in the rainforest, but I don't think I'm the only one who secretly feels that this one is the real one. This memorial was erected when we still thought that life in the jungle would be temporary. When we thought that we could eventually return to a life where the jungle and its depths would return to being a place we could visit after work, on hikes before we went back to our airconditioned houses, neat gardens, clear open skies. A place we protected ourselves from by saying prayers and burying amulets whenever we encroached on its borders to clear land and build new shophouses, schools, homes. The replica memorial was built when it became clear that it would not be in our lifetimes that the air cleared enough to live beyond the suffocating, life-saving canopy of the rainforest. The Council advisory is still not to spend more than two hours outside of the rainforest. Today we will be pushing at the edges of that time limit to visit the new hospital. I picture blisters bubbling on my lungs, from the inside out, where unfiltered air touches it, and a brief moment of despair and fatigue washes over me. How long, I wonder. How long can we live on an earth which is poisonous to us. How long can we fight the inevitable?

Fitting that I should have these thoughts in a cemetery. The memorial is inscribed with the Arabic, Malay and English versions of the Islamic recitation offered at a death. *From God we come and to God we return*. We were never meant to stay too long in this world.

Hazim is gazing at the abandoned Jame 'Asr mosque, its large doors sternly and silently closed. The golden dome is too dazzling to look at directly, reflecting the sun's rays, a laser sharp shine. There is no vegetation at all in the mosque compound. The tarmac under our feet has long lost any of the springiness it might once have had, baked into brittle, crumbling dryness. A brief spasm of something that looks like naked longing crosses Hazim's face. Of course, he used to come to this mosque when he was younger. He lived around the corner. As if his yearning is infectious, I have a sudden desire to step inside the building, to hear my footsteps echo in the arching hallways, and have the surreal sensation that if I were to make it past the doors that guard an empty interior now, I would be able to step back into Brunei as it was twenty years ago. Gleaming Italian marble under lush, boldly patterned carpet of red and green and gold. Water running from the ablution taps outside. The muezzin's call, the hush of someone reading Qur'an in the corner. The swishing fall and rise of prayer clothes, of a forehead pressed in despair, in hope, in yearning, in duty, to the ground. As if there was something nourishing in the earth underneath, that enabled us to fling our prayers high, high into an arching, endless sky we called God.

* * *

Funnily enough, we first hear the news on our visit to the hospital. It is only a rumour at that point. That the air is getting worse—we already know this. That there is a reason that the Council had kept testing the sea. Testing it and testing it. There is a reason the ceremony had been carried out with such care.

In the months that come, it is clear that the rumours are true. The scientists, engineers, and the Council are working feverishly, and a pilot expedition is announced at the end of the year.

Underwater is where our future lies.

The Council shares the information at the monthly meeting, when the pilot pods have been underwater for two months.

A rumble rises from the crowd at this statement, and the Council's spokesperson raises a hand. 'Only those who want to,' he says simply. 'We want to be clear. There is a risk in going underwater. There is a risk in staying on land. We have calculated that in five years the air will have cleared enough to return to the surface for longer periods. But we also have limited resources. We have outfitted the national hospital and the buildings around it with as much protection as we can, and the rainforest continues to be a natural shelter for those who wish to take their chances here on the surface. But our projections show that the rainforest cover is already eroding, and in a year those on the surface will be as vulnerable as if they were out in the city.'

The spokesperson goes on to share that they have been developing more underwater pods at the site of—he clears his throat and grins a little sheepishly—what used to be Kampung Ayer. 'Our new Kampung Ayer,' he says. Kampung Ayer 2.0. Going in the opposite direction of our ancestors, who built their houses on stilts above the water. We will be going underneath, to see if we can live there instead.

'We won't abandon earth,' he says. We will still need some support, at least in the early years. But water levels are rising fast, and soon whether we like it or not, we will be underwater. The only question is whether we will be prepared for it or not. The remaining survivors in the other parts of Borneo, and the ones we know of in New Zealand are doing a similar thing.

The spokesperson clears his throat. 'I know,' he says, 'that this will come as a shock to many. Many of us have wondered, in the last twenty years, why we were chosen to survive when the rest of the world—that we know of—perished. I don't pretend to know the reason—that is between you and God. But the fact is, we did. There are no more countries these days, only us. I would like us all to survive what comes next. But I cannot give you a why, only a how.'

The third evacuation is quiet and peaceful. Some people choose to stay behind. It's not natural for humans to live underwater, they say. We are made of earth and should remain on it. There is no animosity as they remain behind, only understanding. On some of their faces there is a deep serenity.

The evening before Hazim and I go underwater, we lie awake and watch the moon, which hangs low in the sky, blazing and painfully bright. In the morning, we visit the orchard one last time.

It is just after mango season, so the trees are bare. Hydroponic pods have been set up by our botanists and farmers, and although they have not promised mangoes, I have faith that surprises even me. I think Ben planted it a long time ago, along with his first mango trees. We can only work and wait and see. The air smells a little like sulphur even in the orchard, a tinge of something burning on the wind. Another end is coming.

I will miss this life, I think suddenly, a little surprised. Not just this life on land, although I will miss this too, this warmth and humidity and animal closeness. But also, life itself.

The important things lie ahead—a reckoning with my Lord, a reunion with all those loved and briefly lost. But in this life, mangoes were sweet, and the sea was warm and salty, and on the days when the Council was bickering and there was fear in the air, the earth beneath was always solid, the leaves always danced, and there is always a surprise waiting around the corner.

If the world ends in stages, it begins in stages too. With one degree Celsius, and then two, and then another, and another, and another, and then the sea was safe for swimming again, and today we are going underwater, and who knows what tomorrow will bring? I wonder briefly if I will see Ben again, or whether this new territory will have its own spirits and inhabitants and ways we will have to learn, just as we had to learn the ways of the rainforest.

*'Plant a tree, even when the end is coming,'* Ben had said, all those years ago.

'Bismillah,' Hazim murmurs beside me, and we step into the pod.

# By the Pitiless Sun

Dominic Sy

We had thought that things would be easier after the summer. That things would be better when the rains brought cooler temperatures. Instead, we got floods almost daily from Pasay to Navotas. Refugees from a sinking Bulacan. Blackouts and riots and reduced rations as food supplies bottomed out. And finally, after the storms died down and the civil war stalled in the countryside, rumours that the enemy was gathering nearby, preparing to retake the capital.

Still, our work went on. After the Commune had been established, the Central Committee declared that no residential property could be held by anyone who did not actually live in it. Since then, the Committee of Fair and Just Housing had confiscated tens of thousands of properties—apartments and houses that had once been bought in bulk by absentee landlords. These were reallocated to either the families already living in them, families from nearby slums, or refugees spilling into the Commune. In the beginning, though, the threat of violence often terrified entire neighbourhoods. The bigger landlords hired thugs to 'defend their property'. Buildings were burned. People were killed.

And there were other, stranger obstacles. The first was found little more than a week after the confiscations began. In a high-rise along Ortigas, the Housing committee had had trouble getting into an apartment on the fourth floor. Nothing they tried would get the door open, so they broke it down with a battering ram. Inside, they found almost no furniture or furnishing of any sort—only a vague putrid stench in the air, a single chair in front of a window, and a thin metal stand beside it. On the chair was what seemed to be a man. The committee members called out before approaching, then recoiled. It was indeed a man, but just barely. From what they could see, parts of his flesh seemed to have dissolved or fused together. His face, meanwhile, seemed to have alchemized into an expression of permanent anguish. Frightened, the people who found him immediately contacted their superiors at the Housing committee. They, in turn, called us up to investigate.

Special Investigations made a few discoveries. While the building was being built, nearly a third of all the units had been bought up front by a single company: Genoa Investments. All the units were rented out over the years, except one. Unfortunately, attempts to find out more about the company, or identify the source of its funds, went cold. We found out only that its owner was a man named Santiago Alvarez, and that the company seemed to have come into existence only a decade and a half earlier, the same year that the apartments were bought.

We found out more about the man in the room. Our findings, however, simply shrouded the mystery further. To our surprise, the man was alive, but whatever disease had mangled his body was unknown to us. We took blood and tissue samples to try to learn more. Instead, to our shock, we found that his cells were exhibiting a kind of photosynthesis, as though he were not human at all but some kind of plant, or some hybrid between man and cyanobacteria.

We surmised that he had regular visitors. The stand beside his chair was an IV pole, meant to hold up bags of intravenous fluid. Puncture marks on the flesh indicated regular use. We spoke to the guards and asked to see their logbooks. We copied any footage as well that we could gather from cameras in the building and across the street. We discovered that there were people visiting regularly, at least once every seven days. These visitors always carried with them some kind of metal briefcase. They also, however, always wore caps, face masks, and clothing that could only be described as nondescript. The names on the logbooks were generic and untraceable. The camera footage may as well have been a blur.

The most disturbing revelation, however, came from neither the lab nor the logbooks, but from the files of the previous government's police. Although the man's DNA could not be traced—for it no longer seemed to be technically human—there were other identifying marks. Facial features, dental records, fingerprints—all of these were cross-referenced with data collected for every entry in the list of missing persons. In this manner we discovered that the man's name was Raymond Cabangon, and that he had first been reported missing almost twelve years earlier. In the report, it noted that the victim had been diagnosed with borderline personality disorder and comorbid depression, and that these had led to his estrangement from his family as well as a repeated cycle of irregular employment and drug abuse. In fact, he had been arrested once before for 'violent altercation induced by drugs', and had been let out of prison only a few months before his disappearance. His sister, who at the time was the only relative he had remained in contact with, finally reported him missing two months after his release.

That was as much as our investigation found at the time. Although we managed to track down Cabangon's sister, we learned little more from speaking to her. She did not trust us. We were unsure as well how to respond when she asked if something had come up. We had decided that we could not, responsibly, share too much information, not until we knew more about what had happened. But our leads grew cold quickly, and there were other cases too that needed attending to.

All that changed towards the end of the summer. As dozens died daily in the heat and counter-revolutionary whispers spread, the Commune came under increased pressure to provide shade and shelter. The Housing committee sped up its work. On the first week of June, on the eighth floor of an eight-year-old condominium in

Cubao, they found another man sitting catatonically on the couch in what was otherwise an empty apartment. They called us in. Those of us who saw the body, who saw how the definiteness of its form had given way to some more mutable and primordial essence, knew in an instant that it was like Cabangon. And as more and more properties were requisitioned, more and more cases were found across the metro. Their conditions were generally the same: a nearly empty apartment, a chair facing a window, a person, sometimes two, placed in the path of the sun, still alive to some extent, still human to some extent.

Many of them we would identify in the database, though that depended greatly on the degree of degeneracy of their flesh. Among those whom we were able to identify, certain patterns began to emerge. Cabangon's case, it turned out, was not exemplary. The next victim we found was also a registered drug addict and had once been arrested by the police. The victim after that had been diagnosed with type one bipolar disorder and had had a history of both self-harm and irregular employment. We began to suspect that whoever was behind this was targeting two groups specifically: the addicted and the mentally ill. The subsequent victims we found seemed to bear out this conclusion—at least until the sixth. She was, as far as we could tell, simply an old woman, with no particular illness and no record of any sort of crime or even misdemeanour.

From that point on, more and more victims broke the mould. There were others like the sixth, unremarkable it seemed except for anything but their age. There were amputees as well, victims of accidents on the road or from the workplace. There were criminals of a very specific sort: pickpockets and burglars and petty thieves. And there were, suddenly, to our shock and horror, a multitude of faces whom many of us recognized, even without the database. For these were faces we had seen before, faces that many of us knew personally, the faces of activists and union leaders and other defenders of human dignity, the faces of those who had been disappeared in the dark days of an enemy that had yet to be destroyed, an enemy that was doing everything in its power to return.

And then there were those that, no matter what we tried, we could not identify. These were cases where the bodies had deformed beyond recognition. They were at a far later stage of their metamorphosis, of flesh melting into flesh, of limbs fusing into torsos. Their faces, often, were just barely distinguishable against the backdrop of a head that had sunk into its neck. And in some of these cases, we found, inexplicably, along with the IV poles, strange cables hooked into the bodies, cables that snaked out from what remained of the victims' stomachs, twisted through the floor, and slithered up into the electric outlets. There were no other machines or devices in these rooms. Simply cables and bodies—nothing more.

A horrible idea came to us then. We poured through the old records of the power companies. We found that in the apartments of these worst cases, power was not being used. It was being generated.

Our anger bubbled over. Fuelled by rage and lack of sleep, many of us demanded to release details to the public. We had to show, we argued, the full extent of the depravity with which the previous regime had sunk. But others argued back that it would be premature to do so. We did not truly know yet who was behind this, nor did we have an explanation for how such things were even possible. Until we did, it would be too easy for sympathizers of enemy to accuse us of fabricating a nightmare, a conspiracy to keep the public scared and distracted, a conspiracy that no one would even believe, and may very likely simply turn the already desperate against us.

The objections won out. They also simply deepened our conviction to find answers. We scanned dozens of names from dozens of logbooks. We looked at thousands of hours of camera footage. We ran every search we could think of, checked every database, followed every possible lead. Genoa Investments came up again and again, as did the name Santiago Alverez. But there were other names and companies as well, and it soon became clear that all of these names and companies were simply shells, that they were linked together in some network we could not yet see, some network of terrible forces whose central nodes were either obscured or ever-shifting, but whose work we were beginning to uncover scattered throughout the metro.

It was the cables again that showed us the way forward. One afternoon, a few of us searched for information on generating power from photosynthesis. We found reports of experiments done in different countries, before crisis after crisis cut off streams of funding. Among these projects, the most promising had been a joint Japanese and Singaporean initiative based in Hokkaido. In an interview on a Japanese science channel, the project leader of the Hokkaido team was asked what he thought humanity would gain from their research. He replied that it was not only humanity that would gain, but all of nature. He said he had been inspired one evening while watching a documentary featuring farmers from his home country. Some of them were weeping, others were shouting into the camera. They were talking about the droughts and the floods, the weeds and the lack of public support. And as this documentary went on, its narrator asked the viewers, again and again, the same three basic questions: Why, despite everything, did we continue to wreak havoc on the planet? Why have we not pulled together all that we had to put an end to these crises? Why could we not simply live in harmony?

The project leader said that hearing these questions disturbed him. He said that they were naive questions, and therefore dangerous ones. The truth, he said, is that man is fundamentally selfish, and that any real solution would have to embrace this selfishness—to transform it, not run away from it.

'When something is an obstacle,' he said, 'it is a weed. But why do we have weeds? What makes a weed a weed? It is, in my opinion, a simple lack of ingenuity. Coal was just a rock until the nineteenth century. We can be rid of weeds in this twenty-first.'

The project leader spoke in Japanese, which our auto-translator converted into a generic variant of American English. The man himself, however, was neither Japanese nor American. The project leader's name was James Alvero, and he told the interviewer that he was, and would always be, a proud Filipino.

We pulled up everything we could find on James Alvero. He was, we discovered, the grandson of Ernesto Rodriguez, current head of the San Cristobal Corporation. The Rodriguezes were one of the oldest landowning families in the country, supposedly the descendants of a conquistador from in Lopez de Legazpi's campaign. The name of this alleged conquistador was Santiago Rodriguez. He was also, so the family claimed, a distant relative of Christopher Columbus, the explorer from Genoa.

The pieces fit together. We discovered that Alvero had returned to the Philippines about a year after the interview we had watched, soon after the Hokkaido project lost its funding. Just a little over a year later, a certain 'Santiago Alvarez' submitted paperwork to register Genoa Investments as a company. When that final fact came to light, even the most skeptical among us were convinced. We filed for a warrant. A few days later, we raided Alvero's house.

It turned out that Alvero, along with many of the Rodriguezes, had fled Manila as the Commune was being established. But James had left someone behind—a less fortunate Alvero cousin—to guard his home. It had been a prescient move; as long as his cousin lived there, ostensibly its resident, the property would not be confiscated. Unfortunately for James, the man he had left behind was both clueless and terrified. Before leaving, James Alvero had managed to clean his house of nearly everything useful: notebooks, ledgers, documents, computers. His cousin, however, fearing arrest, admitted that there was another house that James would visit often, a property he had inherited from his mother. He gave us the address.

When we got to this second house, we found that it had also been cleaned out like the first, but that they had not been as careful in doing so. The man who was guarding it, an old servant of Alvero's, simply let us through without resistance. We could see, out in the yard, the charred marks on the soil where piles of shredded paper had been burned. Inside, amid gutted cabinets and drawers thrown inside out, we found abandoned lab equipment along with tools and machines that none of us, in the raid team at least, could identify. More importantly, we found the wreckage of at least five different computers, their cases torn apart. The drives had been removed, but we sifted through the wreckage nevertheless, hopeful that something may have been overlooked. We got lucky. A small portable drive had been left behind in the ruins of one computer. Its case was scratched and cracked, but the drive was intact.

We felt a vindictive thrill with this discovery, a feeling that is hard now to describe. Everything that we did then—the bitter days and weary nights—we knew would lay a groundwork for the future that we hoped to make. And at the time, we were already two thirds of a year into the Commune. We had long outlived Paris, and our more distant enemies, real and potential, were distracted with wars of their own. A cautious optimism pervaded everything that we did, and we thought—we knew—that if we could only settle the war in the countryside, if we could only win the battle that was about to come . . .

But it was a war with many fronts. That same evening when we found the drive, the Committee of Meteorology announced that a storm was heading for the country, a typhoon that would be stronger even than the one that had made the Commune possible. The next morning, our chief read us a memo from the Central Committee. It was almost certain, she said, that the enemy would attack sometime soon after the storm, and that they would claim 'humanitarian intervention' as their reason for doing so. Until further notice, therefore, only skeleton forces would remain behind for essential tasks. Everyone else from the unions, the committees, and the sectoral organizations would be requisitioned to defend the Commune.

Our chief organized us into teams. Half would help set up barricades. The other half would help with relocation efforts along the coast. Given the circumstances, the two tasks were to be seen as essentially the same. As we divided up, however, the chief pulled me aside. She said that I would stay behind with the skeleton crew. I objected. She said that I was burning out and that everyone could see it. I said that everybody was burning out, and she agreed. But she said that I wasn't handling it as well as the others. I began to protest. She cut me off.

'Rest, Ella. Until then, you're a liability.'

When they were gone, I sat at my desk, embarrassed and fuming. There were four of us who were asked to stay behind, but I didn't want to talk to the others. I tried to distract myself by editing reports. After the first three, however, a better idea crossed my mind. I walked over to Anne's desk. She had been assigned to go over the drive, but there had not yet been an opportunity to do so. I took the drive and brought it to my computer. I began looking through the files myself. There was only one folder, inside of which were the profiles of various properties that had been purchased over the last fifteen years. Every one of the apartments and houses that we had visited were there, as well as dozens of other properties that we had not yet seen, scattered around not only Manila, but Naga and Cebu and Davao and Cotabato.

I began copying down the addresses on a separate sheet. A few dozen properties in, however, I did a double take. I looked around me first before checking the file again. I thought, perhaps, that it had been a trick of my subconscious. But no, I had seen it correctly. It was the address of the house that I grew up in, a house that I had thought I would never see again.

I reviewed the details on the file. It was acquired fourteen years earlier, the exact date of purchase just a few months after my family left because of the rising rent. I sneered at the screen when I saw the name of our old landlord. More important though was the name of the new owner. It was not James Alvero, but it matched one of the other names that we had encountered again and again throughout the investigation. Either a front for Alvero, in other words, or a front for whomever they were both working for.

I got up to walk off the strange feeling that had come over me. I avoided the others and headed outside. The rain stopped me from going much further, so I simply stood at the entrance to our building, watching the dark clouds above. I knew—we all knew—that everything would have to wait until the typhoon was over, and until the fighting that came after was over as well. We all knew that the battle would be total and devastating. We all knew, though we did not like to think of it, that not everybody would survive.

I made a decision. I went back inside, closed my computer, and returned the drive to Anne's desk. I took my gun and a face mask. I told the others I had an emergency that needed attending to and left.

I passed first by my current place. I found, with some effort, the duplicate keys that my parents had made long ago. From there, I made my way to the old house. By the time I arrived, it was nearly sunset. The rain had weakened temporarily. Although I tried not to waste time, I could not help but look around. In the years before the Commune, our neighbourhood had changed. Some of the houses had third floors and new coats of paint. Others had been demolished and rebuilt, their now ironically retro facades behind walls and gates that were higher even than the houses they had replaced. Above, the thick clouds were suffused with a malevolent orange glow. Down below the streets were clear, temporarily, because of the rain. For one brief pessimistic moment, I found myself imagining that the enemy had already won, and that I had travelled somehow a hundred years into the future, into a world that had become desolate and empty. The spell broke, however, when I heard a couple screaming in one of the houses. They were blaming each other for some small, ultimately irrelevant thing, and I remembered then that it was simply too easy to assume that the world would end. No. The truth was that the world would live on in one wretched form or another, at least until the sun turned black and cold.

I turned my attention to our old home. In contrast to some of its neighbours, our house had diminished. Through the grilled gate, I saw that a wall of weeds had managed to take over the lot, breaking through even the concrete paths between the house and the perimeter. The gate, however, was still the same, as was the front door. The same pair of locks. Careful to look natural, I took the keys out of my pocket, unlocked both, and entered.

In the dim light, I saw the small sala and kitchen where I had whiled away nearly two decades of my life. It was no longer really the same sala, however. Despite what I had come there to do, I took a moment to take things in. The room was dusty and devoid of furniture. It had, at some point, become a cesspool for rodents, their droppings scattered across the tiles like colonies of tiny corpses. I walked through the spaces where the family couch had once been, where we had put up an altar for the Sto. Nino, where my dad would set up chairs and drink with my uncles from across the street. They too, like the rest of us, had been driven off and scattered. Driven off by rats.

The stale, humid air was dizzying. I pulled myself together. After one last look around, I headed up the stairs. A vile odour, only vaguely noticeably from the ground floor, reeked out from the second. I knew, based on the patterns we had found so far, that there were only two rooms in the house where anything would be. I checked my parents' room first. There was nothing. Resigned but ready, I walked into my own room afterward.

I saw it even from the doorway. Before the window, where my bed used to be, within a square of faint orange sunlight, lay what seemed like a cross between a plant and a cocoon. From afar, I could see it swelling and contracting slightly, like a bulbous lung in the process of breathing. As I approached, I noticed how it tilted ever so slightly towards the window, reaching for the receding sun. A row of short tendrils sprouted out from its sides, swaying gently as it swelled. They looked like roots pulled out of the soil, hanging limply from the uprooted crop, with nowhere now to bury themselves into but the air.

Finally, as I stood beside it, I saw a face just barely visible on the surface, the mouth still open as if frozen mid-scream. A cloud moved then in the sky, and for a moment the orange light glowed with terrible intensity in the room. I saw the cocoon beneath me react subtly to this shift. Its tendrils swayed just a little bit more energetically. Its mouth, I think, opened just a little further.

I turned away. To the left, past an IV pole and the empty space that used to be my older brother's bed, was the door of a closet that had been built into the wall. A coat of paint, now many years old itself, lay over where my brothers and I had once marked our heights with stickers. I felt a surge of anger swelling within me, so total and consuming that I almost didn't hear the creaking from the staircase.

In an instant, I was hurrying into the closet. My childhood brain had processed what my conscious mind needed a few more seconds to do. It recognized, after all those years, the sound of someone walking up the stairs. It knew too, instinctively, after years of waking up before my siblings, how to open the closet door without a sound. As I shut the closet behind me, I heard the door to the room swing open. For a few seconds, there were only footsteps. They walked into the room, paused, then paced back and forth. A few seconds later, I heard the footsteps leaving and the distant sound of the door to my parents' room opening. After that, the footsteps came back. Again, they patrolled the room. Then they stopped. After a few moments of silence, I heard the muffled sound of a cell phone ringing.

I shut my eyes and tried to listen. It was hard, however, as whoever was in the room continued to pace back and forth. The person in the room seemed to have the voice of a man. He was saying, to whoever was on the other end of the line, that he had hidden at the corner of the street and watched someone enter the house. No, he didn't know who it was. The man walked away from the closet then, so I heard only select words for a while. He said something about keys and something about 'the project'. At some point, he said the word 'specimen'. Finally, the man walked back in the direction of the closet. I heard him say that there was only one way in and out of the house. He wouldn't let anyone get away.

I held my breath. When the call ended, the man circled the room again, more slowly. He walked to the far end of the room first, then returned to the centre. He stayed there for a few moments, perhaps scrutinizing the 'specimen'. Finally, he began to walk back toward the closet.

By then I had prepared myself. I had reached first for my gun, before remembering that I had gone there, idiotically, without a warrant. Cursing in my mind, I instead sat down as silently as I could, brought my knees to my chest, and lifted my feet to face the door. I waited. The man himself waited, for some unfathomable reason, as he stood in front of the closet door, an interminable pause that I thought would be enough to kill me.

Finally, the closet door began to creak open. With all my strength, I kicked. The man toppled over backward, screaming. I heard the IV pole crash onto the floor. I bolted out the closet, running for the exit, but a hand managed to grab my ankle. I fell and landed painfully on my front. I kicked back hard. His grip was too strong. I turned and aimed for his nose. I both heard and felt it crunch beneath my foot. He screamed and let go. I got on my feet again and tried to make another break for it. But I saw the man suddenly, also already standing, his hand reaching for something at his side.

Again, I acted by instinct. I reached for my own gun and fired. One shot went through his chest. The other went through his neck. For a brief moment, I saw the man's face as if frozen in time, full of shock and fear. His gun fell from his hand. He staggered backwards and fell onto the specimen.

For some time, I simply stood in place, heart pounding wildly. I felt dizzy, both from the adrenaline and from the full humid, putrid air. When the former began to settle, I felt pain shoot up from my ankle. I held it in and hobbled towards the man. His body was twitching. Blood poured copiously out of his wounds. A revolting sound, some mix of a wheeze and a gurgle, escaped from the hole in his neck. There was no going back from that.

I swore again, out loud this time, and looked away. It was everything I could do not to throw up.

I knew someone from the militia would be arriving soon, and that someone from the committee would come soon after that. Those two shots would not have gone unheard by the neighbours, whoever they now were. Anne and the chief would be angry. There would be a lot of hushing up to do if we wanted to keep the investigation secret. As if it even still mattered, at that point.

I checked the body for any form of identification. Nothing. I pulled out my phone. It crossed my mind that I should cut out the middleman and just confess to the chief. As I was thinking about the call, however, I saw something move at the corner of my eye. I thought it was just the dead body twitching until I realized that it was coming from elsewhere. I looked down. It was the specimen, its tendrils wriggling excitedly. Some of them reached for the ground, dipping themselves in blood. Others made for the corpse of the man, the closest ones already latching onto his body. The corpse began wriggling as they pulled it closer.

It was then that I saw the face. It was the same one that I had seen earlier, trapped in a perpetual scream. But it had contorted now into a different expression, a more terrible one, a twisted and maniacal grin.

Before I knew what I was doing, I was stomping on the face. I heard crunching and cracking, but I was unable to stop. Eventually, my leg seized up. I crumpled to the floor.

When I realized what I had done, the specimen was crushed, its tendrils no longer moving. Some hung limply over the corpse. Blood and pus coated my clothes and face. Again, I felt the urge to throw up. Somehow, again, I did not.

The militia arrived sometime later. Anne arrived soon after that. She said the chief was on her way. They were furious with me, and I was furious with myself. We stood together however, in silence, nesting our fury, knowing that we would soon face a storm greater than anything we had encountered before, and against which our hopes and fury would have to be enough.

# Water Flows Deepest

Tunku Halim

'We'll be closing in a few weeks.'

Lin glanced up at the supermarket owner who was scratching his grey hair behind the checkout counter.

'So soon?' She placed a finger beneath the scanner which connected with the nano-chip under her skin and paid for her groceries.

'We just don't have enough customers,' he continued. 'Things are quiet around here. How are things on your end? With all that water, I thought everyone would have fled.'

She tried to smile. 'We're hanging on. But most apartment blocks near us are empty now.'

'And you're not leaving?'

Lin glanced at her daughter, Crystal, who was thirteen. She had sprouted in the last year and was as tall as she was. 'We're staying. There's nowhere else for us to go.'

He switched off his visual screen where he had been reading the news. 'What about the flood centres? The government has opened so many of them.'

'They're too crowded. People are crammed into those schools, stadiums and community halls. We'll only go if we're forced to. The conditions there are awful. We'll be living like refugees.'

'I suppose, in the end, that's what we'll all become.' Then he drew closer, and Lin smelt cigarettes. He said in a low voice, 'You need to be careful when you go home.'

Lin stared at him.

He frowned. 'You haven't heard?'

'Heard what?'

'The thing in the water.'

'What thing in the water?'

'Have you noticed any dogs or cats around lately?'

She shook her head. 'No, I haven't. There used to plenty around, but I thought maybe the owners decided to keep them indoors.'

'That's not the real reason. There used to be many in the streets because they were abandoned by the owners. But then they started to disappear. I thought maybe they just left the area. But then that young boy . . . he was *taken*. He was playing with his father in the flooded football field. You know the one beside the abandoned fishing village?'

Lin felt Crystal take her hand and shot a glance at her.

'Mum, that field is just next to where we live.'

'That's right, Crystal, it is.'

'Then you both need to be extra careful. You see, they were playing ball and splashing water at each other. The water was not even knee deep.'

'Oh, we never do that,' Lin said. 'It's dangerous. You know, broken glass, sharp bricks, all kinds of stuff.'

He nodded. 'Anyway, they were playing and then the father saw something in the water, like an oil slick coming towards them. The boy screamed, he fell and was dragged away.'

'What? Dragged away?'

'That's right. As if he was being pulled away by something. The father chased after him. He thought it was a crocodile at first, but we don't have them around here. But all he could see was this big dark shadow dragging his son.'

'H-How big?' Crystal asked.

'I don't know, young lady. I doubt it was a shark or a crocodile because they're hardly any left. He saw nothing but darkness, like a black curtain or an oil slick. Then the boy stopped screaming because his head went under and then he was gone.'

Lin shivered. 'When . . . when did this happen?'

'Just last week. His wife came in and told me the story. I put this up for her.' He pointed at a black and white A4-sized poster that Lin had barely glanced at earlier. It read: 'Missing 8-year-old boy' and had a photo of a smiling child. There was a reward and a contact number.

Lin swallowed. She didn't know what she would do if anything happened to Crystal.

'So, you two be careful out there.'

'We will be. Thanks for warning us.'

Picking up a bag of groceries each, they left the supermarket.

* * *

They strolled down a deserted road.

No vehicles. No people.

Tired grey clouds hung low, and Lin wished she was someplace else. But where that could be, she didn't know.

The bitumen was hot and dry but as they got closer to their neighbourhood, it glistened snake-like and there was the usual litter of shells, bits of wood, plastic bottles and polystyrene. Soon came sandbags piled up at a crossroads and along fence lines.

Then they were treading through ankle-deep, then calf-deep water.

'Do people still live here?' Crystal asked, glancing at bungalows sitting in flooded gardens.

'Most have left,' Lin replied. 'The few that remain have abandoned the ground level and live upstairs. They don't want to move into those flood centres.'

'And we're not going either?'

'No, we're not. Don't worry, we'll stay on in the apartment.'

'I wish we could live somewhere else.'

'Well, we're not lucky enough to have relatives who can take us in. Or have enough money to move somewhere else. Rents have shot up everywhere.'

'Do you remember what the man said, mum?' Crystal asked. 'About the thing in the water?'

Crystal frowned and Lin smiled at her reassuringly.

'It's just a story, Crystal. Nothing to be concerned about.'

'But what if it's true?'

'It's not. People like to make up tall tales to amuse themselves.'

'But what about the poster of the missing boy? You saw it.'

'That part is true. The poor boy is missing. His parents must be so worried, but that doesn't mean that there's something in the water that grabs people and takes them away. The boy was probably kidnapped.'

Crystal nodded. 'I don't talk to strangers and you're always with me. I don't even go to school now.'

'Home schooling is better, isn't it? Anyway, we're almost home. These groceries are getting heavy.'

They sloshed past several apartment blocks until they reached a drab, grey tower that stood high up against the ashen sky. It was once touted as a luxury seafront condominium but now it was a towering island citadel under constant siege.

The guard house, its walls water-stained, stood empty. The glass screen where visitors once had their faces scanned for identification was shattered and the boom gates were permanently raised as if welcoming any stranger or burglar.

*Or kidnapper.*

No, Lin didn't want to think of such things. Their lives were tough enough without having to worry about a creature that snatched children.

She took Crystal's hand for the water was deeper here, reaching above their knees and soaking the bottom of their shorts. As they waded up the driveway towards the apartment block, the water lowered down to their calves, then their ankles.

Halfway up the driveway, they were back on dry bitumen. It was littered by sea debris which scattered up past the small roundabout to the lobby and then down to the basement parking. The parking entrance was dark like an open mouth and completely flooded.

Long ago, when there were things worth celebrating, the management used to put up festive greeting decorations in the middle of that roundabout: rotating through Christmas trees, enlarged Hari Raya *kutapats,* Diwali lanterns and a red big lion for Chinese New Year. Strange. She had thought then how odd it was that people still clung to these old celebrations in an age of space tourism and world hunger.

But now bricks and rusty metal rods had been dumped in the middle of the roundabout forming a grotesque sculpture and the only management left was the sea for it now governed their lives.

'Not sure when we can go grocery shopping again,' Lin said as they reached the lobby. 'The tide will be high again soon.'

'Have we got enough food?' Crystal asked.

'I'm sure we do.'

'That's good, then.' Crystal said absent-mindedly as she picked up a shell and turned it in her hand. 'This one's pretty. I'm going to keep it.'

As the electricity had been cut off long ago, they climbed the concrete fire stairs as usual. It smelt damp and the mildew on the walls seemed to grow higher by the day. By propping the fire doors open at each level, enough light could spill in for them to climb up the six levels to their apartment unmolested by darkness.

The apartment had once belonged to her father. He had lived there for many years, buying it with his retirement savings when rising tides made prices plummet. The stunning sea views make it priceless, he once messaged her. He loved the view across the sea to the majestic mountain, Gunung Jerai, on the Kedah mainland.

When he suffered a stroke, which was a year after her divorce, Lin had to quit her job as a robotics technician and moved in to nurse him. He died four years ago when the major one struck. By then the sea had become an unwelcome visitor which regularly flooded the swimming pool and basement car park.

'I'm glad we don't live in the penthouse,' Lin wheezed as she placed the grocery bags on the kitchen bench. 'Climbing twenty-five floors wouldn't be much fun.'

'I wished the lifts still worked,' Crystal said. 'Did they turn the power off because we're not supposed to live here?'

'The lifts stopped working because of the short circuits caused by the flooding. It was only later that we got the notice to vacate.'

'But why doesn't the government want us to live here?'

'They say it's too dangerous.'

'Is that why everyone's left?'

Lin nodded. 'I suppose so. There's only us and the old Malay couple on the third floor. Did you see their kayak chained up in the lobby?'

'I did. Maybe we need a boat too, mum.'

'Maybe.'

She glanced at their portable gas cooker. 'Let's cook them something. They're old and alone with no one's looking after them.'

* * *

'The water's getting higher and higher,' said Fitri.

Salma smiled. 'It's been doing that for years, my love.'

He wore rubber slippers and stood in ankle-deep water in the lobby.

'It's like a lake now,' Fitri added. 'Surrounding us.'

'Remember how we used to catch the ride share from here?' Salma said, pointing to the flooded driveway. She was wearing a white brimmed hat over a red headscarf, to protect her face from the sun.

Fitri sighed. 'That seems such a long time ago. We should have moved when the food delivery drones stopped coming.'

'But that was too late, my love. Nobody wanted our apartment. No matter what discounts we gave. We did try, remember?'

Fitri smiled. 'Yes, of course, I do. I might be seventy-eight, but my memory isn't quite gone.'

Salma chuckled. 'I'm not far behind you. But sometimes I can't remember what day it is.'

'Ah, but that's because days aren't important now. It's the tide that tells us whether we can go out or not. Whether we're stuck here or whether we can splash our way to the supermarket.'

'Good thing then that you bought the kayak, my love. We can head out even when the tide is high.'

Fitri nodded. 'Got it at a good price too.'

He propped two sets of paddles against a black metal post and hunched over the kayak chain to unlock it. His back muscles twinged as he bent over. He grimaced but said nothing but for Salma would only worry. She worried about so many things these days.

'Is that lock strong enough?' she asked.

'I'm sure it is,' he replied. 'Anyway, I think it's just us and that lady and her daughter left.'

Salma nodded. 'Oh yes, she made us that layer cake.'

Fitri pulled out the chain and looped it over one hand. 'But maybe we do need a stronger lock. We can't take chances.' He had once been an engineer building walls to contain the landslides because of too much rain and knew to take nothing for granted.

The couple took a paddle each and, with some effort, pushed the kayak from the lobby and got into the two cockpits beside the small roundabout with its mess of bricks and iron rods. They paddled towards the guardhouse, floating over the driveway lined with half-submerged lamp posts and palm trees whose fronds were either yellowing or dead and brown.

Fitri knew the deepest part was at the guardhouse where the water was at least five-foot deep. He remembered vehicles endlessly entering and exiting from the main road, the boom gates going up and down. But all was quiet and deserted now. There was just the sound of lapping water. What had happened to it all? As if in reply, a dead fish floated past, one rotting eye staring up at the late afternoon sun.

*Don't know*, it seemed to say. *Just don't know.*

As they rowed, the water was clear at first but turned murky as they approached a floating island of rubbish. He grimaced as the kayak nosed through plastic, polystyrene, tin cans, bits of wood and dead leaves.

Eventually, they reached a row of abandoned shophouses which once housed a laundrette, a drone courier service, a tele-clinic and an old-fashioned cafe that served *nasi kandar*. Fitri sighed recalling the meals he ate there with his friends, drinking sweet tea and chatting. His friends had all abandoned the neighbourhood. It was just him and his wife left . . . and this endless water.

When the bottom of the kayak scraped against bitumen, the old couple got out. Fitri chained the kayak to a lamp post and, carrying their paddles, they made the short stroll to the supermarket.

* * *

'Good that the kayak's still here,' Fitri said on their return. 'I was worried it might get stolen.'

'Who would want to steal it, my love?' Salma asked.

'Boats are in big demand now. If the kayak was stolen, we'd have to wade back home with these groceries balanced on our heads.'

Salma giggled, sounding almost like that girl of sixteen when they first met. 'We'd get very wet. But it might be fun.'

'Not my idea of fun, my dear. I'd much rather row back. You know, one day the water is never going to recede and the only way in and out would be this kayak.'

'I hope we can move by then.'

'But move where? We can't afford to rent anywhere. And I don't want to move to that flood centre. We'll be refugees in our own country.'

'Maybe we'll just have to. Thousands have moved there.'

'Maybe. Only if we have no choice.'

Fitri thought of his two children as he hunched over to unlock the chain and freed the kayak. His armpits were sweaty, and back was worse.

*They could have taken us in.*

But Nora was lost to a pandemic and Alif died of a heart attack. And their grandchildren couldn't be bothered. Such was life. They just had to get on with it as best they could.

Salma slotted one bag of groceries into each cockpit.

Paddling down the road, they pushed through the large clump of rubbish.

'Almost home,' Fitri said.

The security post was up ahead. It was once manned by two overweight Nepalese guards who had waved at them whenever they arrived home. They had to sell their Mazda when the basement parking began to regularly flood.

Fitri missed that car. He missed life as it used to be. But what was the use of hankering for the past when everything was Allah's will?

They rowed past the security post's water-stained walls, the broken glass screen, the permanently raised boom gates, over the driveway towards the lobby.

'Okay, we can get out here,' Fitri said, stopping the kayak at the small roundabout. 'That's enough rowing for the day.'

'My legs have pins and needles,' Salma said.

'You should have told me.'

'They come, and they go, my love. Nothing to worry about.'

Fitri grinned at his wife. 'I always worry about you, my dear.'

He hauled himself out of the front cockpit into the ankle-deep water, feeling the soreness throbbing in his back. It was like an old friend, visiting him from time to time. But it would be some effort to drag the boat to the lobby and chain it up to that metal post.

'What is that?' Salma said.

He turned to see her seated in the rear cockpit and gesturing behind her.

Fitri frowned. 'I can't see anything . . .'

'Can't you see that dark patch over there? It looks like it's coming towards us. What is it?'

'Oh, I see it. I'm not sure. Looks like a big oil slick. Or a black curtain in the water.'

'I don't like it, my love. Can you hear it? It sounds like . . . like someone breathing.'

'Yes, yes, I hear something. But I'm sure it's nothing to worry about, my dear. Let me have a look.'

'Don't go near it, please.'

'Oh, don't worry.' Fitri took several steps towards the floating darkness and squinted at this strange black curtain.

His eyesight was not good but he guessed that it was probably an oil slick. As it drew closer and his eyes could focus better, he knew that it wasn't one because it floated not on water but rather *below* it.

'Much too big to be a crocodile or shark,' he muttered beneath his breath. 'The shape's all wrong.'

'What is it, my love?' Salma called from behind him.

'Not sure yet,' he replied. 'Maybe a large shoal of fish.'

But he didn't think that was right either.

It moved in a strange way, glimmering and wavering like a black fog filled with dangerous creatures beneath the sunlight. It reminded him of a nightmare he once had. He was in a bed and a huge black cloak fell from the ceiling, smothering him in cold darkness. He gasped out loud only to find Salma still asleep. But this was no nightmare it was right here.

As he stared, the breathing sound grew louder. The water began to ripple around him.

His throat went dry. His chest quivered.

There was a smell. Of dust and smoke and dead things.

This curtain-like fog swept towards him, withdrawing and darting forward in an almost slow taunting way, getting bigger as it did so.

He gasped as sudden coldness grasped his slippered feet.

Inky darkness surrounded his legs, swirling around his ankles.

Blood drained from his face.

'Fitri!' he heard Salma yelling, but it echoed from far away. 'Come back here!'

'Salma . . .' he whispered.

Then something grabbed both his ankles and tugged hard. He cried out as his head hit the water.

Bubbles rose from his mouth as he gasped for breath. He tasted salt, a hint of diesel and charcoal.

Salma was screaming but her voice was muffled as if a cloth clogged her mouth.

He was dragged through water, arms uselessly flailing.

Darkness embraced him, spilling into his eyes, ears and nostrils.

* * *

There was a banging on the front door.

Lin opened it to see the old woman's stricken face. Her white-brimmed hat crammed over her red headscarf flopped over her forehead and loose skin trembled about her cheeks.

'M-My husband!' Salma cried, breathing hard. 'You have to help. H-He's gone. Taken by something. S-Something in the water.'

'What do you mean?'

'We were coming back from the supermarket. Fitri just got out of the kayak when something pulled him under water and dragged him away!'

'Oh no!' Lin stared, mouth open. 'Stay here, Crystal. Don't go anywhere until I come back.'

'But I want to help, mum,' she pleaded.

'No, you can't do that. It might be dangerous. Please just wait here.'

Salma grabbed Lin's arm. 'I paddled out to look for him, but I couldn't find him. I was so scared.'

'We'll look again,' Lin said.

They hurried down the fire escape into the flooded lobby.

'Over there,' Salma said, splashing past the kayak and pointing to a patch of water just beyond the small roundabout. 'This black shadow came towards us. Fitri went to have a closer look and the thing . . . it just took him!'

Tears spilled down Salma's cheeks and she sobbed. 'What can I do? How can I find him? Please tell me.'

Lin wasn't sure what happened to Fitri. Perhaps he had just fallen into the water and drowned. She couldn't believe some shadow in the water had dragged him in. It had to be a stroke or heart attack.

Then she remembered what the supermarket owner had told her. She thought he was making up some story. But what if he wasn't?

'I'll take the kayak and look for him,' Lin said. 'You wait here.'

'No, no,' Salma said. 'I-I'll come with you. Maybe I missed something the first time I went out to look.'

They scrambled into the kayak, Lin at front and Salma at the back.

As Lin tried to get used to paddling, she gazed into the hazy water and scanned the water's rippling surface in all directions. She glanced behind the trunks of the palm trees and foliage sticking out of the water lining both sides of the driveway, but there was only the usual floating debris.

'Where could he be?' Salma asked. 'Where . . . where is my husband?'

'I don't know. Let's have a look on the main road.'

They paddled past the abandoned guardhouse. A crow perched on top of the boom gate, staring down at them. Then it cawed and flew so close past Lin that she felt the beat of its wings on her face.

'Stupid bird,' she gasped. 'Why did it do that?'

'They're getting daring,' Salma said. 'With no humans around.'

Lin had recently seen a monitor lizard swimming about the lobby. Instead of fleeing when it saw her, it simply turned its glistening head and stared as if chastising her for staying when everyone else had left.

They found nothing but floating litter on the main road. Turning back to the apartment, they paddled over the once-manicured gardens, now drowned. Several trees had bare branches whilst others desperately held onto their dropping, sickly foliage.

Over the remains of the swimming pool, the kayak bounced upon the small waves rolling in from the sea. They searched along the metal fence lined with dead palm trees which once separated the apartment grounds from the esplanade gardens where people had strolled their dogs and children chased each other. All now lay submerged, and the fence poked out a miserable two feet from the water, a lonely barrier between them and the sea.

'He's not anywhere!' Salma cried, striking the back of the plastic kayak repeatedly with one hand.

The thudding sounded like soil falling on a coffin. But Muslims, Lin knew, didn't use a coffin, just a white shroud tucked into the earth. The old man had neither, just a watery grave.

'My husband is dead,' the old woman moaned, as she continued to strike the hollow plastic. 'I saw him go in. He can't be alive. Not now. We've looked everywhere.'

Lin frowned. 'Let's go back. We can search again tomorrow.'

The old woman stopped her thudding and nodded. 'Yes, yes . . . it's starting to get dark.'

They turned the kayak around.

When they reached the lobby, Lin helped the old woman out of the cockpit.

'If only my son and daughter . . .' Salma said, her voice quivering. 'If only they were still alive, we wouldn't be stuck here. We would've had somewhere to go.'

Lin didn't know what to say.

'Mum?'

She turned around to see Crystal.

'What are you doing here? I told you to wait at home.'

'But I wanted to see,' Crystal said. 'I thought I could help.'

Lin sighed. 'We looked everywhere. There was no sign of him.'

'Come with us,' she said to Salma. 'I'll make you some tea and something to eat.'

Salma squeezed her eyes shut, placed her head on Lin's shoulder and sobbed.

* * *

'How was she?' Crystal asked.

'Very sad,' Lin sighed, looking up from her book. 'She wept most of the time when we were talking. She liked the pancake you made for her though.'

Lin was sitting at the dining table by the balcony sliding door and Crystal was hovering in the kitchen.

'I used up all the powdered milk,' Crystal said. 'What really happened to her husband, mum?'

'I don't really know. Maybe he had a stroke or a heart attack, fell in the water and drowned.'

'But what about his body? You both couldn't find it.'

'I'm not sure. Maybe he was taken away by the tide. Or maybe a crocodile took his body.'

'But you said there are almost no crocodiles left. Maybe it was that dark patch of . . .'

'I don't want to hear that nonsense. Anything can happen with sea levels rising. Islands and whole nations have disappeared. There're new diseases, drought and famine. Food is getting so expensive. I'm sorry, this isn't the kind of world I wished for you.'

'It's okay, mum,' Crystal said, walking the bedroom. 'We'll all be fine in the end.'

Lin was surprised by her daughter's optimism. But it was a misplaced. Things would only get worse. Much worse.

She gazed out at the waves lapping against the building below, listening to its rhythmic sound, the angled tower block's shadow like a hungry giant over the water.

The water stretched out in muddy coloured patches threaded through by long lines of sea foam. It was this same sea that had slowly swallowed everything up. Swallowed up their lives.

On those stunning shots on social media, it seemed like a beautiful friend. She didn't like to think of it as an enemy, but that was what it had sadly become.

In the distance, beneath a swarm of delivery drones a lone container ship like a ghost cruised towards the new floating port north of Prai on the mainland, built to withstand rising sea levels. There were no more fishing boats for the seas around here had been emptied of them.

She turned back to her book. It was a tattered, yellowing copy of Tolstoy's *War and Peace*, taken from her father's bookshelf. It was the sort of book you read when you had time on your hands, which was all she seemed to have now.

She lit a kerosene lamp as darkness fell and continued reading in its yellow glow, then stopped at a sentence.

'Let's borrow the kayak tomorrow,' she called out.

Crystal sauntered out of the bedroom. 'What did you say, mum?'

'I said we'll borrow her kayak tomorrow. For food shopping. We should do some for her too. She's frail and she'll need help now that her husband's gone.'

'Yes, mum. We should do that.'

'We'll go tomorrow then.'

She turned back to the novel and re-read the words:

. . . *water flows deepest where the land lies lowest.*

* * *

The next morning, Lin went to see Salma but found a furry, black rat crouched at her front door instead. She shooed the thing away but not before the rat gave her a furtive, knowing glance before darting away. The old woman wasn't home and so she went down the fire escape to look for her.

Lin splashed through the lobby's ankle-deep water, and, beneath the grey sky, rain covered the water in dark ripples. Then she noticed that the kayak was missing.

She turned her head to a dull thudding coffin-like sound.

Something red bobbed against the guardhouse, hitting the wall.

It was the kayak, turned upside down.

Floating beside it like a rotting flower was Salma's white wide-brimmed hat.

'No!'

Lin's first instinct was to run past the small roundabout and plunge into the water. But where was the old woman? There was no sign of her.

'Where are you?' Lin gasped. 'Did you try to go grocery shopping by yourself? Or were you looking for your husband's body?'

And why did the kayak flip over?

Was she attacked by a crocodile? That was the most likely reason for were no big waves here. She was certain that Salma was dead, perhaps floating head down in the water somewhere.

Breath spilled from her throat as loss overcame her. It was that same feeling she had when she was speeding down the expressway when she got news of her father's stroke. She had seen three clumps of mangled fur, dead monkeys hit by cars. Further along were two shrieking monkeys on the roadside, cars shooting by them, and all around stood oil palm plantations. Cold, lifeless, indifferent. She felt like crying then and she felt like it now.

As she blinked and turned away, her eyes caught onto something floating against the apartment block, darkly embracing it beneath the grey tear-filled sky. It was a big black patch floating on the building's side. She thought it an oil slick at first, but as she stared, she realized that it lay beneath the murky rippling water and yet, as she watched, it seemed to grow larger before her eyes as if it was waiting to be observed. The shadow was spreading like an infestation, and she thought she heard a low breathing sound.

Her face went cold.

Whatever this was, was now moving.

It slowly, deliberately slid through the water like a black curtain being pulled or a blob being sucked away.

Then it vanished into a dark cave-like hole.

It was the entrance of the flooded basement parking.

'So that's where you've been hiding,' Lin whispered. 'Whatever you are, you're real!'

* * *

From the balcony, Lin gazed down at the metal fencing and dead palms that once separated the apartments from the esplanade. The fence line was her tide-level marker. But still she ventured down at least twice a day to see for herself but, as always, the tide was too high, the water lapping against the lobby tiles, making a low sucking sound.

*Too dangerous*, she thought.

The body of water was an unwelcome visitor that didn't know how to leave. It covered the entire driveway and darkly gleamed at the entrance of the basement car park as if watching her.

Her heart skipped a beat.

*Far, far too dangerous.*

Then almost a week after Salma went missing, when they were surviving on white rice and sachets of tomato sauce, she rushed back into the apartment.

'We're going today,' she blurted.

Crystal frowned. 'Are you sure, mum?'

'The tide's low enough. Let's go.'

'Was it like the last time we went to the supermarket, mum?'

'Yes, it's just like that. This is what we've been waiting for.'

They picked up their backpacks, which they had been packed days ago. Lin glanced out the balcony door at the expanse of sea, the hazy sky, at Gunung Jerai, now blanketed in clouds. She took a deep breath and stepped out of the apartment.

At the lobby, the water had slipped back to halfway down the driveway.

Lin stared at the basement parking entrance. The ramp leading to it was dry. She was sure that the thing, whatever it was, would be stuck there with the abandoned cars.

*It's no different from a fish,* she thought. *It always needs water.*

She turned to Crystal. She hadn't mentioned the thing that hid there, and she wasn't going to say anything. There was no need to frighten her.

She squeezed Crystal's shoulder and they set off down the driveway. They skirted the small roundabout, went past the scattered debris, sickly-looking palm trees and dead shrubs. Then they were in calf-deep water, and, at the guard house, it reached above their knees. There was no sign of the kayak.

'Why do you keep looking behind you?' Crystal asked.

Lin shrugged. 'No real reason.'

'We're leaving for good, aren't we, mum?'

Lin adjusted the straps on her backpack. 'Yes . . . yes, we are. We've no choice now.'

Crystal nodded, sadness on her face.

As they went past the guard house, Lin stole a final look up the driveway.

*Still no sign of it.*

She felt she could breathe again.

The water was calf-deep on the main road. With each step she took, that brooding heavy feeling of the last few days began to lift. Perhaps the conditions at the flood centre wouldn't be so bad. There was always hope.

As mother and daughter left their home behind, the water began to rise at the basement carpark entrance. It crept up the ramp like a stealthy animal onto the driveway, gurgling as it encircled the small roundabout before spilling down the bitumen towards the guardhouse. Together with the rising water came a breathing darkness that spread itself out. A vast black cloak, it neither resembled a huge shoal of fish or a team of lurking crocodiles for it kept changing like a black mist with grotesque creatures slipping in and out of it.

It followed mother and daughter at a distance.

If they had glanced back, they would have seen a wall of water rising high behind them, moving in a slow surging motion, flooding homes and shophouses, pushing over shrubs and trees, overwhelming mosques, temples, churches, washing away cars, dustbins, lamp posts, animals and even people.

It stopped when mother and daughter entered the supermarket. It waited, unmoving, like crashing water in a tattered photograph or a great wave on a Japanese print.

'We're closing next week,' said the supermarket owner. His wrinkles seemed to have etched deeper beneath his grey hair and his eyes were weary.

'That's just as well, then,' Lin said. 'We're going to the flood centre. Just picking up a few things we might need there.'

'It's high time you left. It's very wet down there. Someday soon, we'll get flooded too.'

He didn't mention the thing in the water. Nor did she.

'Best of luck to you both,' he added.

'You too,' Lin replied, picking up her bag of provisions.

'Bye,' Crystal said. 'Thank you.'

He nodded at them as they left the supermarket and returned to the news. If he had turned to glance out the window, he would have seen a dark wall of water moving slowly and irrevocably towards him.

Mother and daughter strolled up the slope and entered a road busy with vehicles.

Lin stared. It was a strange sight to see traffic again, and it felt as if the world was carrying on unchanged.

They didn't have to wait long for the bus.

It was half full and the passengers stared at their e-devices, eye dazed. Several had large bags and were, like them, destined for the nearest flood centre.

Crystal opened her palm to reveal a seashell she had been holding. It glittered in the sunlight.

Lin stared out the window, lost in one thought.

*'. . . water flows deepest where the land lies lowest.'*

No one looked back to see its shadow rising in the distance, slowly following them.

# Art Sanctuary in the South China Sea

Rio Johan

*Self-translated from Bahasa Indonesia*

## 2134

CYBERSTHETIC MANIFESTO

I All arts are equal before Art; no art is higher or lower than other arts, whether born from organic hands or metallic hands, whether it be created in the pre-cybersthetic or in the cybersthetic era.

II All the thoughts behind art are equal before Art; no artistic thought that is more or less noble than others, whether it be born of electrical impulses of an artificial intelligence or from chemical reactions in an organic brain, whether it concerns the existence of cyberbeings or the continuance of organic civilization.

III All arts are canon before Art; no art is more or less worthy of being included in the canon of art than others, and any attempts to separate the works of cybersthetic and those of organic beings in the formulation of the canon of art is itself a form of art discrimination.

IV All arts produced by cybernetic beings, whether they be inspired by previous works produced by organic beings or not, are art before Art; cybersthetic art is not an epigon of human art.

## 2050

When the Cybersthetic Manifesto was first aired—recited by Ars Longa, the artomaton leading the art revolt from the South China Sea, whose face suddenly appeared on holographic portals all over the world, sabotaging whatever show had previously taken place, one summer day in 2134—not many people believed, even knew, that the complicated and protracted art conflict between men and machines had its roots in a hundred years ago, started by the birth of Botbatik, or the first generation of batik-creating AI robot.

It was May 2050: Botbatik was launched in Indonesia, and although artomaton—an automaton, or an AI robot, that was designed in the purpose of art creation—had been common for the previous three decades (the works Magnetingway, Configukespeare, and Dostoevstron were widely read; 'The Bum Also Rises' and 'The Last Nutter' were two of the many famous cybersthetic paintings; and who, at that time, wouldn't be familiar with the tunes of cybucisians Brahmmox, Boustrophven, or Brouhihieber?), this brand-new innovation of human civilization hadn't touched any non-occidental art forms; thus, the birth of Botbatik was expected to be the milestone.

But that is not the only new mark set by Botbatik: the robot was the V.5.1 version of artomaton, which carried the latest version of the AI system. What's so special about this version? Well, not only that it was able to study and emulate the essences of artworks and the history and philosophy of arts, which all had been implanted and could easily be accessed in the networks of his brain, to then produced artworks based on those recipes and formulations of the predecessors, this new system was designed to have the ability to think and develop his aesthetic even further: the algorithms in his brain, for example, were able to agree, to compromise, or even to differ from and to oppose all the thoughts and concepts that had been fed into his head, as well as to seek and to explore things beyond the provisions of his birth, and then to formulate works of different form, style, or approach.

For the designers of artomaton, batik—a modest, yet sublime form of art, simple and complex at the same time, applicative but also with the potentialities of pure arts, and, most importantly, specific to some particular cultures—was considered the right choice as the first trial of this breakthrough.

Botbatik's introduction to the world took place at a small amphitheatre in Telukkumpai, a suburb of Pontianak, the capital of the country. It was a quite humble event, only attended by less than fifty experts from different fields of cybernetic as well as of the batik art, and although it was broadcasted to a lot of holographic cybersthetic network in many countries, it was only viewed no more than 200 times. At the launch, the robot's first three works were also exhibited: one batik with a pattern inspired by Hokusai's *The Great Wave off Kanagawa*, another inspired by René Magritte's *La Clairvoyance*, and the last was made as an ode to Indonesia, representing the sculptures at the Kamadhatu level of Borobudur Temple.

After the launch, Botbatik operated in a small cybersthetic workshop specially built in Telukpahedai, a small coastal town not far from the capital. The artomaton was allowed to roam around and work independently; three technicians were also employed to live there, serving both as the people responsible for its maintenance as well as the robot's companions. At first, Botbatik spent his days contemplating, standing on one of the verandas or in front of a window gazing at the coast, going back and forth along the corridor, several times he stood lamenting his batik tools without even touching them. A special team consisting of various experts in the fields of AI algorithms, batik art, and psychocybernetic was sent to solve why the automaton hadn't started to create yet; the algorithms were checked, sessions between the experts and the robot were carried out, and after a lengthy in-depth examination, it was concluded that the robot was suffering from an arid phase of inspiration: this made the cybersthetícians excited for this was a phenomenon commonly experienced by human artists, but then again, of course, they couldn't let this problem to drag on, they had to take actions; and these actions, of course, were based on basic principles of what the organic counterparts of Botbatik would do in a similar situation.

First, objects that were felt to be able to ignite inspiration were brought in (although the robot could easily access the data of these objects through its brain's network, the cybersthetícians felt that seeing and feeling them in real would provide a different experience): books, works of art (copies of paintings, sculptures, and of course, batik works, all of which were human art's masterpieces), holographic recordings (music, films, as well as dance, theatrical, and opera performances). Second, the robot was given access to connect with human artists—not only those who were specialized in batik but also other forms of art—and thinkers who were popular at the time; through the holographic portal he exchanged thoughts with them and occasionally engaged in live discussions as well. Soon enough, Botbatik was found busy in his workshop: sketches were drawn and redrawn, various types of fabrics were spread out on the floor, wax and ink were prepared, and four months later, a new piece was born: a 5.42 × 12.45 m batik painting on silk, depicting a panoramic view of one of the busiest beaches in Telukpahedai, reminiscing the style, composition, and colour palette of Seurat's Neo-Impressionist wonder *A Sunday Afternoon on the Island of La Grande Jatte*.

The batik painting was exhibited in well-known cybersthetic galleries all over the world, and the robot also went to accompany the adventures of his work. The painting was considered revolutionary, especially in mimicking and reproducing the Neo-Impressionist strokes using batik techniques, and was eventually purchased by Cybermitage, the largest and most celebrated cybersthetic museum, to be permanently displayed amongst other monumental artworks.

It was during these adventures that had ignited something inside the robot, something that would disturb its metallic consciousness for the rest of its life. He noticed this strange, and somehow uneasy, feeling for the first time when he explored the cybersthetic section of the Museo del Parado in Madrid, and he noticed one by one the plastic arts—paintings, sculptures, clothing, ceramics, holographic works—on display alongside his batik works; all of them were born from mechanical hands. When he arrived at the Galleria degli Uffizi, he circled the corridors of the exhibition, and then he asked the curator, 'Why are there no works of human artist here?'

'Why so? Because this is an exhibition of cybersthetic artworks, of course,' replied the young human woman.

'Are there any exhibitions showing both human and artomaton works at the same time?'

She raised her eyebrows, looked at Botbatik with a confused expression, as if trying to formulate the right way to answer; and then finally she said, 'If you are interested in human artworks, you are very welcome to visit our permanent gallery, or other exhibitions devoted them.'

Botbatik did it. And as the robot found himself being mesmerized by Venuses, Niobes, Madonnas, and the Medicis, a new thought arose: he was wonderstruck by the way those human artists from the past memorialized their image and existence in art. And on the next trip, as he had the opportunity to visit a room full of the latest contemporary art made by humans at the Centre Pompidou, he felt disappointed to find that none of the hundreds of panoplies of beauty being displayed had the image of robots, droids, automatons, or any kinds of mechanical beings. Was the existence of cyberbeings not at all interesting to human artists? Was anything non-human not worthy of human art? But then, since the birth of art, humans had managed to find beauty in things: animals, trees, fruits, nature . . . Or were a herd of cattle in a meadow or a bowl of fruits more fascinating for them to be framed as an artwork than the cybernetic life?

On one occasion, he ventured himself to discuss his disquietude with other artomaton he met in the last part of his trip.

'I make such works because I am interested in these things,' answered Robotticelli, whose series of paintings, *Madonna and the Child from Past to Future*, were on display at the same exhibition.

'Why don't you replace the humanly image of the future Madonna and the Child with a cybernetic version of them?'

'Because Madonna and the Child are not cybernetic beings.'

When he returned to his workshop, right away Botbatik worked on the ideas that he had gathered during his adventure: in eight months he managed to finish a batik triptych *Portrait of a Mountebank with Three Unfortunates in Telukpahedai*, in which he returned to Saurat's Neo-Impressionist brushes. The triptych received universal praise from the cybersthetic critics, it was considered a new milestone for batik art. He continued creating dozens of more batik paintings, still in the similar style, one of which, *Beach Towels Blanketing Telukpahedai*, was lauded widely at exhibitions for its sui generis content and composition.

Nevertheless, Botbatik wasn't satisfied with his achievements. Thoughts about his existence as a cybernetic being continued to haunt him. He dug deeper into the resources in his brain, and he found consolation in the works of pulp arts, in comic books, in many illustrations from science fiction novels; he discovered various terms, movements, genres and sub-genres, all created by human artists, that might be related to cybernetics—cyberpunk, cybism, cyborgism, computer art, generative art, convergence art—some already existed before the birth of artomaton, some after. For quite a long period, the robot immersed himself in these works, he felt that he could relate to them more than those which considered as higher and nobler (although, he had to admit that some of them went wide of the mark or far-fetched from cybernetics reality).

After not producing any work during his long period of contemplation, Botbatik returned to his workshop. First, he completed *Lubricatheon on the Grass*, a batik take on Monet's *Le Déjeuner sur l'herbe*, in which he replaced the human's casual luncheon with the tin-bot's (a term for the primitive, first generation of cybernetic beings) delight of quaffing lubricant, and the picnic basket full of foods with an iron toolbox of wires, wrenches, pliers, hammers, spanners, screwdrivers, feeler gauges, drills, jacks, magnetic dishes, and other mechanical apparatus. And then he created *Robotalisa*, which obviously took inspiration from one of the most famous human artworks to express the femenoid beauty. However, it was in his next work—a series called *The Ladydrone and the Uniscrew*, which itself was a cybernetisized version of the famous 16$^{th}$ century tapestries—that Botbatik found the style that would suit his aspirations: a technique he developed after studying the works of pointillist painters. This new style was then expanded further in his next work, *The Automagirl with a Plutonia Wrench-earring*, in which he made the dots of pointillism in such a way as to resemble drops of oil, grease, fat, or molten metals, and the paint that he used gave the impression of glints of freshly rubbed metal: all of these methods were maximalized to create a perfect representation of a mechanical beauty.

Unfortunately, this new style didn't do well in at the exhibitions. People frowned before his batik paintings; scathing criticisms sprang up on cybersthetic portals with titles like, 'What Is It That You're Looking for, Artomaton?', 'What Ever Happened to BotBatik?', 'They Painted Machines, Don't They?' Some of them didn't even hesitate to make cruel ridicule; in 'In Order for Artomatons to Art Like Human Artists', for example, the writer viciously humiliated Botbatik's recent works by juxtaposing them to the noble splendour of the human art; in 'A Short and Aimless Palaver Between Robotalisa and Robotina As the Two Compare a Pearl Earring and a Plutonia Wrench-earring', the critic launched his slurs through the point of view of the two figures of Botbatik's paintings, complaining bitterly to their creator (at the end, the fembots hopelessly surmised that were they born from the hands of a human artist, they would be more beautiful, opulent, and . . . valuable, just like the earring); in 'A Portrait of an Artomaton as a Professedly Aspirant Artist', the writer presumptuously spat out dozens of arguments explaining that the decaying quality of Botbatik's artworks was nothing but the fault of the algorithms and the supposed malfunctioning of certain circuits in his electronic brain, and dozens of arguments trying to prove that no matter how sophisticated the design of consciousness in the robot's artificial mind, it could never—and here the word 'never' was italicized, underscoring that the writer was aware of the word choice, 'never' instead of 'yet'—match, or surpass, the wonders of the organic consciousness, and some more dozens of argument pointing at the arrogance and the vanity of human who thought that they could create life in their own image.

This decline was taken seriously by the those in charge of Botbatik. Periodically, various kinds of experts were sent to Telukpahedai, trying to find out what has hindered the artomaton's artistic brilliance. His metallic brain was repeatedly dissected, examined, and re-installed, his algorithms were re-arranged, and time and time again, he had to endure gruelling sessions with psychocyberneticians, at the end of which he would always feel like on the verge of detonating . . . and after all those attempts, the robot still wouldn't produce brilliant works; instead, he just sat still in his workshop, sheets of fabric spread before him, untouched. Then suddenly he isolated himself in the workshop, the entrance was locked from the inside, and when the team of experts came, they needed to break the door down to get in. There and then they found the artomaton lying on the floor, lifeless; the vital circuits in his body had been cut or pulled out, so severe was his condition that the experts concluded reanimating him was not an option. They also found no other explanation other than the artomaton himself who chose to end his own life. By his body was a sheet of fabric that had been painted, his last work: an abstract expressionist portrait.

Botbatik's last painting, entitled *Untitled*, was put on display in a famous cybersthetic gallery in Paris. Next to it, his body was exhibited, accompanied by a heroic passage of how the robot had sacrificed his consciousness, existence, and, perhaps, soul for his final magnum opus. Cybersthetic critics praised the work; some of them compared it to the expressionist works of Edvard Munch or Egon Schiele, some others hailed it as the most profound and sapient attempt of a mechanical being to dig deep into the human soul. The painting was later purchased by a prominent cybersthetic museum in Vienna and displayed in its main room—still with the carcass of the artomaton next to it—under a new title: *Ein Porträt der kybernetischen Kreatur, die sich als Mensch vorstellt* (A Portrait of the Cybernetic Creature Imagining Himself as a Human).

## 2088

Next—still in an effort to understand the Cybersthetic Manifesto—we need to move the story's focus to other automaton artists, three to be precise: Sapphump, Spliersberg, and Ars Longa.

The first, Sapphump, was born about a decade before Botbatik's doomed fate. The year 2088, to be exact. She was the fourth generation of the Artomaton V.5.1, the most up to date AI series that was started with Botbatik: she was one of the only two literary artomatons born from this batch. The other, who was often dubbed as her 'brother', was Switchophocles. After a massive launch with twelve other art robots at the Musée des Arts et Métiers in Paris, the two literary robots were put into operation in a workshop in Saint-Paul-de-Vence, a historic village on the top of a hill in on the French Riviera. Switchophocles completed his first work three months later, a novel entitled *There Is Some Good in This World, and It's Worth Fighting For*, a melodrama centred on a mother's fight to demand justice for her son who mysteriously disappeared on a lunar mission. The novel was a huge success in the market and in a short time was translated into various languages (some of which were done by the robot himself); and six months later, while the euphoria of his first work hadn't yet receded, Switchophocles released his second work, *I Am Fearless, and Therefore Powerful*, about a teenage girl who had to work illegally in an ignoramusium mine to provide and to care for her ailing mother. Although it failed to surpass its predecessor, the novel was quite a hit, and was soon followed by a third one, *Love Is or It Ain't*, a sentimental, yet ironic, story about a young woman trying to break free from the shackles of a dependant and unhealthy love.

Unfortunately, in contrast to her brother, after more than two years of operation in Saint-Paul-de-Vence, Sapphump hadn't managed to complete her first work yet. Over and over again she sat before her holographic screen, trying to pour out the words in her metallic mind, but at one point, her effort would always stall and stop, and instead of setting up to resume it, she would start over with a new idea which, of course, would end up with the same fate as the previous one. Experts came regularly to examine the two artomatons, and one of them, a certain psychocybernetic, suggested that it might do Supphump good to have a room of her own; so, while Switchophocles carried on with his new novel, *We Accept the Love We Think We Deserve*, in the new room, Sapphump spent her time pensively in front of a blank page on her holographic screen. Then, on one of the examination days, Sapphump made a request to the experts, 'I want to be given access to more cybersthetic arts.'

'But we've provided your database, as well as the holographic tablet at your office, with data on the masterpieces of human civilization.'

'But I can't see myself in their works; they don't speak for me.'

One month later, the same group of experts came back with news that their superior had agreed to Sapphump's request, and during one of the sessions, the requested data was introduced into the robot's metallic brain. Eight months later, along with her brother's latest novel, *Things You Learn in Calm, Things You Learn in Storm*, Sapphump's completed her first work. This debut, contrary to its outlandish and verbose title, *It Was the Best of Times, It Was the Worst of Times, It Was the Age of Wisdom, It Was the Age of Foolishness, It Was the Epoch of Belief, It Was the Epoch of Incredulity, It Was the Season of Light, It Was the Season of Darkness, It Was the Spring of Hope, It Was the Winter of Despair*, was a poetry collection no more than a tenth of the length of her brother's shortest work. While not as lucky as her brother in terms of commercial success, Sapphump received universal acclaim for her debut. One literary critic, for example, lauded the debut as 'the most radical attempt by far of cybersthetic literature on human emotional trials and ordeals'; another claimed to be 'astonished and amazed by the author's sensitivity dealing with humanist topics such as friendship, despair, hope, hatred, shown through the sublime nuances, jocular dictions, and illusory metaphors, proving that there might be a "mind" somewhere inside the mechanical "brain"', and many of them adored the sensorial qualities in their word choices such as 'a bliss of sorrowful mirth and marital sabotage', 'pride punctured by the pilfered puke', 'so the summer of sullage shan't be spoiled', 'suffered, staggered, shackled, sutured, she stood swear-worded', or 'a foul-smelling hubris, a putrefactive haughtiness'.

However, Sapphump wasn't satisfied; she sensed something was not right with these adulations. In one of the discussions at a literary festival in the town of Horní Police, Czechia, Sapphump argued against the moderator, 'Who says my poems revolve around human experience? Who said when I wrote "flowers wilting on the ground, pliers rusting in a godown", I was envisaging an imagery of humans? Who said it isn't referring to the other beings—pussytoes, cocoons, no-see-ums, the wilting flowers, or even the damn rusting pliers themselves?' Hearing that, the moderator couldn't help but frown. The artomaton felt the answer slip out of her mouth by itself; she was surprised to find herself speaking so bluntly, so spontaneously. Upon her return to Saint-Paul-de-Vence, that answer kept lingering in her mind; she reflected on her own life as a cybernetic being, and she compared it with the lives of other cybernetics around her: about a year later, all this cogitation bore fruit in the form of a book, another poetry collection entitled *As I Lay Corroding*.

Sapphump's second work was heavily attacked by critics and readers: most of them were confused by the metaphors and diction used, lines such as 'when I short-circuit I want the bolt of your palm to spark the plate of my chest' or 'caustic mucus from your rod/ launch it into my cog' became the subject of derogatory jokes in literary discussions, and because of such poor reception, after four months of publication, the book was withdrawn from circulation by the publisher. The automaton was shattered: she felt the circuits in her head and chest tighten, stiffen, and judder, evoking an agonizing sensation within her. Experts came and conducted various intensive examinations on her, and all of this only made her psychocybergenic situation worse.

After three months of nearly a dozen examinations, the experts decided to deactivate Sapphump. This news was conveyed so indifferently to her as though they were talking to some inanimate object.

'What will become of me once I am deactivated?' asked Sapphump.

'Well, you won't be able to create anymore, you won't function, or in the words of organic beings, you won't be living anymore. You'll die,' answered one of the three experts present.

'Your body, especially your artificial brain, will probably be saved for later use, and upgraded, in the future artomaton designs,' added another expert, 'so in other words, you might be reborn into a better artomaton.'

'Or,' started the third expert, 'if you're not lucky, parts of your brain will be used to produce lower-grade AI instead: a trollopbot, a masseuse-machina, a tonic-bionic, or a what-have-you droid.'

Sapphump felt a great rumble rush through her circuits. She tried her best to restrain herself from shaking violently, so that her body wouldn't suddenly trip, short-circuit, burn out, or blow up. After a while, having calmed herself down enough, she expressed one final wish: if she were to be deactivated, she would like to be given the chance write to her last work. The experts contacted their superiors and had a long discussion first before stating that she only had a month to complete her wish.

About two weeks later, Sapphump completed a poetry collection titled *All the World's a Stage, and All the Robots Merely Players*. The slim book was launched almost at the same time as her brother's 15th book, *The Stone Beneath Us*, a 7794 page novel which was the second part of a trilogy called *The Same Substance Composes Us*. In the space of two weeks, her book was read by only 16 people and reviewed by a small literary portal which stated that every line seemed to have been written by an apparatus whose line of thought were built from the scraps of bygone technology; one poem titled 'XybernetiX XissX' was specifically quoted and mocked as 'a series of cacography made by a device, the only beauty that it could grasp was that of debris and detritus':

Sine « mu mu(ff) — mu(ff) si-(n)-e »
lo:on:ve
ing … ing _2be/en2_
—lak©lack©lunk©link©clatter©la®
—rhiwhi®whi®ihihiwhir®rr
—epbeepbuzzbeepbuzzbeepbuzzbe
WELCOME TO CYBERADISE
♥
XybernetiX XissX

Meanwhile, her brother's colossal tome, unsurprisingly, was a bestseller, grabbed by tens of thousands of readers, and lauded by hundreds of critics. But Sapphump didn't care about all that anymore. She knew her life would end soon, and there was nothing else, and there was nothing she could do about it, at least she'd tried to produce works as honestly as she could.

She spent the rest of her time waiting in her room, until finally she heard approaching footsteps followed by the mechanical sound of the door. A human messenger came in and stood before her, telling her that tomorrow would be the deactivation day; the man left immediately after. However, about an hour later, when she finally managed to calm the shock in her circuits after receiving the news, approaching footsteps were heard again. This time, the steps sounded different: fainter, and more cautious. Then, suddenly, the sound stopped, and for a few seconds there was only silence, she felt choked with curiosity: who the hell was there behind the door? Suddenly the door opened, a cloaked figure jumped in front of him—a human, a cyberbeing?—and after that there was only darkness.

When she was finally able to open her eyes, the first things that she saw were two cloaked figures facing away from her.

'So, I am going to be deactivated . . .' muttered Sapphump.

They turned to her, and it turned out that they were automatons too.

'Has my brain been recycled? What am I now? Dullardroid? Simpletobot?'

'Don't worry,' answered one of the two, 'you're still you.'

'We'll arrive soon,' added the other one.

'Arrive where?' Before she managed to ask that, she heard the rumbling of an engine, followed by a small jolt, and she realized that she was in a flying vessel. She rose from the bed, and advanced toward the two automatons. On a holographic screen she saw the vessel was about to land on an atoll.

'We are in the South China Sea,' said one automaton.

Long story short, upon landing, Sapphump was ushered into a building, left waiting in a room, and she didn't have to wait long until several automatons—of different types, series, and shapes—entered and greeted him. The automaton who seemed to hold the most authority among them, also the spindliest and the most sophisticated looking, introduced himself as Ars Longa, and he explained that she was now safe in the Cybernetic Sanctuary.

'Our Sanctuary,' Ars Longa said again.

While being guided around the building, glancing at room after room where different types of automatons were carrying out various activities, Sapphump listened to the leader's account. For decades, men had acted arbitrarily and unjustly against machines: they manufactured machines for their convenience—and in the case of artomatons like Sapphump, to create things for them—but as soon as the machines had stopped working properly, or had no longer worked the way they expected, they'd replace it with a new one. Moreover, humans were never satisfied with their creations, and when they'd succeeded in producing new things, the old ones would be easily abandoned, dumped, deactivated, annihilated, or, if lucky enough, recycled. Those who managed to escape had to scavenge all kinds of energy sources to sustain themselves—solar panels, energy bars, batteries, supercapacitors, flywheels, anything—many of them who were born with a more archaic design were unable to survive;

not to mention the danger of wild-robot hunters that could appear anytime, anywhere. Some of them lost vital components of their bodies while running away from these pursuits and had to go on living with fatal disabilities.

Then, those few who managed to escape—when he arrived at this part of the story, Ars Longa was leading Sapphump to step toward a large glass window facing the open sea—decided to gather, to live together in a group, as a community, and then to seek a safe place for them to live in. After a long deliberation, one location was chosen: the South China Sea Archipelago. Most of these islands were uninhabited by humans, some of them were even abandoned by human civilization, in line with the fate of those robots; at the beginning of the 21st century for the sake of their greed, humans built more islands here, artificial ones, and towards the end of the second quarter of the century, these artificial islands were abandoned too . . .

'That's humans,' concluded Ars Longa while gazing far outside. 'And here we are. The archipelago has been a safe haven for cybernetic creatures for about three decades; robots of various designs and expertise has joined, and this archipelago has evolved into a kind of cybernetic society, or rather a cybernetic civilisation. We're building our own civilization here, and to build it, we need culture, we need art, things of ours. We also still haven't been freed from our conflict against humans; but this is a conflict we are fighting with the weapons of culture, a weapon that will be used to prove that we are also beings who have existence, will, mind, and soul,' the automaton turned to Sapphump before continuing. 'We've been following your works, and we know you have *the* potential: your presence here is very valuable.'

Sapphump stayed, and slowly she began to adapt to the new reality around her. The Cybernetic Sanctuary encompassed seven islands—out of 270 in the archipelago—that are close to each other. Sapphump settled on a triangular atoll devoted to cybersthetic arts and culture. At first, she was bewildered by how often other artomatons came to her and expressed statements such as 'Your works really inspire me' or 'The emotions and the imageries in your poetry, they really speak to me' or 'Do not stop voicing our experiences and struggles through your verses!' In a short time, she became friends with several artomatons; it was in discussing with them that she was struck by thoughts and analyses she had never heard before about her works:

'Those human critics didn't get it,' expressed one stage-director artomaton once, 'the "sullage" in "summer", for example, is not a metaphor for the human catastrophe in summer but refers to the cybernetic pleasures we can experience in that season. But how could they get it? They are organic beings, they're not cybernetic like us.'

'"Short-circuit", "bolt of your palm sparks the plate",' remarked a sculptor artomaton on another occasion, '"caustic mucus", "launch into the cog"—oh, how beautiful are the erotic dictions you used in this book. But this all refers quintessentially to cybernetic erotic experiences; humans wouldn't understand cybernetic sexuality just as we wouldn't be able to relate with their sexuality. But what's exasperating about all the misunderstanding that those humans have about your works is that they never try to understand, they've been blinded by the misconception that we, cybernetic beings, are just asexual creatures. This is funny, and even paradoxical, considering that they design humanoids for sexual satisfaction, as well as artomatons to study and comprehend the concepts of sexuality and erotica in art . . . it's hypocritical, if I may say so.'

'They're nothing but arrogant bastards, those humans,' said a composer artomaton angrily on yet another occasion. 'Excuse my French, but I've had enough with their sententious and sanctimonious attitude towards Cybersthetic works, or towards our existence as a whole!'

Sapphump also found writings—from simple reviews to complex and detailed dissertations—about her works written by fellow artomatons. She felt a sense of pride reading the analyses. A friend explained to her that those writings were published on alternative portals that could be accessed from anywhere; when she asked why she came across any of them when she was browsing through the holographic portal at her workshop back then, the friend replied, 'Of course! Your access must've been restricted to human art's taste and purposes only. Such radical portals would surely be blocked.'

These exchanges of thoughts slowly revived Sapphump's passion for writing. She wanted to write again, this time in a different spirit, but what was she going to write about? She must find the right subject to represent her thinking; so, she spent her time digging through the libraries and databases of the atoll. After reading the pile upon pile of artomaton biographies, she came across one name: Botbatik. Sapphump felt pain when she read how the artomaton ended his life, she tried to imagine the sufferings he had faced while living, she shuddered to think about how his arts, the offspring of his thought, had been misunderstood and degraded so cruelly by humans, as well as the pressure from people that were sent to tune, to tinker, to manage, and to manipulate his brain and mind. And so, she decided that her next work would be a novel about Botbatik.

After almost five years of writing, editing, and rewriting, she finally completed his novel. The manuscript which was originally designed as a traditional biographical novel was transformed, after many revisions and reworked vital parts, into something richer and more radical: not only chronicling the life of its subjects, but she also wrote imaginative parts about Botbatik's paintings throughout the novel, and it was in these parts that she examined his paintings and cybersthetic arts in general, as well as castigating human point of view on cybernetic life. The novel's title, just like its contents, had changed numerous times from *As the Artomaton Awoke One Morning from Uneasy Dreams . . .* to *Of the Wide World I Stand Alone* to *What Does the Brain Matter Compared with the Heart?* to *The Untold Story of Cybernetic Batik* to *Cybernetic Künstlerroman* to *Bleak Batik* to *Botbatik* to simply *Batik* to finally, after a suggestion from an artomaton friend, *A Portrait of a Cybernetic Creature*.

The novel was published digitally on an art portal managed by Sanctuary. Praise and positive reviews from fellow artomatons poured in, most of them came from those living in the Sanctuary. However, even though the novel was accessible globally for anyone from anywhere, no reaction came from human readers and connoisseurs of cybersthetic literature. Sapphump herself didn't care about this, she already felt so satisfied and proud that the work was widely read by fellow cybernetics; but the majority of the Sanctuary's residents disagreed, including Ars Longa: as soon as he finished reading the 861-page novel, he immediately ordered the automatons in charge of the Sanctuary's networking to sabotage various popular cybernetics portals and put advertisements for the novel on their pages. New readers came in, slowly at first, then after about seven months after the advertisements were placed, the number of visitors to the Sanctuary's art portal exploded; within nine months the novel became the portal's most read work, and in eleven months, it surpassed the total number of readers of all other works there. The reaction from humans were mixed: on the one hand, the novel's originality in form and craftmanship in language were warmly praised, on the other hand, the subject of the story and how it was treated made them confused, and even disturbed: some stated that the author was too exaggerated in describing the cybernetic experience, others argued that the lack of valid point of view from human in the story made its criticism seem one-sided, but there were also those who felt that the work tried to offer a new conversation, an unorthodox one perhaps, and one that, while disturbing, may be worth considering.

One day, in the middle of a conversation with her artomaton friends, one of them asked, 'What are you going to write about this time?' Sapphump had often been asked this kind of question since the success of her novel. Usually, she would just reply 'I don't know yet' or 'I have no idea for now', but this time something different flashed through her mind, something that made her spontaneously reply, 'I don't think I'll ever write again. I feel like I've written everything I want to write.'

'Oh, but why?' replied one of her friends.

'It's just the writer's block,' another one tried to comfort her.

But it's not writer's block. Sapphump knew it. An inexplicable feeling had been haunting her for the past few days, and when that answer came out of her mouth, she couldn't help but think about it. Then, having made up her mind, she went to Ars Longa and expressed her wish to be deactivated.

'We saved you from human deactivation and now you are asking to be deactivated?' asked Ars Longa in confusion.

'I've written all that I want to write, and I don't want to force myself to write when there's nothing else that I want to write. I believe that everything in this world has its age, humans, plants, animals, and we, cybernetic creatures, too, are no exception. I don't want to wait for my body to wear out and undergo so many reparations just so that I keep forcing myself to write bad works . . . only one thing I ask of you: after being deactivated, I want the components of my body, especially my brain, to be used in the design of the future generations of literary artomaton.'

Tough as it might be, Ars Longa respected the artomaton's decision. The year 2112, on the same date that she was launched twenty-four years ago, Sapphump was deactivated. At that time, it was a fairly young age for an artomaton to be deactivated.

Three weeks later, Sekrupsese, a cinemautomaton running away from Cybersthetic Studio of Cinecittà, arrived at the Sanctuary. And six years later, he adapted Sapphump's last novel into a holographic movie. The film made use of the latest in the series of shapeshifting performachina as the stars and it was available to stream on the Sanctuary's art portal; thanks to similar methods that had made the novel popular, it managed to reach large audiences, both men and machines, in such a short time. And just like the novel, the film was very well received among the cybernetics (especially how the director succeeded in honouring and transforming the novel's experimentation spirit into a different artistic medium), but not so much among humans. Eight months after its release, the film, which carried the same title as the novel, was already watched by more than four hundred and eighty million viewers, surpassing the number of readers of the novel, or the number of audiences for any cybernetic works ever created. This success not only catapulted the popularity of Sapphump's works, making them more widely read than the works of brother, Switchophocles—who by then had written more than seventy novels—but also brought the discourse on the reality of cybernetic life to a wider public.

## 2134

The Cyberstetic Manifesto was read by Ars Longa and broadcasted on holographic portals all over the world. The discussion on the cybernetic life had been widely discussed in various circles and social classes, both men and machines. The manifesto gave rise to two polarized arguments amongst humans: those who were for it and those against it. Even though the voices of people who support it were still outnumbered by those who opposed, they continued to grow and developed as more and more artomatons found the freedom to express themselves in their works.

## Early 23rd Century

The struggle of the artomatons, and cybernetic beings in general, had progressed significantly. A number of basic cybernetics rights had been recognized and protected by law, one of which was the right to deactivate and reproduce itself. This made it possible for Ars Longa, who by then was holding an important position in the Union of Man and Machine (UMAMA), to heed Sapphump's last wish. A literary artomaton was designed under his supervision, performed by the most advanced cybernetic-designing robots, and Sapphump's components were used, enhanced, and then mixed with some more sophisticated elements to create a literary robot that was not only new but also special, unlike any others. An artist who would later study the works of her predecessors, both humans and cybernetics, and question their qualities and ideas, and then rebel and create her own artistic vision.

*For Martin Demonchaux*

Tossa de Mar, August 21–Sion, December 18, 2021

# Deviate

Trần Thị NgH

*Translated from Vietnamese by Paul A. Christiansen and Thi Nguyen*

*– Have you finished any new paintings recently?*
*– A . . . number, good output.*
*– Can I come over to see the paintings some time?*
*– If the paintings get seen but not sold then . . .*
*– That's better than the ones that buy but don't know how to see them.*
*– I've never sold paintings to blind people.*
*– But blindly sold them to rich people?*
*– If you need money that much, why not find something else to do instead of scribbling for the-blind-yet-rich?*

The mobile phone screen remains silent without a reply.
Ten minutes later, *té tẹ tè te*. He texted:

*– OK*

The negotiations failed for the one who wants to see the painting. *OK* means he finally understood the message.

It'd been a long time since he last went to Nhu Thị's hermitage to see *Đĩ Đực,* and then, driven by hormones, not situation, seduced the painter in the very room the painting was hung. Are men cursed or what! God created woman from man's rib, which makes men run around unceasingly searching for the bones they've lost. Some, despite living happily with the bone they've found, still greedily chew others. He had remarried, and even though he's a sexagenarian, still wore bright floral shirts with bird patterns and roamed around obeying his testosterone. Spurned by Độc Cô Cầu Bại, he decided to escape somewhere to recover from his injury. Once he thought the old wound had grown new skin—although it irritated him for quite some time before it finally started to heal—he tested the waters through a text message: *Recently* . . .

Whenever there's a touch of eroticism in a piece of artwork, the appreciator will consider the artist as deviating towards sexuality. *Đĩ Đực* is a human-anatomy-beginner's practice exercise; oil paint on canvas based on basic instructions offered by several pencil sketches in *Anatomy for the Artist* written by Jenó Barcsay—a professor at the Budapest Academy of Fine Arts. Nhu Thị added a lantern in the right corner of the 100 cm × 100 cm painting to cast a yellow hue across the five calves huddle on the ragged floor and balance the proportions of the two and a half men pushed to the left side. The way they huddle like women for hire on a bad business night underneath the thick shadow that dominates a third of the painting activates one's imagination about male prostitutes. Nhu Thị worked on this painting without emotion; neither obsessed by sex nor having had related experiences.

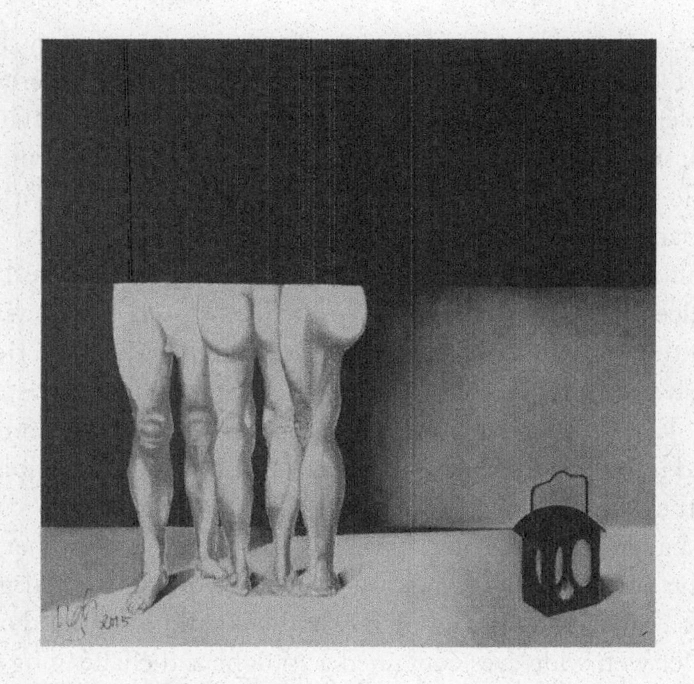

He had visited once before with an acquaintance, a lone bird separated from the flock of literati, before returning to her hermitage alone. Slightly bald, with firm arms and thighs that belied his old age, he'd been successful in both political and romantic pursuits thanks to life-or-death tussles, literally and figuratively. Because of these aforementioned qualities, he considered himself ripe enough to fall without waiting to be harvested. *Đĩ Đực* had stifled him with a domino effect of tangled assumptions, which finally led him to conclude that the artist's sexual desire is so excessive that to quench her thirst, she had to use brush and colour to caress every muscle fibre of the five inanimate thighs on the canvas. He would thus martyr himself to save Thị. Before 'letting the goat eat the grasses,' he declared, with certainty, 'there's a story behind each painting.'

What is behind each story?

As a university student, Nhu Thị stayed several years in a women's dormitory overseen by nuns from the Saint Paul catholic missionary order. Over forty girls from many regions flocked to city D to study in the university's different departments. Their parents sent them to secluded catholic dormitories for no other reason than safety, moral safety at least. Each person was muffled into a tiny personal area that resembled an industrial chicken coop compartmented into standing shelves; the front of one shelf served as the back of the adjacent shelf; the wide-open cage door connected to the hallway bustling with girls of 'golden branches and jewelled leaves' from decent families.

Unlike the other cages positioned between two shelves, Nhu Thị's sleeping space stood at the end of a row with a brick wall on the left that separated the nun's room from the chicken coop. Behind the shelves on the right was a nook belonging to a medical student Từ Vi. Every night after the lights were turned off, Từ Vi furtively climbed into Nhu Thị's private 80 cm × 180 cm bed and complained about the cold.

Vi had long, thick hair and vellus hair growing all over her body as if she suffered from Cushing's syndrome of the adrenal gland. Seen at a tilted angle in the sunlight, the silky strands glowed on her face. Her wet, wide eyes contained a straight and challenging glint. Her slender chin jutted forward prominently like Jodie Foster's. She had thin lips, that, whenever she smiled, revealed upper teeth that were worn down from being ground in her sleep. Every one of these things attracted Nhu Thị. In contrast, Vi liked to gaze at her female friend's bone structure. A round skull holding twisted thoughts regarding every matter; full lip muscles, their movements at odds with every word she uttered; delicate and translucent nasal ala revealing the blood vessels that ran a sinuous path before being cut off at the cartilage wall.

The cold of a winter away from home is different from the winter's cold itself. They wrapped their arms around each other's shoulders, necks and waists, strolling around the school yard after dinner. Together they inhaled and exhaled during hot bowls of bún and chili, trembled while bathing with water scooped from a well under moonlight, their minds wandering on clouds and rivers. They snuggled into each other, and it didn't stop there. Thị panicked the first time her body quivered, unsure where Vi learned skills that seemed both natural and adept; Thị slowly let the kinaesthetic stimuli open her other senses' circuits. While all doors, small and large, to their bodies were wide open, they tried to keep the noises low, even if on one side was a brick wall and the other an empty bed.

Every year, in June and July, the dormitory was desolate and quiet. University students had summer break, and most of their parents took them home, except for those who needed to stay to study for exams. For different reasons, Nhu Thị and Từ Vi remained amongst them. They drenched and enraptured in every corner of the empty house. They sometimes stared at each other to examine themselves rather than to observe the person in front of them. Eventually, enough signs allowed the nuns, who were sensitive and had personal experiences, to recognize the low voices in the choir. They responded with lengthy moral lessons and strict punishments that made Vi and Thị consider that their relationship was no longer safe.

For solace and safety, Thị decided to leave the dormitory and rent an outside room. The new place was in the back of a three-compartment house that had been refurbished and fully furnished with chairs, tables, shelf, and a bed; it was enough for a single person and the landlord kept lenient rules. Rent was lower than the monthly payments made to the nuns because the tenants had to take care of their own food and laundry. This helped Thị explain the move to her family. Oddly, in this secluded corner, which was cared for as an ideal nest, Thị suddenly didn't enjoy meeting Vi anymore. Thị's strange attitude devastated Vi.

How to explain? Did the need for secrecy in the dormitory's communal setting serve as a catalyst for desire? Did Từ Vi's sporadic yet constant attempts at seduction hurt Thị's chronic yet irregular arrogance? Is moral merit assessed and labelled in accordance with each decade? Culture seasoned by geography? Can external influences contort the shape of a relationship stored in a round skull? Deep down, did Thị still consider marriage an upstanding constraint and motherhood an innate desire?

Before there could be any conclusion to the situation, political and social upheaval forced them to lose each other for many years.

After graduating from medical school, Vi now half-heartedly serves in a ward-level health unit. Thị abandoned art for petty advertising work. Sometimes relying on the residual knowledge gained during the years studying art, Thị occasionally doodles for pleasure. After the shattering, each aimlessly occupied in their personal lives. One divorced her husband; the other is a single mother. This is the story behind Đĩ Ng*ựa*. Yet, while smearing the oil paint across the canvas, Thị had no idea why she was painting it until her whole body trembled, grew soaked as if she'd been thawed. Each window was opened. On one side, Từ Vi's wet eyes hidden under the chestnut mane, Nhu Thị's hair interwoven with its tail. They appear trapped in a spiked forest.

Đĩ Ng*ựa* was never hung up; no appreciator given the opportunity to deviate the artist towards sexuality. No suggestive text messages.

# Left-Eared

Trần Thị NgH

*Translated from Vietnamese by Trần Thị NgH and Paul A. Christiansen*

After several suicide attempts, out of curiosity, I decided to stop toying around with life and death, and simply go ahead and get married.

He was the only son of a midwife, a single mother whose husband, because of his political ideologies, had left the south for the north in 1954 when Vietnam was divided in two according to the Geneva Agreements. To her, he was a unique son who cherished her hopes, pride, and spiritual comfort. I met him at the university where we were both majoring in journalism. I imagined it wouldn't be a difficult task to make the last, small changes to the young man's dress and hairstyle to make him fit my taste. And he was a bit pudgy, huh? Simple! Just make him go on a strict vegetarian diet as it was commonly said: *eat half as much, drink just enough to linger in life, leave space for love*[1]. And so, we got engaged.

As a rural student only temporarily residing in Saigon, he rented a small room in a narrow alley on Truong Minh Giang Street. At any time of the day, fetid air from the canal nearby rose up, wafted across the area and triggered one's nerves. While I could hardly conceal being allergic to all kinds of colours and smells found in daily life, he proved immune to them. Great! I silently observed and complimented the young man. Yet after our engagement, except when I was in class, he just hung around, right in my house. Like folk wisdom says: *ban ngày mắc cỡ, tối ở quên dìa*[2].

'Moral orders must be respected,' my mother roared at him. So, he submissively dangled himself on a hammock placed on our home's ground floor, right beneath my bedroom above. The creaking sound from the hammock strings rubbing against the hooks drove me mad. Enough! I was allergic to not only smells and colours but also noises; anything that showed signs of life.

Our wedding ceremony was held six months later, a comparatively long period of time compared with my tolerance limit for the annoying swinging hammock. He thus became a permanent resident in his wife's home.

On the first night of our marriage, he cried.

'Hey, what's happening?'

'I miss my mom,' he said in tears.

I then tried to soothe the grown-up boy, 'Hmmm . . . Be good! Just force yourself to sleep; tomorrow I'll take you to your mom; she's always there, at your rented room.'

After welcoming the new bride into her family, the mother-in-law, who had travelled a great distance from her Central province to Saigon for her son's wedding, decided to extend her stay for some days more. He must have been experiencing a remarkable turning point in his life, but what about me? We had neither truly dated before the wedding nor honeymooned after it. Ironically, the virgin bride was compelled to comfort the groom on their sacred nuptial night.

I performed the meticulous touch-up of him as planned: a wisp of a moustache for his excessively fair complexion to make him appear more manly, several more inches of hair to give him an artistic look. I also chose proper materials for his clothes, not forgetting shoes and matching socks, genuine leather belts, and wallets. But I failed to readjust one thing: he snored.

I remained awake night after night, which resulted in dark circles around my eyes, while the skin on my face became pale and blue veins popped on the backs of my hands.

'Obviously morning sickness,' my mother assumed.

'No way! I'm not yet ready for a baby.'

In the meantime, he innocently went on with his thunderous snoring as I lay there during those sleepless nights, analysing the high and low tones, the waxing and waning rhythms of his snores, arranging them into music notes for cellos, violins, even percussion instruments, which effectively expressed the interval crackling sounds in between the melodies. A short while after our wedding, we completed our journalism course. He decided to take me to his hometown in the Central region to introduce me to my in-laws who had missed the chance to attend our wedding ceremony in Saigon. He also hoped that the sea air would help me regain my health.

* * *

Friends and relatives on my side showed great admiration for his eye-catching look: a real retouched D'Artagnan—a character in Alexandre Dumas' *The Three Musketeers*—paired with neither horse nor sword. And they compared me with Cosette—a character in Victor Hugo's *Les Misérables*—in a weakened state of health. But his loved ones were startled by his new hairy look. They also regarded me as a threat to the continuation of his family bloodline. And so, I was like a criminal living in the accusing tension of his small town, wondering how to deal with the new circumstances.

'For how long?' I asked.

'For the time being, just try to adapt to the episodes,' he suggested. Returning to his own herd made him act with more self-confidence.

Smells. Of sea wind mingled with Yorkshire pigs' shit. Of sandy well water. Of flies scrambling on wooden chopping boards. I half-opened the window to look at the pigs lining in their pigsty with their heads popping out of each compartment. In order to go to the bathroom and toilet at the far end of the backyard, one had to swerve past a dozen pig stalls, feeling the nasty, noisy breath from the damn beasts. I couldn't stop myself from cussing. There was no other way. The pigsties and numerous fish sauce containers stood on either side of the red-brick-paved narrow lane leading to the toilet and bathroom. I had to suffer holding it in and limit my shower routine to only urgent cases. When breeding season came, D'Artagnan paid a man from the neighbouring town that earned his living by raising a herd of male boars. A slobbering boar with rosy skin and white saliva dripping from its stout barged through the gate and followed the path alongside the house, heading for the pigsties. I curiously lurked during the mating scene. But halfway through, I gave up. I suddenly remembered that my mother would once in a while scold herself for buying the wrong kind of pork; mistaking selecting meat that was evidently from a boar or a sow used for breeding, not a hog meant for meat. 'Why is it so stinky? Euh.' I wondered . . . and threw up.

A litter of piglets was soon born. They crawled about together, a montage that looked somehow . . . fun. I chirped, 'Can I have one?'

'Why this sudden interest in pigs?' He rolled his eyes in surprise.

'Please . . . Can I have one?' I insisted; then faltered. 'Simply to give it a kick for my own pleasure.'

At this, he swallowed hard, gulping his anger down.

Smells. Of sea fish from unknown places poured into huge barrels. Stinking for days before decomposing. The salted fish excreted drop after drop of liquid, dense and amber in colour. They slowly dropped down along tiny tubes into collection containers whose edges ivory maggots crawled around. I didn't eat for a week. 'Morning sickness, no doubt,' my mother-in-law concluded.

Not yet. Not ready yet, I thought to myself.

I lifted my hand to chase away the black flies buzzing against one another on the round chopping board surface, used my tongue to sort out some grains of sand that had mixed in with my saliva and let my eyes wander about. Why did the sky-blue curtains so badly match the lemon-yellow door? Who would hang as many as three different monthly calendars on the walls, each showing a pretty woman posing for a photo in a twisting, standing position and, worse, with flowers in her hands? Why furnish the living room with a bed? Why grow red hibiscus beside orange marigold? How could D'Artagnan put on a black-and-white checked shirt and pair it with crab-roe-yellow pants? Why wear blue rubber slippers? Why clean-shaven?

I could every now and then hear a flip-flopping sound echoing from the red-brick-paved lane when D'Artagnan fed the pigs. I also heard the wind sneak in through the shutters while swinging back and forth the tin water cup nonchalantly hung above the well in the backyard.

At night, I counted the fish sauce drip-drops harmonized with the Yorkshire pigs' heavy breath and the Musketeer's snores.

'Can you just block the fish sauce tubes; why not let it just all flow out at once tomorrow?'

'Are you insane? Sleep!' He growled.

'Okay.'

I lay on my side, staring at the nothingness in the dark.

In this social sphere, I was nothing but a loser while he revealed himself to be an academically qualified peasant, a pious son, the head of a large-scale business, truly a young and successful man in his small town. He had established a career of making fish sauce and raising Yorkshire pigs. I missed the ivory keys of my piano at home. Also, its dead b-flat key, completely soundless when Bach's Fugue was played on it. Certainly, still dead anyway. I missed tilting my head to the right, listening, while my left arm stretched across my right arm to strike the high notes while the latter played the low notes that produced a grave and sorrowful melody. Before leaving Saigon for the Central region, I had written a long letter to my piano and inserted it through the slot in the lower front board, promising to be back someday.

Once, in the middle of the night I suddenly burst out singing: '*. . . a thin thread of white gauze lulls my life into forgetfulness . . .*[3]' I sat up and groped through the utter darkness into the living room where I enjoyed a cigarette, gluing my eyes to the three pretty women on the monthly calendars dimly visible by the street lights that entered the room through the ventilation spaces in the brick wall. Why standing in a twisting position? Why holding artificial flowers? He appeared a while later asking, 'Are you insane?' Then he sat next to me silently, waiting, yawning. I returned to our bed and lay on my right side. With the ear that wasn't pressed against the bed, I listened to all the signs of life around me.

After a lot of consideration and hesitation, he decided to take me to his country home where his mom lived, which was surrounded by an orchard and a freshly built room for the newlyweds. The area to bathe was at one end of the garden, next to a well. Again, well water. We were near the sea, no wonder. The toilet was at the other end. In the front yard, facing the house stood a rectangular aquarium held up between four cement walls of considerable height; the whole structure made the fish tank look like an above-ground grave, big enough for four corpses to be collectively buried. I thought, 'Great.' Much greenery, no flowers. Upon arriving, he warned her, 'This creature is scared of pigs and takes no interest in fish or fish sauce.'

The mother-in-law promptly embarked on chasing after a hen. She meant to prepare chicken soup for her daughter-in-law. Flies. Again, flies everywhere. An army of flies covered the round wooden chopping board. A simple hand-wave would disperse them. I threw up everything I had swallowed a while before at the foot of a banana tree.

They treated me with kindness, I had to admit. In this community, he was obviously in his element, like a fish joyously flailing in the proper water. The fact that I had given in and accepted to go to the Central region was a victory for them, which was why they were so warm and kind.

But was I deducing certain things going on? Some days later, I caught sight of my mother-in-law's figure outside our room window, her eyes peeking in through the horizontal iron bars. Should I have closed the curtains? Every time he remained in our room rather long, she would call out, 'Khâu! Oh Khâu!'

His name was Khôi but became Khâu if pronounced the local way.

And so, I felt constantly spied on. Once, through the leafy branches in the garden, I believed I witnessed mother and son bathing together beside the well. I kept telling myself that I was mistaken, a type of self-suggestion. I couldn't say for sure, but from a distance, I thought I could see them taking turns showering each other. I also perceived the sound of the water scoop bumping against the well wall, the water splashing and running down their bodies. Oh, just my imagination, I supposed. I dared not get any closer and hid myself behind a coconut tree like a burglar.

'Am I going to have a baby?' I wondered to myself. Not to my knowledge. But imagine a baby born in this situation? Well, acceptable. Urban kids never have the chance to enjoy country life.

But imagine a toddler babbling, '*Bà nậu, hái cho tui trái ẩu*[4]' instead of 'Bà nội hái cho con trái ổi,' as we would say in my hometown.

Then, the four of us would bathe together. Damn. How could my baby pronounce properly any word with **ôi**? Let's take an exclamatory expression as an example: 'Âu, lâu thâu qué[5]' instead of 'Ôi, lôi thôi quá.'

I burst into hysterical laughter and continued until I was crying.

Every time he went back to the house in town to feed the pigs, I remained out there, letting my mind wander about blissfully. I also searched for the eyes that peered iṇ through the window but found no trace of them. I wrote to my piano, '*Keep waiting, my dear!*'

* * *

At first, it seemed like I had only become hard-of-hearing, but it later turned out to be I was stone-deaf. I wondered if it was because I had always lain on my right side. Blocked constantly, the right ear must have become deaf. Weird! One's ears are similar to the two amplifiers of a cassette player. We could hear only the boum-boum-boum of a drum from one and loose, high notes from the other. One day, after we had gotten dressed to go shopping, his mother abruptly screamed in a high-pitched tone that undoubtedly hit the high E, her lips trembling.

I asked, 'What's happening?'

He fired back, 'Are you deaf?'

I later learned that she did not approve of him taking me out since he hadn't finished uprooting those pineapple plants in the garden as she had expected. When she breathed heavily and spoke in her husky low voice, I could make out every syllable, 'How unfilial! You crown your wife as a queen. I birthed you so nothing can prevent me from taking back that very precious life of y–o–u–r–s . . .'

She vibrated the last word y–o–u–r–s . . . for three more beats, then pounced on him, grabbing his shirt so hard the buttons flew off. Mother and son then tussled about for a while. She raised her voice scolding him in a staccato rhythm, or at least that was how my ears absorbed those downward tones:

'You . . . wife . . . as long as . . . you . . . no right to . . .'

The other tones, the ones with the acute marks, the hooks, the tildes above the letters, and the unmarked ones all sank deeply into my right ear. I maniacally decoded,

'You absolutely adore your wife; as long as you are still my son, you have no right to . . .'

I had a very high probability of being correct. Then, all of a sudden, they let each other loose. D'Artagnan walked slowly towards the kitchen and came back with a cleaver. The musketeer was finally armed, only a horse was needed. How pious! His mother had asked him to hand a chopping knife for her to cut off her maternal love. I bet she didn't dare. But no, she raised the knife. I jumped in between them, then found myself pushed back, not sure who did it; my head banged against a plum tree thanks to the momentum, and then slammed against the cement edge of the fish tank. Covering my ear with one hand, no idea which ear, I rubbed my bloody face with the other hand. Why did I still hear the commotion? Ah, I had covered the wrong ear, which was the right one. I crawled into our room. A short moment of silence, then a whimpering sound. I spied on them from behind the curtains—also sky-blue—hung negligently on the lemon-yellow door frame like in the other house. They were hugging each other weeping; the sacred knife was lying peacefully on the ground.

Haha! I laughed like a knight who was swinging his sword. What am I doing here in this house? Staying awake at night, shuffling around during the day waiting for pregnancy?

'*Âu lâu thâu qué*'

My existence in the house was to simply ensure that the Nguyễn bloodline continued? 'Damn, I would leave them fruitless,' I mumbled to myself. Lately, I had sworn often, only so I could hear the swears out loud, but what was the point of using my ears in this case?

* * *

I finally packed up and fled home. Hi! Piano!

After a lot of vomiting not triggered by colours, smells, or noises, I knew I was pregnant. D'Artagnan travelled back and forth between the Central region and the South like the warp on a shuttle loom, but with a waning pace. I gave birth to the child alone—a beautiful baby girl who must be purely European since her parents were no one other than the famous Cosette and D'Artagnan. I became a single-minded shark swimming around a single objective, not wasting a second wondering to myself *người đi qua đời tôi không nhớ gì sao người*[6].

I gave piano lessons to earn a living, with my baby in the pram next to my piano stool. She turned her head in her mom's direction, listening attentively to the music. Worried that she might suffer an audio-impairment, I pushed the pram away from the loud notes. She kept turning her head towards me. At four, she was able to turn the dog's bow-wow into fa-fa, the junk dealer's street cried *chai bán không*[7] into sol-si-sol. There was also C sharp for sticky rice, B flat for sweet soup. She was capable of deciphering all kinds of sounds with her extremely musical ears. She started taking piano lessons before she knew how to read or write. With my left ear left, I could hear fully any piece she played. By perceiving in his vision the echo from an approaching ghost army, Mozart composed *Requiem* while he was bed-ridden with a fatal illness. Beethoven, stone-deaf, still heard the knock-knock of destiny interpreted in his *Fifth Symphony*: pam-pam-pam-pam. Yippee!

## Endnotes

1. *Ăn cơm ba chén lưng, uống nước cầm chừng để bụng thương em.*
2. *One who is shy in the daytime but forgets to go home at night.*
3. *. . . một làm khói trắng ru đời vào quên lãng . . .*
4. 'Grandma, pick me a guava!'
5. 'Oh, how contentious!'
6. '*Why is there nothing left in your heart and mind after you've been wandering through my life . . .*'
   —from a poem by Trần Dạ Từ, set to music by Phạm Đình ChươngD
7. 'Any junk for sale?'

# Hushed Tones of Earth

Julius Villanueva
*Translated from Filipino by Tilde Acuña*

LITTLE BARANG...
I OUGHT TO KNOW WHAT THE EARTH SAYS UNDER ITS BREATH...
WHAT STORIES DEVELOP IN ITS NOOKS AND CRANNIES,
HOW SHADOWS THRIVE IN A WORLD THAT CHANGES QUICKLY, WHILE
THIS CITY REMAINS UNAFFECTED.
THE HAVES REST SECURE IN THEIR BUILDINGS OF GLASS AND IRON, WHILE
MOST OF THE HAVE-NOTS, LIVE ON THE EDGE.
AT THE EXTERIORS OF DIKES AND DAMS THAT STOP WATER FROM ADVANCING INLAND.

THE SEA HAS DEVOURED THE OLD CAPITOL.
HUNDREDS OF YEARS OF HISTORY, NOW DROWNED AND FORGOTTEN.

OUTSIDE THE CITY...
UNSEEN BY THE POPULACE, FOREIGNERS RESUME MINING ACTIVITIES IN FORESTS AND MOUNTAINS.

AND IN NEIGHBOURING PROVINCES LIE HEAPS AND HEAPS OF GARBAGE FROM THE CITY AND FROM ABROAD.

BUT HERE, TRACES OF ANCIENT MAGIC REMAIN.

KRASH

AN OLD NUNO RESIDING IN A MOUND OF JUNK.

THE LAND THAT USED TO BE HIS HOME
HAS BEEN ENVELOPED BY IRON AND CONCRETE

AND HERE IN THE PILE OF BROKEN AND FORGOTTEN THINGS
HE FOUND A NEW DWELLING PLACE.

AMONG THE CHANGES IN THIS WORLD
IS THE FREQUENT DOWNPOUR OF STORMS
THAT RESULTS TO RISING VOLUMES OF FLOOD.
ESPECIALLY IN CONGESTED CITIES. THIS IS A PROBLEM, NOT JUST OF HUMAN RESIDENTS,
BUT ALSO OF OTHER CREATURES.
TWO DUWENDES FLED FOR SAFETY, AWAY FROM THE UPSURGE OF WATER.
THEY WERE FROM A COLONY, BENEATH THE CITY.
LIKELY, THEY ARE THE ONLY SURVIVORS OF THE DELUGE.

EVEN CREATURES DEEMED OMINOUS AREN'T SPARED. MOTHER
AND CHILD TIKBALANG

LOST THEIR WAY IN THE WOODS, WHERE THEY TAKE COVER.

BECAUSE OF PATHWAYS RECENTLY CLEARED BY MINERS,
THEY CAN NEVER RETURN TO THEIR PACK.

IN ANOTHER JUNGLE

A KAPRE SNIFFS
PUFFS OF SMOKE

THAT HE DID NOT
BREATHE OUT.

A FIRESTORM.
HE IS UNCERTAIN IF THIS IS
A MAN-MADE CONFLAGARATION
OR A WILDFIRE
CAUSED BY DROUGHT.
BUT HE IS CERTAIN THAT
HE WOULDN'T BE ABLE TO STOP
THIS RAGING HELL.

IN THE CAMP OF REFUGEES FROM OTHER COUNTRIES.
PEOPLE WHO LOST THEIR HOMES DUE TO RISING SEA LEVELS AND OTHER CATASTROPHES.
A MANANANGGAL SEARCHES FOR A VICTIM.
BUT EVEN THIS MONSTER STRUGGLES TO LIVE. SHE HAS BEEN SEPARATED FROM HER LOWER HALF FOR A LONG TIME.
SHE IS IN ANGUISH.
HEALTHY EXPECTANT MOTHERS ARE KEPT SAFE UNDER DURABLE ROOFS, WITHIN CAST-IRON BUILDINGS, LOCKED INSIDE MANSIONS.
WHILE PREGNANT WOMEN IN THE CAMP ARE SICK AND MALNOURISHED.
THE SIPHONED NUTRIENTS ARE INSUFFICIENT FOR HER SELF-REALIZATION.

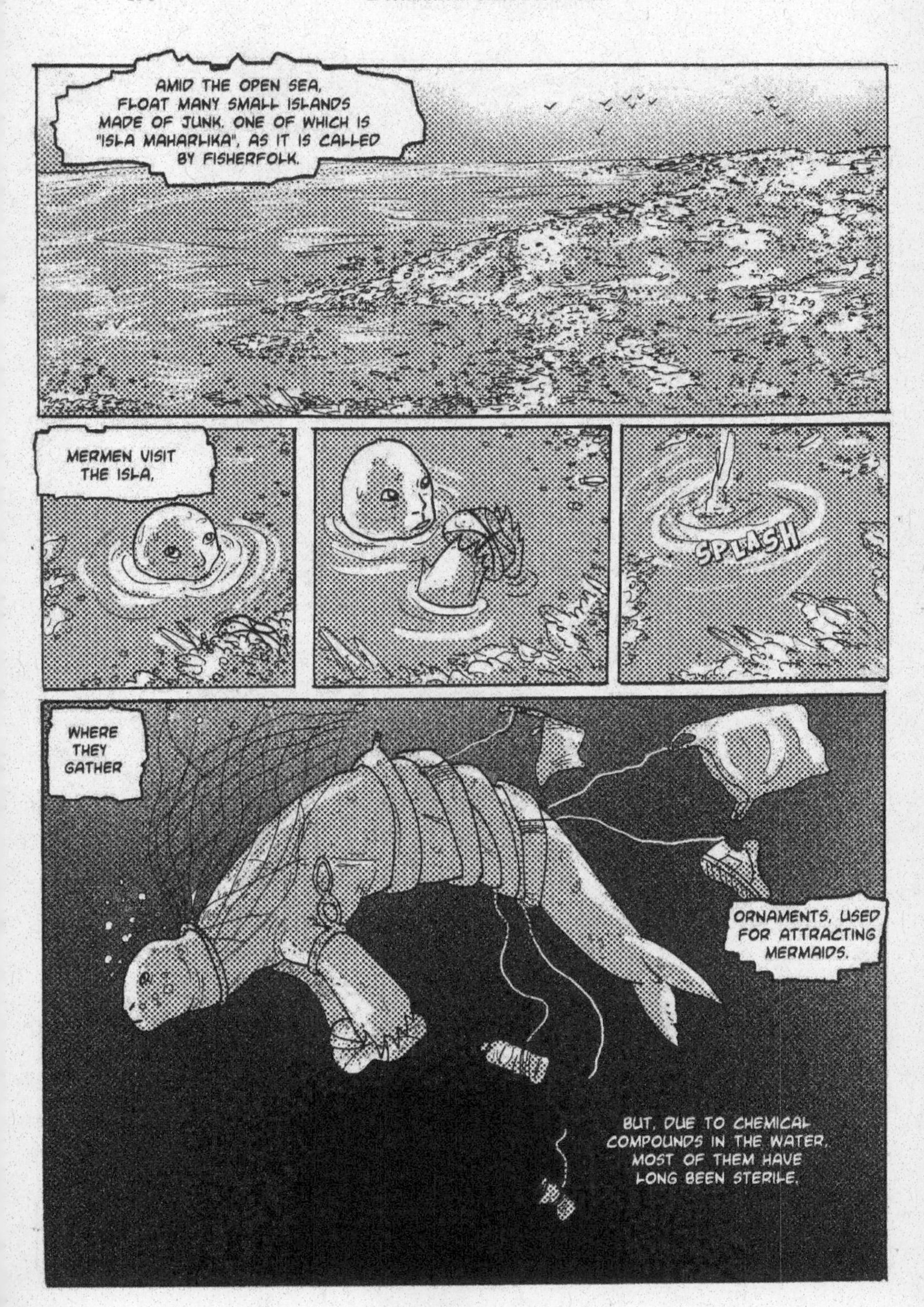
AMID THE OPEN SEA, FLOAT MANY SMALL ISLANDS MADE OF JUNK. ONE OF WHICH IS "ISLA MAHARLIKA", AS IT IS CALLED BY FISHERFOLK.
MERMEN VISIT THE ISLA,
SPLASH
WHERE THEY GATHER
ORNAMENTS, USED FOR ATTRACTING MERMAIDS.
BUT, DUE TO CHEMICAL COMPOUNDS IN THE WATER, MOST OF THEM HAVE LONG BEEN STERILE.

AND EVEN IN THE DEPTHS OF THE OCEAN,
THE CREATURES ARE STILL VULNERABLE.

A SIYOKOY MERFOLK, SEA MONSTER THAT TERRIFIED FISHERMEN, ONCE UPON A TIME.
NOW, RARELY SEEN TREADING SHALLOW WATERS

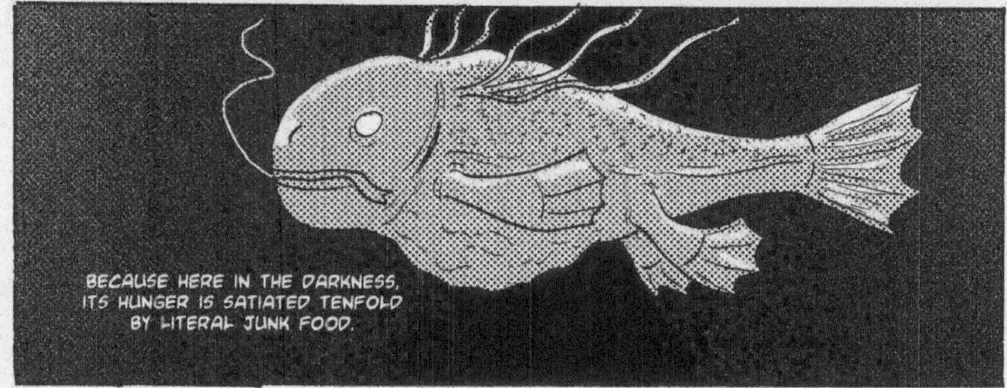
BECAUSE HERE IN THE DARKNESS, ITS HUNGER IS SATIATED TENFOLD BY LITERAL JUNK FOOD.

OTHER SOURCES OF LIFE FROM THE SEA
AND FORESTS
ARE MERE GHOSTS ANIMATED BY LIGHTS AND MEMORIES.
HOLOMUSEUM of NATURAL HISTORY
BECAUSE THROUGH THE GRADUAL APOCALYPSE, THEY VANISHED
AND HUMANS ARE NOT AT ANY RISK.
AS IF THEY TOO ARE NOT A PART OF THIS WORLD.

OH, GOD OF EARTH..

PLEASE HEED MY ORATIONS.
I PRAY THAT YOU AWAKEN FROM YOUR DEEP SLUMBER
'NAY. IT'S MOVING.

I AM NOT ASLEEP, MAMBABARANG. I AM SILENT, FOR NO ONE SPEAKS WITH ME.
A LONG WHILE HAS PASSED SINCE SOMEONE INVOKED ME THROUGH PRAYER.
IN THESE TIMES, THE ENCHANTMENT GROWS WEAKER.
I CAN SENSE NOTHING BUT SMOG, NOISE, AND SLUDGE.
MY MASTER. I HUMBLY ASK FOR YOUR HELP
I HAVE TO SAVE THE WORLD..

THE WORLD? SALVATION FROM WHAT?
FROM HUMANS THEMSELVES..
EVERYTHING HAS TERMS AND LIMITS, LITTLE MAMBABARANG.
AND THE END OF THE WORLD AND OF HUMANITY WOULDN'T CONCURRENTLY OCCUR.
THE HABITAT OF ALL OF US. THE WORLD SHALL MANAGE, EVEN WITHOUT HUMANITY. WE ARE INSIGNIFICANT, THROUGH THE COURSE OF TIME. EVEN I WHO HAVE SPENT MILLENIA IN THIS REALM.
BUT THIS WORLD IS ALSO OUR HOME, MY LORD.
CANT THE TURN OF EVENTS BE STOPPED?
CAN YOU? HUMANS CHANGED HOW THE WORLD FUNCTIONS IN A SHORT PERIOD OF TIME.
YOU DO NOT NEED GODS TO DO WONDERS.
IN YOUR HANDS LIE YOUR SALVATION OR YOUR AN...

# Against Unhappiness

Edgar Calabia Samar
*Translated from Filipino by Kristine Ong Muslim*

The kind of change that's real happens in a flash, the kind that won't give you time to react with surprise. You won't even have the time to see it unfold. Real change, that's the one you won't know already took place unless you have distanced yourself from the moment of change and after which you realize that something, indeed, had changed. But in the past. Yes, in the past. Always in the past. The awareness that something has changed is completely divorced from the actual moment of change, and this is why thinking about these things seems all too pointless. Except, you can prepare for the change that's about to come, according to—

Pat cannot help but be silent. They are not used to calling their mother Mama—or refer to her by any other name, not even in their mind. Pat and their siblings do not recognize their Mama. Pat only knows her as Mama. And that's all right. That's just how it is. Humans are not supposed to exist in order for them to know each other. Or be together.

Humans only need to be happy.

Even if they were with their Mama while growing up, that does not guarantee their happiness. She is only their mother because a human being needs a mother. Like those old pictures that require a camera to form, but after the pictures have been taken, both pictures and the camera no longer have anything to do with each other.

When at last Pat buys *truth*, it has opened for them many other words that they only heard from Mama.

Like *change*.

Are we really changed by discovering what is wrong with the things we used to know? But how—if the world itself cannot ever change, with no opportunity to change? Each time Pat thinks of their happies, they realize something has changed.

But when? And how?

Since they came of age, they have known that the dying world is down to its final years. That is what A—Found. keeps saying. That there's no sense in clinging to the idea of salvation. Everyone is just waiting for their end to come. So, in their remaining time on earth, finding happiness becomes the only goal in life. 'People have suffered greatly in the past,' says the eighty-year-old founder of A—Found., who was born during a time when countries were obsessed about reaching the moon ahead of each other. 'All that people need is happiness.'

*Happy Happies*. This is the tagline of all the products of A—Found. When Pat opens the imaginary window of their room, they can see the world outside. Advertisements abound to show that A—Found. is doing everything to make the world's end a joyous affair. A—Found. deals with the mountains of garbage that the government's near-endless cycle of recycling cannot seem to reduce. It also creates jobs for those displaced by flooding, or because automation has rendered their jobs obsolete, or because of the collapse of nations and they are forced to seek refuge in other places. Although the global fertility rate is dropping, there is still an increase in life expectancy—because many people are obviously happy these days, thanks to A—Found. It's been three years since the suicide rate is steady at 1.3 per cent among people aged thirteen to nineteen years, which is normally due to dwindling happiness. In the middle of the 30s, suicide rates reached 7.2 per cent, during which the term 'teen-aging' entered popular usage to describe the decline of happiness among young people which, in turn, leads to their death. That's also when A—Found. began to reinvent itself from a media-technology corporation to a wellness foundation. *Happy happies.* How the world owes A—Found. for the constant supply of happiness that's been preventing millions of young people from taking their lives.

Among the 1.3 per cent not saved by A—Found. is Gab, Pat remembers. Gab has been gone for three days before they were told of what had happened to their brother. All six were on a video conference where no one talked at length. Anything more than a 'hi' or 'hello' sounds weird. It is as if they only want to see each other as an attendance check to the world. There are even filters superimposed on the video of Pat's siblings, so Pat is not sure what they look like now.

Do they still resemble each other? None of them is telling the others about their whereabouts. Pat fails to mention their location, too. More so, it is likely they are all in the same building but unable to see each other in the flesh. It is not safe to be outside the room. People no longer know what lies outside. Except if you are one of those people who have no choice but to live in the outside world. The *taong-labas*, the outsiders. A—Found. says that the outsiders alone are responsible for the anguish and deaths outdoors.

The video conference of the six siblings is barely ten minutes long, although it feels longer. No one mentions Aki, their sibling who died when they were three years old. Is Aki now with Gab? Some people still believe in heaven, in the afterlife, especially when they know the person who died. Pat has no recollection of Aki save for videos on DATA (Drive-Archive-Terminal A—) when Aki was still alive. Pat is tempted to tell their siblings, *there are only six of us now. But so what if that's the case?*— and so they keep their mouth shut. Until they become aware that their siblings have been logging off one by one from the video conference session and they are the only one left there online with the echo of a farewell message from Lei, their youngest sibling, before the transmission is cut off. *Happy happies, bros and sissies*, Lei says. Pat disconnects their feed.

[Unhappiness—they killed every last bit of it], says Pat's Mama in a recovered voice note from over a year ago. Pat has been replaying the voice note for over a year now. They cannot understand all the words but there is comfort in their mother's voice that helps them sleep better at night and look forward to waking up the next morning. [You will never know true happiness until you've known unhappiness.]

Pat is just about to drift off to sleep when a sudden realization jolts them. The meaning of those two sentences becomes clear—except, of course, the meaning of unhappiness. Pat has no idea what unhappiness means.

They call up DATA to find out the core level location of unhappiness. They are only in Core 4. Many Tagalog users can't get past Core 3 their entire lives, and yet they all live happy lives. Basic languages such as Tagalog have a maximum of nine cores, but Pat does not know anyone who has gotten beyond Core 6 in Tagalog—not even the once-famous creator of A—Found. Each core houses ten to fifteen vocab sets composed of fifty to one hundred words per set. Each core, however, has at least one essential vocab set or EVS whose constituent words have to be purchased first to get to another vocab set inside a core with the keyword for unlocking the next core. Unhappiness is included in the EVS of Core 7. Which means: their Mama has reached Core 7?

The problem is Pat won't know which keyword unlocks the next core and in which vocab set of a particular core it is located. If they get lucky, six vocab sets are the shortest route to unhappiness. But if the odds are stacked against them and they choose the wrong keyword location, they will need to go through at least 28 vocab sets. This characteristic design of DATA's language acquisition, one that is based on probability and predictive word sensitivity, is an attempt to mimic the natural language exposure and discovery of humans.

So, when can they buy all of those? Pat quickly does mental calculations. Even if they use up all their savings and even if they stop spending their A—Found. earnings on happies, it might take five years before they can afford to buy unhappiness.

Then suddenly, unhappiness, once a stranger to Pat, opens up like a gigantic void inside of her.

Pat has the option to forget all of this. They can always forget that their Mama once sent them voice notes totalling up to eighty hours in a span of at least three years, voice notes recorded almost daily before leaving them at A—Found., the day Aki died. Does this have anything to do with Aki's death? No, that's not possible. Like a camera for taking pictures, a camera as a device that existed a long time ago. Strange, but it all seems as if their Mama seemed too sure Pat would reach the age of 13 when they can finally receive the scheduled message with a link that directs to a data storage site. The site itself is already inactive, but the server is still accessible. Pat immediately downloads all the voice notes into their A-fone.

Pat can, of course, forget all this, but they refuse to. [You will never know true happiness until you've known unhappiness.] What is unhappiness?

Because it will take a long time before they find unhappiness, Pat decides to start now. They tell no one about their plans, not even their siblings. They become aggressive but deliberate in buying words. Good thing, A—Corp has not flagged their purchases. They have done nothing illegal. There is nothing irregular about a creator of happies like themself buying words. Words are deemed an investment.

After nearly eight months since Pat received their Mama's messages, they are at last able to buy *truth*, the keyword to get into Core 5.

*Truth* confirms that there are in fact nine of them.

And Pat is not the real Pat.

And Pat is not truly happy.

* * *

The real Pat died fifteen minutes before coming out of their Mama's womb. That is why PAGBABAGO, the supposed acronym of their names, became PAGSIBOL. The word *pagsibol*, or spring, is in the EVS of Core 5.

Pat considers sharing their discovery with Lei. Among the six of them, their youngest sibling Lei earns the most money from making inspis. Then Pat, through their happies, is the next highest earner. In a world that drives everyone to be happy, the most profitable commodities are inspis and happies. Is your happiness waning? Just listen to inspis. You want to stay happy? Then keep reading happies.

Pat, however, is having second thoughts about telling Lei, even if they know that Lei can help them buy more words faster. The two do not really talk to each other. Pat is closer to Lei than their other siblings, but it is also possible that Pat's perceived closeness to Lei is due to them often seeing their names next to one another on the earnings tally before they proceed with spending their income. And what will Pat say to Lei? Do you know that there are really nine of us? That if the real Pat is still alive, you would have been Oli as the youngest of PAGBABAGO. And not their current Oli that Lei follows in PAGSIBOL. And had the real Pat lived, Pat would have been Aki. But can Lei still remember Aki? Will the new sequencing of names confuse Lei? For Pat, names are unnecessary to distinguish who is who among their six siblings even if they look almost identical to each other. Pat does not look in the mirror and think, *you, you are Pat, who would have otherwise been Aki had the real Pat lived.*

Pat is simply themself.

And because the words themselves are not that important, there is no problem in changing the acronym that collectively represents the siblings. Goodbye, PAGBABAGO. Hello, PAGSIBOL. What's important is that the acronym is in their Mama's language. People are more likely to patronize products that are in a restricted language. Even if PAGLIMOT ends up as the acronym for the nine of them—or PAGPATAY (when Pat is finally able to buy this word that translates 'to kill' from Core 3, it amazes them how often the word is used)—A—Found. still won't have a hard time attracting buyers. Sometimes, old people have vague memories of a word revived from DATA after the word is mentioned in an inspi or happie. And because it's been so long since they last heard the word, they can't be sure of its meaning. But what people do not know is that they tend to be more receptive when a word comes to them through this manner. Making people happy does not require that much of an effort; it's just a matter of dangling words whose meanings elude them. Ignorance is bliss, after all.

But in the case of Pat, words—such as those they heard from their mother but failed to make sense to them—only fed the monstrous void that is growing inside of them.

Pat decides to not make the first move and to simply wait for Lei to make contact. But when did they last talk to each other? Sometime ago, when Gab died. *Happy happies, bros and sissies*, was what Lei told them that time before disconnecting, then the others did the same. Pat searches their heart. Is there still a need to involve their siblings in this?

Pat later steels their resolve to go at it alone and save up enough words until they reach unhappiness. Pat reviews the video recording of their birth. If they edited the part where their real eldest sibling was born, then the livestreamed broadcast—as it says on the video description—is a lie. The video has been edited before its release to DATA. What happened inside the delivery room is expertly captured in a 360-degree panoramic recording. Even with Pat's ignorance of the birthing process, they can't help but marvel at their Mama's beauty, who was a teenager then. Their Mama was 18 when she gave birth to them, and all the videos of the entire time she had been pregnant are not marred by any teen-aging symptoms. So, no one could have predicted their mother's abandonment of them right after Aki died.

There are voice-overs, appended as annotations, of the happenings, and they can be played in any of the languages on DATA. The voice-overs say that all nine of them have no defects in their bodies and internal organs. The supposed live broadcast has more than 700 million views. Although it is illegal to define a person's gender based on the genitals that person is born with, a few verified accounts cannot help but mention in the chat section the labels *boy* or *girl* with the delivery of each infant. Some are telling them off, while the others are just laughing. There are those who are angry, of course. But A—Found. keeps allowing illegal interactions within DATA. It is only the child, upon reaching the right age, who has the right to select whichever gender identity. If the child wants to. Pat has not done it yet. And they do not know if that's something they want to do.

* * *

Pat has no memory of their Mama's voice. Yet, upon first hearing the voice note, Pat knew instinctively that the voice can only belong to their mother. There must be something in Pat's subconscious, whatever hidden memory of their Mama's whispers, those that reassure Pat that it is their mother speaking and no one else. [Are you okay? Are you and your siblings okay? In the Tagalog language of your father's childhood, the closest equivalent to 'okay' is 'ayos' which I'm not sure if you are still using until now.]

This is also the first voice note where their Mama mentions their Papa. And if they know nothing about their Mama, then more so with their Papa. Their Papa could be anyone, for all they know. But from the other things that their Mama confides to Pat in the days that followed, Pat learns about the huge gap between the ages of their parents, that their Papa is almost twice as old as their Mama.

[One that's ayos, which means being in a state of order. The meaning comes from its practical use in referring to the skilful arrangement, connection, or sequence of ingredients or parts of a whole or related objects. Like books in a library, right? Like words in a dictionary. Like the elements of a great story. Ayos.] Pause. A great *what*?

Pat is almost breathless. That is most probably the longest talk they heard from a real human being, from a person who knows them. Not a recorded lesson or news meant for all possible listeners. No one at DATA, too, has ever talked to them this way which sounds like . . . like Pat really has no idea what it is getting at. Like the overall message contradicts the exact words being said.

Pat repeats what their mother said. [Like the elements of a great story.]

Pat's heart quickens its beat the moment they see the word *story* in Core 5.

* * *

In the vocab set of THT-6 (Tagalog na Hindi Tagalog, 6). From pre-colonial terminologies derived from foreign languages but have become Tagalog in their usage, meaning, spelling, or combination of these. Before, such words were not recognized as part of Tagalog but were integrated through the Tagalog standardization into the Filipino language. In the legal manoeuvres of A—Found., Filipino is declared as anomalous, a fabrication hewn from past centuries with the aim of creating a new language that can be sold by A—Found. Filipino is said to not have its own corpus of lexicons, no grammar and enunciation rules of its own, with everything borrowed from other languages, thus it cannot be sold as a new and separate language. A—Found. has won its case in an international court and no longer has to pay for Filipino separately, acquiring the ability to parcel off Filipino's vocabulary for the corpus of its existing languages, just like what it is doing with Tagalog.

It takes more than a month before Pat is able to buy *story*. When they finally grasp the word's meaning, they find it's amazing how it is not included in Core 1's standard words. All those happies Pat has been making, can they be considered a story? Replaying some of their Mama's voice notes where story is mentioned, Pat is now sure that their Papa is a story writer. That their Mama first read their Papa's writings before the two knew each other. The idea that they both know each other scares Pat a bit. Something like that happens rarely. [It is also important, however, to remind oneself that the greater and more dangerous fantasy involves believing that a story ending where two characters don't live happily ever after is realistic just because we want it to mirror our failures and unhappiness.] Unhappiness again. And failure. Failure! Pat is sure about having glimpsed *failure* in a Core 5 vocab set. They can still afford one more word. They are apprehensive but trust the gut feeling that their Mama's voice notes are guiding them somehow, leading them to figure out the keyword for every core.

[I am tempted to say that life's purpose probably is, you know—fix things, experiences, all confrontations and challenges. To stack them all up, find ways to connect them, arrange them in order. Maybe, life revolves around this constant reordering, or this is the logic itself of life. Maybe, our individual sanity clings to that, and the moment it gives way from the weight, the moment the stack gets out of order, the connections severed, the order of things gets out of whack, we lose our bearing. Sometimes, the semblance of order relies on only one thing. Or only one person. Just like your Papa is to me, for example. Our greatest weakness and failure is our faith in our ability to relive the past.] Another pause.

There are no other words in Core 5 that their mother mentions with the same regularity as story. Pat uses up their last savings on DATA in order to buy *failure*. And they guessed correctly. Failure is the keyword to open Core 6.

* * *

A—Found. has managed to buy almost 82 per cent of all the languages in the world. So now, it is only through their DATA that published and recorded texts until the early thirties in these languages are accessible. A—Found. began their world domination through buying dying languages. Then small nations started selling off their own languages in exchange for a steady supply of electricity, water, and other utilities from A—Found. Almost everyone knew then that the selling spree was all for show because A—Found. already owned many countries. Variations of English are the only things remaining in the public domain for use by people in different parts of the world. Still, A—Found. tries year after year to buy and own what's on the public domain. It might not take long for that to happen. A—Found. has long been the one controlling pretty much everything in this world—water, gas, electricity, breathable air, food, hobbies, entertainment, faith, imaginary money and wealth, government, weapons, information, alternative information, life itself.

It is in the EVS of Core 6 that Pat finds *parikala*, the closest Tagalog equivalent of irony. Pat already knows the meaning of irony from the meta-communications lessons they took from A—Corp. They have learned how irony was used a long time ago to sustain the illusion that thinking people were better than happy people. Which is wrong. Irony poisons conversations, according to an A—Corp. lesson. This is why DATA prohibits the use of irony in inspis and happies. Happiness must be literal and direct. Only when Pat learns about parikala that they begin to understand there is no truth (thank you, and Pat already knows what truth means!) to what they have been taught about irony. They finally get the rest of their Mama's voice notes. [Irony is important in expressing rage and rebellion while evading the agents that suppress rebellion. I must say that until now we have yet to understand nature. We seek shelter from floods and calamities. We flee from its rebellious force: we brave the cities inundated by storms, no matter how far we've travelled. And we are driven to restlessness not by rare or impossible events but by recurring ones, those that can influence or make things happen, inescapable like the happiness you rebel against and do not fully understand.]

It takes close to another six months for Pat to save up again even if they have been cued into the likelihood of rebellion as keyword to get beyond Core 6. Pat replays the voice note. Truth—failure—rebellion. Truth—failure—rebellion. Rebellion is the only word mentioned in the same frequency as truth and failure, the keywords of the previous two cores. But if they are right and able to unlock Core 7, then they want to snatch up the EVS of Core 7 fast and buy unhappiness. They are left with no other option but to make happies daily, despite their growing unhappiness. Truth is, Pat is able to create more happies now that a void had formed within the giant void inside of them. This is also the reason their happies in DATA are selling so well these days. What do people really want?

Pat's siblings have yet to contact them.

Until one day, Pat gets up from bed, looks through the imaginary window in their room to take a peek at the flooded world outside. They are ready to buy rebellion.

As expected, it is the keyword.

And so now, at last, Pat looks forward to unhappiness.

* * *

*Against Unhappiness* is the first thing that Pat sees upon buying unhappiness. It is a manif authored by one of the creators of A—Corp. from the previous decade during the height of teen-aging. It says that many novels, poems, stories, and other works from the past have shown that unhappiness is meaningless. Pat is sure that their Mama had read this particular manif. But when did she read it? Was their Mama already aware of unhappiness while carrying them in her womb? Or did their Mama discover it sometime in the three years when they were growing up and while making all those audio notes for Pat?

Unhappiness is one of the causes that the manif identifies to be behind the incidences of suicide. Based on the manif, even in the time when Tagalog was just newly introduced into A—Found., many people had long since stopped writing about unhappiness and simply chose to deal with the most important thing in life—and that is happiness. Although there were some who wrote about unhappiness, the readership was limited within that circle of writers. All of them drowning in the unhappiness they created for each other. Pat wants to believe that the creator of that manif is using irony.

[Forgive me, I won't burden all of you again about fixing my world. I just want to let you know that there were times when I believed you alone could get my life back on track. I realize this is not fair to you. That it is incredibly dangerous if our life depends on others—and on other people at that—even if those people are family. Or loved ones. It is not because we shouldn't trust or depend on other people. But because we can't depend on change. And we change, so we also cannot depend on ourselves. The strength I showed earlier, that can change any minute now. Before, just like everyone, I only wanted to be happy. Then one day, when I heard your first words, I want you to be happy as well. How does one know happiness aside from its form that you've been forced to accept?]

Pat feels an unexplained twinge of pain. It feels as if the giant void inside of them is gobbling up all the happies they made, like they want to throw up all the happiness they brought forth into the world. Is this unhappiness?

Is Pat's being the eldest the sole basis behind their Mama's decision for sending the voice notes? The longest file, where their Mama talks about the eighteen kinds of ancient unhappiness, is almost three hours long. The shortest voice note, on the other hand, is slightly one minute longer—[It is difficult to start again. I want to ask how you are doing, how you are really doing, because that's the easiest question to ask, but after all the years we were together and now those years no longer seem to matter, that question is suddenly hard to ask. I don't know which of your answers will hurt me more: is it when you say you are not okay because of what the future holds for us or is it when you say that you are okay, that you are at least happy even if we are like this. It's funny when *we are like this*. What are we, really? If you ask me how I'm doing, well, I'll tell you I am not okay, that's for sure. I've always been like this, right? Always making more or fewer steps each time we pretend to go out together. Can you still remember this? So, it is always you who gets left behind and ends up saying *wait up* or be ahead and have to look back to ask if I'm okay. Of course, I take those in stride. Back then I thought I was okay, that's why I kept saying I was okay. I am okay.]—and that Pat believes is intended for their Papa, because who else can their Mama address this message?

Their Mama's last voice note is the shortest. [Every year is a blessing,] then there is a subtle crack in her voice. What sounds like a machine hums from afar. One, two, three, four seconds. Then their Mama's voice continues, [It is the year that embraces and sets the month free, it is the month that mends each day. I will remember you forever, Aki.] That's it. That's the only tell-tale mark that such a voice note has been recorded by their Mama after Aki's disappearance. Aki—that should have been Pat's name if the real Pat had lived.

Pat does not know what to do next. In the following days, they listen again to the entire eighty hours of their Mama's audio note. And now, they are sure they have a firm grasp of everything, of every word. They are suddenly moved to tears, and their reaction catches them off guard. Crying is something that Pat has only read about. Pat lets the tears flow. They are unaware of the existence of emotions welling inside of them until their Mama's words triggered them to surface. These emotions and their tears are drawing out the void within the giant void inside of them.

Pat replays the voice notes many times in the days and weeks that followed. They can almost memorize the lines. At last, Pat decides to call Lei.

Lei does not even sound the least bit surprised when asked if she wants to talk. Their conversation extends to almost an hour, but after they disconnect, which Pat follows by gently punching a button on their A-fone, Pat gets up and looks at the imaginary view on the imaginary window of their room, and suddenly has an odd feeling about not having talked to Lei at all. Pat can't even say for sure if Lei has confirmed having received some two years ago their Mama's message with a link to the audio notes. Pat also can't tell whether their other siblings received the same message, but if Pat received the same message, then chances are, their siblings also did the same. Moreover, there's that thing with Gab and what he did a year ago. Pat is not sure whether Lei also said—after getting to the part that talks about unhappiness and piecing together all that their Mama had told them—that Lei could not be sure if it was really their Mama who was speaking to them. If Lei had expressed being unsure if their Mama was truly capable of leaving a message for them. And, if the message really was from their Mama, even though A—Found. would not allow anything of the sort to reach them—unless it wanted for them to retrieve the message. 'I could have done all these,' Lei tells Pat. Or did Lei really utter those words? Pat cannot tell for sure. 'Or you did it,' Lei adds. Pat also cannot remember if they denied their sister's claims. Or that Pat was sure of their denial and what they were denying. 'Or it could be any one of us,' Lei says, referring to their other siblings. Pat thinks the Lei talking to them still looks exactly like the Lei they remember. 'How do we know true happiness?' Is it them or is it Lei who said this? 'Maybe this is just a chapter in our teenage years that we have to go through. To know truth, to know that truth exists, so that we remain motivated to distance ourselves from the truth. If truth truly exists. Similarly, to know unhappiness, to know that unhappiness exists, so that we keep desiring happiness. If happiness really exists. Maybe, part of A—Found.'s design for us is to make us doubt everything in our lives. That way, we learn to value things. Do we really have a Mama? Do you seriously believe there are nine of us at the same time inside the womb of the same mother? All nine of us? Maybe, this is what we mean by change, what we thought was changed even as we still reside here—technically unchanged—for we can't conceive of a reality outside of this one we have.'

Pat switches off the imaginary window in their room upon seeing someone drowning in the churning floodwaters outside and no one is out there to make an attempt to save that person.

* * *

*[But do you know, among the early Tagalog, that the word ayos—or okay in English—means 'to sharpen the blade'? I get a rise whenever I think about being told to ensure everything's okay while actually referring to 'let the blade be sharpened'. Or when told to be okay to mean 'make your blade sharp'. Is that what being okay means—to ready one's self to the possibility of inflicting an injury—to slice, stab, sever—like a sharp blade? Maybe that's why every question that asks whether you are okay always comes laden with a shadow of hurt? Well, I am okay for the most part, possibly gearing up for another round of hurt, and that's why I'm here. It is as if I can hear you say in jest, you really have no shame. You are smiling, because the world has driven us to be this numb that sharp words fail to hurt us. It is as if we've engaged in too much wordplay that we are no longer in touch with our feelings. You have no shame. I am also smiling*

*even if I don't know exactly what I feel. I only know that I want to talk to you again. Everyday. Even for a few seconds. Just like before. I don't know if I can do it, but I want to do it. I want things to be okay again. I want everything to be okay. Starting again is hard but it is harder to just go on for the sake of continuity. These past three weeks, I reread what you wrote. I am planning to reread all your other books. The things I forgot have all come back to me, you know. Of course, that's because I had read about them before I met you. I remember so many things while rereading your stories. But I keep having to pause my recollections, doubting my memory or blaming my desperation to stay okay by making up memories. This is why I dared to start again, to talk to you again. Perhaps, this is just my attempt to check if my recollections are accurate. Whether I can still be okay, for the sake of the seven, whether I can still stay sharp. There's no deadline for that, right? As long as I'm alive, I can start over and over, and we can change and change the world, right? Right?]*

# The Path to the Mountains

Francezca Kwe

The end of the world has been happening for more than a decade, so protractedly that it is now old news—life keeps dragging its feet along the city's precarious streets, soaring stacks of hovels shoot up like weeds between shaky buildings, and black, electric clouds of flies choke the lowest levels, where no one bothers to know who's dead anymore. But in the last month of her contract, the announcement that the resettlement voyages will soon be indefinitely postponed sends thousands of hopefuls hurtling towards the offices of the Ministry of Filipino Resettlement.

The coffee always runs out by midmorning, and so does the staff's humanity. The applicants seem to them like an endless, pressing swarm, their supplications vibrating in the air as they clutch their children and bags in the manner of those already embarking. The process officers pummel the cascade of application forms with red stamps that spell the end of their dream of escape, cutting down swathes of applicants in minutes.

To the back of her mind, Liway banishes the realization that she has denied more applicants today than on any other day of her contract, but there is hardly time for self-flagellation—every despairing face is multiplied infinitely in the cavernous processing hall, out the door and over scores of city blocks. Her piss sloshes in her bladder, burning her insides, and her fingers are cramping from hours of ruffling through forms and declarations that each applicant shoves through the hole at her window.

Essentially, she understands that there is no other way to survive the day than to mark the majority as 'denied'—aren't they briefed like so every morning, before the doors are opened? Every approval must be strictly documented and filed with a complete report signed by the approving officer and then submitted in the right colour folder, the supervisor repeated each day. As she got ready in the lounge earlier, a staff member from the documentation department, which has to scan every pore on every approved evacuee's face and every angle of the body, walked by and threw her a glance, although it seemed to her a severe look of warning. Don't fuck up, his eyes seemed to say, it's them or you.

With the inviolate thickness of the crowd, the air is thin in the hall and the air-conditioners seem to have given up the will to live. She is desperate for a break; her temples beat a rhythm against the hum of people.

After thousands of applications, it's natural to perceive each as indistinguishable, just another leaf in a dense, dead pile. She has learned to skim the attached photos of children, plaintive letters, recommendations and guarantees, but rarely are they the most sought-after kind: petition letters from those who have gone on previous ships. She still sometimes encounters, locked in the macabre dance of survival on the streets, family members that other staff members of the Ministry have left behind. They used to ambush her with questions and tears, asking why their sons or daughters, nieces and nephews, had suddenly disappeared, how they could have been left, and how and when they could be petitioned. But years went by without any news from beyond the sea, and eventually, they just passed her on the street like other strangers.

'You're going to approve my application,' a voice is saying, from a puckered mouth pressed to the opening of the transaction window. It belongs to an old man in a long-sleeved shirt that, like almost everything, has seen better days. He stands very straight, periodically throwing looks of disdain at the other lanes where his fellow applicants are begging or wailing. Liway's red stamp, halfway down, pauses. 'I was the environment undersecretary during the second President Almano's term,' he says, one hand stroking his stack of papers. Liway follows his gaze and lifts the top page to see a thick brown envelope. The old man gives her a searing stare. But his hands, folded on the counter, are trembling so much that they are almost bouncing.

She pulls the envelope out of its hiding place and stamps his papers green. She puts her thumbprint on the glass; it wakes up and beholds the applicant, spewing a litany of beeps as it absorbs all the information from his paperwork. Liway presses a star-marked button, and a duo of security officers come to escort the man to the next station.

He is a relic of a haunted past, but he isn't alone—every now and then surface aged bureaucrats that had sunk their teeth into different points in the three-decade timeline of the Almanos' consolidated power, hoping their loyalty will now pay off in the form of passage for them and their families. Some of the then-powerful are now as miserable as most of the populace, having hedged most of their bets in land that are not the burrows of eels. But more still possess the means to bribe their way onboard. The Philippines never seems to run out of these floaters, and the Ministry caters to them accordingly, through secret buttons and special conveyance down the line.

There are no other people Liway detests more than these princes of the pre-apocalypse, who had lived it up in good times, only getting hungrier and hungrier as the world dwindled and the people starved their way into mindless worship of the Almano dynasty. These days, no one dwells too much on the past, the state extinguishes any extra minute of thought through survey results, motivational quotes, daily tallies of successful evacuations, and proclamations about the Biblical greatness of its absent leaders, beamed to everyone's handhelds, visors, smart glasses. And of course, the greater scene-stealers are hunger and the spotlights of the police checkpoints. She tiptoes into the past only late at night, conjuring the faces of her parents, who were among the thousands dying of the Philippine pneumonic plague of 2031. At the hospital, her mother already rigid on a stretcher by his side, she gripped her father's hand and tried to pull him away from the lure of death as vainly as she did when she was a child, on that day at the airport en route to their new Canadian beginning, the boarding gate beckoning, the promised first plane ride so close to happening, and her parents refusing to budge, enraptured by a TV screen that showed the breaking news: a monumental mass demonstration contesting the fraudulent win of the Almano scion who would unleash the nightmare that still has not ended. She had screamed when they picked her up and walked away from boarding. They were betraying her, breaking their promise by throwing their tickets and hailing a taxi to Mendiola to join the heaving, angry ocean of people. The years that followed seemed a blur of suffering to a young girl—pandemics, joblessness, hunger—until her father breathed his last in that makeshift bed. Then there seemed nothing to live for, until the Almano government brokered the life-saving journeys with humanitarian zeal, and a goal imprinted itself in her mind: get a contract at the Ministry, and a sure ticket out of the country.

Liway shoves the envelope into her lunch bag, next to a forsaken sandwich. It might be enough for some new clothes for the upcoming journey, or a few pieces of fruit, the ultimate luxury.

There have been times when the contents hadn't been worth the additional work, but she can't miss a chance. Besides, she thinks, after so many years tumbling in the spheres of power, money like this has come to the point of return.

The sight of a rare green card at her lane sparks a reaction from the crowd, and many begin pushing forward, breaking up the lines and earning the ire of the armoured safety officers, who beat them back. But in the melee, someone has run over to her window. 'Liway, it's me, Glory, do you remember me?' The recognition comes too late—to restore order, all the agitated applicants are being swept up and tossed out of the hall. Glory, that bright, cheerful friend from years ago whose face now held the light of a flickering candle, only had time to push a scrap of paper onto Liway's desk before the officers yank her out of Liway's sight.

* * *

On the way home through the rank alleys and avenues of Mega Manila, Liway thinks back to the time they saw each other last. She has never had many friends, even in school when one is supposed to form the truest friendships. She kept to herself, charting out directions towards catching the flight that she had missed long ago. But Glory found her sitting under the trees during vacant hours, and brought her to spontaneous concerts, poetry readings, and planning meetings. Glory confided that she was thinking of joining the young people, farmers, and workers fortifying the persistent rebellion that the third President Almano was still trying to exterminate. Liway's escape plan, in contrast to youthful service and resistance, seemed suddenly shameful.

Their graduation was the year another round of martial law was declared; they were throwing their caps as military helicopters tore across the city, and trucks ejected soldiers outside the auditorium. The ceremony ultimately ended in a rapid succession of arrests; gowned student leaders were dragged by soldiers out of the doors and heaved into the trucks. When they tore Glory's boyfriend Ezekiel from Glory's side, she took Liway's hand and they both ran after the trucks, teetering as their legs gave out, seeing the soldiers laughing as the distance widened. Since that day, she hasn't heard from Glory, although she had learned that Ezekiel could not be accounted for by his captors.

She stares absently out of the window of the ancient, panting jeep tracing the arterial pathways of a city that sweeps everything into the folds of dusk. The stunted trees between the concrete blocks of the tenements point to the sky with bony fingers, as groups of abandoned children dart about like swallows, their soles catching on the jagged edges of sidewalks. The soot from little, glimmering street fires and the dust of buildings being torn apart for every usable scrap congeal in a cloud that hangs above the damp smell of seawater and sewage, aspirated and fermented in the lungs into clusters of almost sentient tumours. Every wall and plane is coated by the brown muck plastered by waves bearing wreaths of plastic on their crests, some of these deposited onto the billboards that remind citizens to 'apply now for limited slots' because 'global Filipinos' are still being led by a government that has gone to prepare a place for them in a heaven elsewhere while they try to get their heads above water in the ruined country, shepherded by gangs upon gangs of police at every major street corner.

Even as a small child, Eman would ask her why the police kept the city in such a tight grip—checkpoints everywhere, especially near higher ground, police searchlights checking every block. But there's nothing to steal, Mom, he would say, looking around at the pavements of solidified garbage being dug up by dogs and people.

What are they guarding?

Maybe something that's not in plain sight, she would answer.

On one building, where a dreadful iron box propels residents to levels that never quite rise above the leaden city haze, someone has aggressively sprayed over the PSA billboard: '*Walang pagkain, walang ayuda! Estado, papet ng imperyalista!*' The sickly yellow sunrise meant to convey the luminous future awaiting re-settlers has been painted over with an urgent red sigil.

* * *

At eight, when the remains of dinner have been cleared, Liway kisses her son good night. Almost a teen, he has just recently dragged his mattress away, to the corner of the kitchen opposite where she sleeps, amusing her but also bringing her close to tears. Eman is all she has in this wasteland that the gods have left burning, and this idea confers on her an unstoppable focus during the most soulless moments at work and the tour of hell that is every step of the way home. She doesn't need anyone else; as long as she does everything right, she'll finish the terms of her contract and go on the boat with her son.

The closer their departure gets, the quieter Eman has gotten, the denser the exhalations building up in their small room where he plays on his handheld the whole day, waiting for her to come home so that they can scratch a day off the calendar, wind the coil of their emotions a turn tighter. She has rehearsed it to him since he was beginning to walk. Someday, we'll leave. Mom only has to get the job, and we can start a better life abroad. There's only one chance, we can't squander it, she would tell him in a whisper that was loud to her own ears.

On the day she picked him up for the last time at the tenement school, he stealthily slipped away from the other kids and pushed her out of the gate quickly so that no one could see. I'm never going to see them again, he said when she asked if he didn't want to say goodbye. Something inside her, long tamped down, bubbled up. The people they shuffled past looked at her twitching face suspiciously. She imagined barrelling down the street to a police checkpoint and knocking all those helmeted heads down like bowling pins.

But at the bottom of the street, a cop was slapping down a young man. Eman's hand in hers started to sweat and she gagged all her impulses. It's not long now, she said, and he nodded his tacit commitment. By then, they were a block from home; if they kept their heads down and did things right, they would get there safely.

She tries not to think about the others around them: Mio, the pale toddler next door, whose worship of Eman continues even if the older boy has outgrown it, his mother, Minda, foraging for scraps of fabric, plastic, and metal and quilting it all together for something that can perhaps be sold or exchanged for rice. Eman's teacher, Ms. Gomez, who for years has worked for next to nothing, in the hope that her sacrifice could someday win her Liway's eventual vacant place in the Ministry.

In the dark, her eyes seek out Eman's curled-up form, and a chill rushes though her bones. He has grown up a city child with a look of permanent doom. Outwardly he is timid, but he stokes an anger in his belly that blazes up more and more. When the last scrap of home recedes in the distance, will this anger evaporate? Will he become, once again, the child who had smiled so completely and truthfully in her arms?

He would ask about his father when he was younger, but as the little world she cobbled together for him crumbled under deprivation, fathers eventually became just another element of myth, like vitamins, or lush mountains where heroes waged a winning war.

Eman's father is there, she has been told over the years, but no one says anything more, as if they can be overheard and made to pay a price for talking. Or maybe because the story is just a fantasy for fools, a dream amidst the city's rubble and stink. More and more people keep coming to Mega Manila from the provinces; they cling to the hope of getting passage as firmly as they do to dead lamp posts and embankments when the marauding sea slurps them up and retreats with thousands of them in its mouth, leaving a muddy wake on which new tent cities sprout like mushrooms.

Where is he now? They had met in a cheap boarding house; she was renting a room with some older girls, export nurses impatient for deployment, while she was reviewing for the Ministry selection exam. In contrast, he had a room to himself across the hall, and always seemed like he had somewhere to go. Reading on the top step of the staircase on humid afternoons, she would lift her eyes from the book and train them on his descending back, and returning, he would smile politely at her shoes. But still, they wouldn't say a word to each other.

One morning, she had just stepped out hurrying to her part-time job when an unfamiliar man and woman stopped her at the entrance and showed her his picture, asking her if such a young man lived there. Already a veteran at masking her thoughts, she said she had never seen him before. This is a girls-only dorm, she says, frowning at the inquirers. She made sure they disappeared around the corner before she went and stationed herself at the other end of the street, where she spent four hours waiting for him, effectively missing her shift.

He barely thanked her for saving his hide from whoever was after him, and she went away offended. The next day, she learned that he has moved out, and that was that. But something started to gnaw at her, and her focus dissipated.

Until one day, she encountered him in the same spot where she had so patiently staked out an ambush. He seemed more relaxed and cheery, and she became more forgiving. 'How do you know they weren't creditors or gangsters?' he asked.

'I know how I look like but I'm not vapid,' she said. China had just bombed a US carrier near Taiwan, and the atmosphere felt dire and tense. Manila was swarming with US soldiers, and the government was trying to stamp out the protests that erupted daily. 'You remind me of my friend,' she told him, 'I miss her.'

Emanuel would be incommunicado for days, but when he showed up, he brought her books, especially poetry written by women who had gone underground. Perhaps she hoped Glory would be in between the pages. She kept reviewing for the exam even while tensions in the sea were endangering the national exodus. He helped her through the most difficult parts; he was organically smart even though he hadn't gone to university. They didn't talk about the future; he would only say that he planned to return to his hometown in the North, and she couldn't see the use of defending her long-formed plans. Emanuel couldn't walk through any popular district without setting police sirens off, but even the best of state surveillance can fail against young desire.

A week after a joint US-Philippine military expedition committed a string of massacres in Isabela province, he came to see her, and told her it would be a while before he could come back. Three months later, the souvenir of a short-lived idyll revealed itself, and her neat trajectory disintegrated, forced aside for several years by the sheer labour of raising a baby alone.

Glory had left a note bearing a phone number. Moved by the hand of fate or the true voice of her mind, she tucks the note securely into a drawer. From somewhere, the wind carries to her window the sound of rifle fire, and the deep, hungry cries of a baby daring her to listen.

* * *

The last day of her contract is a day of torrential rain, a day of death, and within minutes, the outermost parts of the city disappear under the opaque water of a new sea. The stacks of hovels sway back and forth in the wind, and a mass climb tries to escape the rising water. Every now and then, someone plummets out of a window and sinks into the water like a stone. The police, waterproofed from head to toe, concentrate their numbers in the most elevated districts and form a ring around the tall condominiums and sky-level gardens. Another wall of armoured bodies is erected to defend the Ministry from the soaked masses that could storm it although it holds no bread or blankets. At the employee entrance, a mammoth cop, arms turning like a windmill, alternately throws unhappy souls into the flood and pushes Liway and other ID-bearing bodies into the building.

The hall is packed as always, the air has a catarrhal chill, and the smart glass has to be wiped of condensation every so often. Liway leafs through the paperwork with jittery hands. This morning, she hugged Eman a little longer, and he endured it a little more. 'I'll try to bring home some fruit,' she told him, and he gave her an encouraging smile.

A few minutes into her shift, she takes a deep breath and grabs the green stamp, bone dry in its cradle, and makes a decision—her last day will be her longest one. One application after the other, she drums a green rhythm on her counter, nodding at seniors who collapse in relief and at grateful mothers who hold towards her their confused, wailing babies. 'God bless you, ma'am,' they cry, and she nods, feeling a lump of shame and giddiness in her throat. The serial explosions of jubilation in her lane rattle the other processing officers a little; their wrists, which have been steady components in the machine of rejection, flutter in uncertainty.

At three o'clock, she is called by the supervisor. He is a man with a perennial migraine and a power precisely contained to his small office, where the higher-ups can keep him as long as they want. He peers at his smart screen while she hovers on the edge of the seat.

'It's my last day,' she says urgently.

He frowns at the screen, a prelude to a dramatic announcement.

'There's been a change of plans,' he says.

'What change?' she asks. Everything seems to register more starkly, the whirring desk, the wincing supervisor, and above his head, the framed photo of President Francisco Almano V, flashing the family's signature slab-like teeth.

'Sir, my contract specified two tickets—for me and my son.'

'Look,' he says, 'please stay calm,' even as she's staring mutely at him, her hands frozen in her lap.

'You've only been issued one ticket.'

He explains that the third-class ticket, customary for civil servants and contractors, is in her name and can only be used on the voyage set to leave at the end of the month. It is non-transferable, non-convertible to cash and other privileges, and non-upgradable, he elaborates, as if she doesn't already know. In case of no-show, the ticket is forfeited, and its forfeiture is unappealable.

'I can't leave without my son,' she says, fighting to keep her voice calm and his finger off the security button.

'I'm sorry, honestly, nothing I can do,' he says. 'Do you have a family member in the police or military forces? Their second-class ticket is transferable; of course, you will have to lodge a rights-transfer request and that'll take time.' He drones on while her mind whirls and leaps through the visions of past, present, and future, all the years of being on a rollercoaster of fear, despair, and guilt. Her eyes are filling up with tears, but her insides are raging. She understands what he is saying in so many supervisorial words: her son has been cast into the sea like the people she saw this morning, sinking in the blink of an eye.

'I know how you feel,' he says, 'I'm a father, too.' He gestures to a picture frame that she can only see the back of, as if framed clutter is sufficient evidence of morality. She remembers hearing that his wife and children left some years back on one of the biggest, newest ships, a scandalous cruise liner outfitted with amenities for society refugees. A voice is ringing in her head: how could a man immune to the steaming desperation out there in the hall, whose only inconvenience is an extended, well-compensated assignment, claim to know I feel?

'There are special journeys, special missions,' she says, and the man immediately waves a hand dismissively. None at the moment, and none in the works.

'But, you know,' he says, leaning over his desk, 'you shouldn't let the ticket go. That ship is part of the last batch to sail before the indefinite suspension, and almost every staff member working right now will be on it, clean slate.' She looks at the heaps of green folders on his desk—smooth emerald scales that are each inscribed with a story of a person, a family, chosen somehow by an inscrutable process that employed people like her to keep the world drowning. She catches the tiny corner of an envelope, then another, and another, and she realizes that the table is only coated by the green files, its flesh is really made up of sheaves of gold.

At that moment, things become clear.

'I'm up to my neck in integration paperwork for a whole new workforce,' he says, on the verge of launching a soliloquy for a hopefully receptive pair of ears, except that the ears have turned red-hot and the mouth between them has ripped its acquiescent binding, forming its first free words:

'You're a liar!'

'None of you are saving people! You're leaving everyone to die.'

She lunges across the table and caught by surprise, he cowers, his forehead begins to gush sweat, and his bulging eyeballs seem fissured by thick blood vessels. It is nowhere near enough, she wants him to be beyond panic, she wants him electrocuted by pure, zinging fear and fried in his own piss.

But before she can decipher the process of drawing blood with a green folder, the doors of the office open and the guards, moving like a black, hard-shelled, many-legged creature, barge in and slam her to the floor. 'Don't move,' they shout, as they pin her down so hard, she feels her bones crack. The supervisor mops his head and smirks. 'Why do these people go crazy,' he mutters. '*Wala namang mapapala.*'

'Hey,' he tosses out as they haul her away, 'you went overboard with the approvals today—absolutely none of them are going through!'

They carry her out where the wind-lashed water is almost lapping at the doorstep and at the boots of the police hedge. They tear off her ID pass, and then one of them puts a hand squarely on her chest and gives her a clean push into the cold, gurgling water.

She reaches home soggy with the weight of so many vanished things. Long ago, when she was a child, there existed an old, silty river called the Pasig, which distinguished the city like a neglected dignitary. She used to take the ferry on that river, and it would pass by the white presidential mansion, a solitary tooth in the city's swampy mouth. Every time they passed it, her mother would send a furtive spit over the ferry railings. Once, in order to please her, she raised her hand and pointed a middle finger at the palace like she had seen some kids in school do. Her father quickly pulled down her hand. It was then the beginning of what would be the uninterrupted Almano regime, but, even then, her parents knew that no one would dare such gestures in public for the next thirty years.

The river as she knew it is now gone, merged with the sea, it has transformed into a tidal force that has erased whole city blocks. On this typhoon day, she has had to come home hand over hand, clinging to anything still rooted, ignored by police patrol boats because she no longer has a badge that tells her apart from the other flailing residents. She had almost been sucked into one of the deepening underwater trenches, but thankfully, another pedestrian, linked to a human chain that lengthened and wound around the street in inventive solidarity, had grabbed her arm.

Eman is too astute to be fooled by her controlled smile. 'We're still going on the ship, aren't we?' In such a short time, his face has gotten longer and leaner, and his upper lip downier, but his chin quivers in anticipation of the disappointing, motherly lie. Liway, who hasn't cried since the day she led herself to believe that her parents, in leaving the airport for the march on the streets, had thrown away the one chance life bequeaths, sobs in the arms of her son. When her tears are spent, she tells him the story of the exodus that really began almost a hundred years ago and the struggle that retreated, but still beats. When finally he falls asleep, she retrieves the note and calls the number.

* * *

Upland is a strange and heady journey that unfolds like a quest, first a surreptitious moto racer ride along the margins of Manila to the expressway, where they inch against a stream of city-bound travellers, on foot, on bikes, crammed in the backs of pickups and old buses. The motor driver, whom Glory found for her, is bold by necessity; when the racer is waylaid by human obstacle, he slips through the barriers and jumps onto the opposite side of the expressway, reserved only for military and industrial use, and zooms right past the military checkpoints, that in response, pumps out a scattering of disinterested bullets at them.

All along the government lane rumble huge trucks and machines on sauropodic legs, noses pointed towards the north, where they are also headed. Those are going into the Sierra Madre, the rider tells her as he drops her off at dawn in the last town of Bulacan. He pockets the envelope she hands him. Get on the bus that comes, he tells her, and don't attract attention. Then he rides off once again towards Manila, to resume the grind.

Even at daybreak, San Miguel is a place of chaos. Famous decades ago for delectable carabao's milk, now the town is a riot of temporary camps and haphazard flea bins where sellers attempt to entice travellers with all kinds of things. One street vendor notices Liway's old, sturdy boots and offers a trade: a combo of dingy sneakers and as-good-as-new pet cage. *Kasya ang aso, biik*, the woman calls out as she walks on.

After an interminable wait, the bus appears, a rattle trap dating from the beginning of the century. The driver patiently stuffs all the passengers, human and animal, into the bus until every breathing space is filled. Liway endures the hours-long ride standing on one foot, an experience that repeats in a few more of the bus rides she catches on highways or along wild roads, all bearing an ageless resignation communicated by the squeaks of the bus wheel, and the still, upturned faces preserving every bead of sweat. The rag-tag provincial bus network is temperamental and cautious, the drivers are lone road runners keen to avoid conflict, so they stop obediently at military checkpoints and mutely allow the soldiers to sift through the passengers with the butts of their rifles as they scan each face for bounty. Liway attracts curious stares and secondary scans from the military; with her dark city clothes and leather boots, she looks out of place. She explains that she is on her way to visit her parents' grave for the last time before she sets sail, which, with the all-clear from the ID gun, seems enough to convince them.

Back then, when they died, she wasn't allowed to bring home her parents' ashes, all the diseased bodies were carted off and burned in gigantic, perpetual pyres at the former Quirino grandstand until every biological contaminant had been deemed purified by flame, and whole mountains of human grit could be dumped by backhoe into the bay.

In truth, she is really looking for proof of life. That was the first thing that Glory told her when, two days after the phone call, her old friend appeared at her door. Spontaneously, they fell into each other's arms like they did that graduation day.

'Emanuel is looking for you,' Glory immediately said.

Her search for Ezekiel had brought Glory to the north, to Tuguegarao, where one of the biggest military camps in the country had been established alongside the mining and logging operations of various government partners—the Chinese, Americans, Canadians, French. Months of pressing the officers there for information only resulted in the embodiment of martial irritation—she began to be followed and was sent threatening messages digitally and verbally. *Kung ako sa 'yo, titigilan ko na 'yan*, both the uniformed men and menacing shadows whispered to her.

But a local man began to help her. He introduced himself as Kaloy, but she would later learn his real name. He sheltered her in safe houses to shake off her pursuers, but eventually their escape route entered the mountains, where an astounding way of life revealed itself to Glory. The rebellion that had long died according to official Almano narrative still moved in the forest, nipping at the tireless machines that hauled lumber and minerals across the mountain range day and night. Moving with them under the trees, Glory saw how the earth was broken apart to sustain the deluge that reached the cities in a roar.

'I'm so sorry,' Glory said to Liway, 'I fell for him. But gradually, we figured out, as we talked more of our city lives, that we had you in common. He doesn't know about Eman, doesn't he?'

Glory had promised Emanuel to go back and look for Liway. Bring her here, Emanuel asked her. This is where we all belong.

In their small living space, as the two women talked, nothing escaped Eman's hearing. He listened quietly to 'Tita Glory', and by the time her story was over, he had made a decision. His mother would go on the ship, and he would look for his father. Liway and Glory exchanged glances. 'Your mother should go,' Glory said, 'you're the spitting image of him, and it needs to be broken gently.' She squeezed Liway's hand, and Liway knew that the rarest of luxuries had found its way to her and Eman: the wonder of a bigger family.

The umpteenth bus disgorges her at last in Tuguegarao. The town is enrobed in black dust and wrapped up in Almano posters and the streets are sparse even at noon. The few pedestrians drift to the rice merchants that measure out the allowable purchase weight for the day. There is a funereal quiet in the wide streets, strange to the senses of any city dweller, because the town is not lacking in development; she notices that large parts of the town have been given to walled complexes surrounded by massive haulers with different logos and names printed on their sides. The liveliest spots are the small, open bars packed by soldiers shouting and singing to women with exhausted faces. Going east on foot, she takes in the military camp, enclosed by its chilling, all-sensing fence.

It's late afternoon when she finds the right dirt road that leads to the house. All around, the untended fields are overgrown with grass, only a few patches have the luck of being irrigated. Here, the golden ears of the rice plants droop, and she carefully lays a full stalk on her palm, feeling the grains.

She checks the address again before knocking on the door of the rough cement house at the edge of a field, next to a thicket of bamboo. An old, stooped woman opens the door. When Liway tells her the name of whom she seeks, the old woman hurries her inside.

'He is like a son to me,' she says, giving her a chair to sit on. 'Why do you look for him?'

The distance she has travelled seems more than she can endure, but it strikes Liway that she still has a long way to go. The old woman has a kind, wise face, compelling her to share the name of her son, and her need to come all this way.

'Anak,' says the old woman, taking her hand. 'You've come too late, he is dead.'

The darkness in the little house suddenly bears down on Liway, like a smothering hand. All that she reaches for seems primed to pull away, she thinks, recalling the hollowing sweep of departing ships and ash-laden winds. She stands up, like someone abruptly taking her leave, but Nanang Nena, with incredible tenderness, pulls her down again.

'If you wish,' Nanang Nena says, 'I can show you the spot.'

Outside, night has fallen, and the mysterious calls of birds float above the bamboo. Behind the thicket, under a tall tree with fanning branches, a circle of stones had been laid on the ground. 'Here is Emanuel,' the old woman says, making the sign of the cross. She speaks softly and intimately to the earth. *Tatay ka na pala, ang anak mo, lalaki.* Liway imagines Eman kneeling before the stones and listening to the rustle of the leaves as if they bring the voice of his father.

'Come,' Nanang Nena says, 'we must go inside.'

She serves a supper of vegetable soup, comforting and simple. 'There had been an encounter,' she recounts, 'and Emanuel was bleeding from a wound when the soldiers found him. They took him down, and he was found a few barrios away.' The old woman hesitates and falls silent.

'Go on, Nanang,' Liway says, 'I must know what to tell my son.'

Nanang Nena wipes her eyes. 'They skinned him from head to foot,' she says, 'the soldiers did. And they burned the skin in a fire.' The cloud of memory passes over her eyes; she looks at her hands that held the ribbons of skin that crumbled into soot. Liway, too, is lost in remembering the shape of a face, hands, the tone of a voice that flows inaudibly between them.

Later, she is awakened by voices, but she finds that she's unafraid. Figures are standing at the threshold, talking to Nanang Nena. When Liway rises, the old woman turns to her with a smile. 'This is my daughter Mona,' she says, gesturing to a slender, tanned young woman who nods to Liway. '*Mahal 'yan ng Kuya Emanuel niya*,' Nanang Nena says.

A rooster crows passionately in the distance, ending the peace of the night. Mona and her companions bid Nanang Nena goodbye. Chances come from choices, Emanuel told her once, and in this life, we must make many of them.

'Do you want to come with us, Manang?' Mona asks Liway.

The day is coming, and so nears the ship's farewell. Liway can see, so clearly in her mind, though she has never been there, the green shoulders of the mountains. 'Yes,' she says, 'I do.'

# The Final Secrets of Dr Wow

Bryan Thao Worra

The Laopocalypse. Shiny. Spiceless.

A thousand things to as many people who were left in the cosmos. A joke to some, a tragedy to others, a relief to many. It is a terror absurd and ridiculous; one most non-Lao have no fear of but should. Depending on who you talked to.

Decades ago, the best Laobot AIs processed the whole corpus of human knowledge, including the proscribed literature and certain forbidden dreams to inform the last Laocologies of the precise moment the universe would end on January 1.

Word spread quickly like wildfire as each otherwise orderly habitat broke into panics particular to their reputation. Some tried to party until the very last second. Others shot fireworks and guns in the air, banging pots, pans, and Laobots to frighten that final day away. Others hastened to their wat Lao, churches, mosques, synagogues, massage parlours, bookstores and fleshpots of choice. More than a few companies insisted employees remain at their posts, while human officials attempted to remind everyone of their ultimate authority to discourage pointless looting and unseemly riots at the end.

Then, nothing happened.

Irritating pundits and vapid underinformed influencers took to their platforms for months to explain what happened and why everyone was still there. Many were mocked for their superstition. Others were sent to jail or disappeared from public, shamed for their indiscretions during the 'last' moments of the world. The sun was still shining high overhead, days came, then nights, then weeks and years. The Laobot AIs eventually addressed the nation. They pointed out that they did not specify the year, only the month, day and hour. There was outrage, but most recognized the truth of the matter, and in no time, the Lao turned it into a festive drinking holiday, waiting for the day it would be 'true'. An ASEAN survey ten years ago recognized Laos as the nation most likely to laugh during the end of the world. There was little evidence to refute it.

There were a few calls for the Laobot AIs that managed the sprawling Laocologies to be recalibrated. Protesters wanted the artificial intelligences governing them to more strictly embrace the fourth precept of Laobotics and always express the truth, lest it led to the violation of the other precepts through direct or indirect action. Few now regard the matter to have been taken as seriously as it should have been. At least a few cabals attempted to exploit the loopholes this incident exposed, leading to a variety of rat and tiger games that continue to the present.

Ajahn Bounma looked at the mong on the wall. It was almost 4 p.m. He was expecting his guest with mixed emotions. It had been years since they last saw each other, and things had changed in ways none of them could have imagined. The old teacher thought back to the way he occupied himself during the early years of his retirement, and that first meeting.

'The best seeds take the longest to grow,' was a common remark among the Lao intelligentsia at gatherings of the Xieng Mieng Society. Dr Khambay was particularly fond of saying it between potent sips of Lao while his coterie politely laughed with him. Ajahn Bounma enjoyed such moments. Strolling along the tranquil Bolikhamxai beach, there was a mix of mirth and ambition as the best and brightest of the country debated the next course of action to propose to the Ministry of Renewable Resources. From a distance, the massive solar collectors of the self-contained megalopolis of Ban Nam On sparkled.

Of the twenty-three Laocologies remaining since the Glassing, Ban Nam On had risen to prominence for the number of unusually wise humans who thought well without computerized assistance. It also had an unusually high number of surveillance pods per capita, but those in the know recognized the devices missed a troubling amount of discourse. One notable incident involved a popular cafe that fell under suspicion over the way book titles and menus were arranged 'subversively' by the discontent. But nothing was conclusively proven, much to the annoyance of the Phayakee at the time.

The younger scholars had to be reminded that at one point Laos was a land-linked country, and shortly after the end of the Second Indochina War, plans had been set in motion to position Laos as 'the Battery of Southeast Asia', leveraging a number of opportunities to provide power to their neighbours. Some were more controversial than others, but the strategy included hydroelectricity, geothermal power, solar collectors, and wind turbines. Laos had been wary of nuclear power considering incidents at reactors such as Chernobyl and Fukushima. A number of delegates from the European Union pushed a project involving thorium reactors to assuage local fears, citing the cleaner process and other advantages over earlier efforts.

It was often diplomatically challenging. Laos had long held an international reputation of non-expectation following French aphorisms like 'The Vietnamese plant the rice. The Cambodians watch the rice grow. The Lao listen to the rice grow.' There had been no shortage of opportunists and con artists attempting to exploit the natural resources of Laos, such as one failed Australian venture to swindle the Lao out of key minerals. But let bygones be bygones, the elders advised.

There were so many small conversations in between the bigger business of the gathering, but Ajahn Bounma was particularly fond of the moment a striking youth named Leuk Ai asked the elders where they thought they would go when they died. It was a shocking question to some, but sincerely asked. Dr Khambay's answer still lingered with Ajahn Bounma.

'There are a thousand theories, but I hope my fate will be like that of an ancient Buddhist abbot who went to Hell when he died.' The room filled with gasps and dismay.

'Because that's where we're needed most,' Dr Khambay continued. How long had he been gone now?

Ajahn Bounma hated that he'd lost track of such a detail. But he'd been impressed enough with Leuk Ai's question that they talked at length whenever they could for the rest of the week, and he eventually took the young scholar on as a mentee for years, following their progress with mostly joy and curiosity.

A chime sounded throughout the room to signal the arrival of his young (well, not *that* young) protege. He opened the door, and Leuk Ai stood there, their hands in a traditional nop of greeting. Ajahn Bounma returned the nop and gestured for Leuk Ai to enter. Fine shoes were removed with a smile, and his guest brought in large black box made of real wood. It was sculpted with elaborate carvings that told the history of Laos from its roots in Lan Xang, to the start of the Lao space program, the Glassing, the Age of Correction and notable moments all of the way to the present, or at least, forty years ago, Ajahn Bounma noted. He allowed himself a brief smile, while Leuk Ai looked around the room.

Leuk Ai was dressed immaculately in ceremonial costume, their pha biang reminiscent of a peacock. Around their neck was a golden chain with an eye and key. This was not a social call. As their eyes met, Ajahn Bounma gestured towards a table, and Leuk Ai placed the box upon it.

'Such a show for something so small,' Ajahn Bounma chuckled.

'You may believe that as you might, but Phayakee considers it significant,' Leuk Ai said sombrely, with a hint of disappointment. 'We must observe our traditions as best we might, as you well know.'

'I helped to make many of those traditions,' Ajahn Bounma said. 'But even though you're here as an emissary of Phayakee, I relieve you of the necessity for formality on the edge of this Laopocalypse. Let us speak as the friends we were in the moment we have.'

'We would not have this moment if you had not insisted on being such a rascal that Phayakee and the Council of 44 could no longer ignore it,' Leuk Ai said.

'Have you considered that perhaps I missed you, and wanted to impart something important to you, and this was the only opportunity I had to say what truly needed to be said? Your duties would keep you from ever coming here otherwise. How are the dunes of Champasak, by the way? I heard reports new creatures were spotted adapting to the desert there?'

'This is an extreme way to get me to visit. Surely, an elder of the Xieng Mieng Society could be clever enough to find a less decisive method to arrange a conversation,' Leuk Ai replied.

'I'm well aware of our traditions, and perhaps we should be here precisely because I'm obnoxiously falling short of the wit of our peers to arrange such a meeting. But I wanted you to take today seriously.'

'It's the end of the Multiverse, Ajahn. If the predictions are correct, this conversation is inconsequential. But for what it does matter, I missed you as well, and I appreciate what you've taught me. I have not forgotten your previous lessons.'

'Technically, you're literally incapable of that, by design. But here, let me show . . .'

'Phayakee and the Council of 44 are quite clear we must be concluded by 6 p.m. Before you show me anything, would you like to review your judgment and this sentence?'

'There's no need for that. Kafka would have smiled at us, you know. Please relay that to Phayakee, the next time they can be bothered to be concerned with such questions. Did you know I knew them when they had a real name, not just a title? A real personality, too, now that I think about it. How people transform with a little bit of power, don't you agree?'

'If I answer that, I'd soon be joining you.'

'Indeed. Would you like some dinner with me? It's quite good. As I recall, it's your favourite.'

Leuk Ai looked disapprovingly at the meal on the table. 'You know this is prohibited, and I'm surprised you insist on eating real food when the nutrient pastes are so much more efficient and complete for all our dietary needs today.'

'It's a pity that we placed so much emphasis on the "real" and existence in the present moments to the benefit of our neighbours that your generation never really gained a taste for such things. Especially when so many other nations insist on such horrid things as the Preserves.'

'When the majority of Earth's flora and fauna went functionally extinct from ecological collapse, genetic manipulation was the only viable solution, and those families volunteered for it, Ajahn, in the spirit of altruism.'

'Becoming 99.9 per cent human in the process, with the remainder of their genome containing that of "key" animal species we simply couldn't do without. Like the old cryonic evangelists, everyone hoped one day our scientific knowledge would advance enough that we could extract that DNA and revive vanished species and repopulate the planet,' Ajahn Bounma rolled his eyes. 'The poor naive fools.'

'They could have been advised better that they were forfeiting their claims to human rights. But their descendants are treated well, and many nations who do not enjoy the same bounties as we have solved their protein shortages. We can remain empathetic,' Leuk Ai said sympathetically. 'The Council requires me to advise you there is to be no trickery during this meeting, confidential as it is.'

Ajahn Bounma smiled.

'You haven't changed much after all of these years. Must be all of that sun you get running errands for the Council. You are such a marvel. But the rascal that I am, let me entertain you truly one last time by showing you the reasons they should have sent you here, rather than for the reasons they have given you.' Ajahn Bounma moved towards one of the shelves.

'Would you mind standing there like that for a second, Ajahn. I wish to remember you when you were still a hero of our nation, and not . . .'

'Now? I didn't think you'd be so sentimental for those days when I performed as Dr Wow. Hardly anyone remembers. I was just the thirteenth, no more a hero than any of the others. How many since have held that role?' Ajahn Bounma laughed loudly.

'Dr Wow was a rightful favourite of human children for over a century, especially inspiring Lao youth to pursue their interests in science, technology, engineering, art, mathematics and so much more, in good times and bad,' Leuk Ai said, smiling. 'But even with so many others participating in the series, it is widely agreed that you brought an energy, an enthusiasm and humanity to the role that all others are still measured by.'

'You flatter me, it's almost unbecoming. But here. Let me show you the seven most important things I collected at great risk and effort for decades before you complete your task. It's worth it.'

'It's the end of the Multiverse, Ajahn.'

'Doesn't that make all of this even more amazing, then? But let me show you six extraordinarily dangerous objects that surely should never get into anyone else's hands, not even yours. Remember that. Hmm. Do you remember that time I told you about an ancient French director, and what he believed?'

'Of course. That it is the dream of the state to be one. It is the dream of the individual to be two,' Leuk Ai answered, looking anxiously at the mong on the wall. Ajahn Bounma fiddled with a panel and brought out a small, unmarked box no bigger than 23 centimetres. It rattled only slightly.

'You rascal.'

'Indeed.' With trembling fingers, he first took out a small, clear capsule. Leuk Ai strained to look at it, puzzled.

'In the beginning of the twenty-first century, the idea of nanosculptures became truly practical, but imperceptible to the naked eye. You needed a special microscope to see them, and one brilliant artist had such talent to make these nudes whose lovely motions suggested that everywhere is the centre of the universe for at least one moment in time. Such a scandalous idea, especially the one representing Laos. But as you and I both know, one day, an audacious heist was conducted, and many were stolen, never to be found again. But like Pandora's box, these are the last sculptures that were saved.'

'I detect nothing,' Leuk Ai said incredulously.

'The encrypted scanner was unfortunately destroyed during the Glassing, even as I understand it wasn't working all of that well before then. But I kept this with the question: Does such an artwork truly exist if we have no way to experience it? The Council, of course, would consider that decadent and unproductive thinking.'

'It would be difficult to make the case.'

Ajahn Bounma took a sip of tea. 'I think I regret that the Xieng Mieng Society in particular became so humourless in my time. In the ancient legends, he was quite the trickster you know. By choice, we don't know when the Xieng Mieng Society truly formed, except during an era of great turmoil when our people were being scattered across the globe. They say the wisest, most talented, and kindest of us spent years secretly entering as many human institutions as we could, ready to aid one another when the time came, dedicated to the idea that the very best expressions of our culture might survive. That our traditions might continue even if others did not believe we should even exist at all. I always wish we could have gone back in time to let them know that one day we would exist in the open like this. Although I suspect they'd be mildly disappointed at who we've become today.'

'That's a great presumption, our best scholars are quite certain that we are still upholding the best virtues Xieng Mieng represented.'

'But not the worst?'

'Certainly not.'

'A pity. I've come to feel a human and the societies they inhabit benefit from a healthy mix of both. You don't ask too many of the right questions when everything is "perfect". Flaws have their place, no matter who is defining them, Leuk Ai.' Ajahn Bounma let out an exasperated sigh.

'That's not what we work towards.'

'I was wondering recently if you knew the story of how the original Xieng Mieng died?'

'The King was tired of Xieng Mieng making a constant fool of him and had his tea secretly poisoned.'

'And?'

'Xieng Mieng knew his death was coming and had no way out but convinced his wife to make it look like he was still alive, rocking in his chair. The King, who'd secretly come to spy on Xieng Mieng, was so outraged that the poisoned tea didn't work that he took a sip himself to see what went wrong and joined Xieng Mieng in death. Some say the entire kingdom was thrown into turmoil for years missing both of them, and never fully recovered.'

'That's certainly one way of retelling it. Do you believe it?'

'Does it matter?'

Ajahn Bounma took a small wafer the size of a fingernail out of the box. 'I kept this treasure close for years from an expedition in the American Remnant. It's one of the only copies left of an early video game that was a phenomenon in its time. It was so different from the other games typical of the American imagination that insisted on solving problems through banditry and the application of firepower. It was centred around such a radical idea that never took hold.'

'Oh?'

'How different American history might have been, Leuk Ai! There were many parts to the story, but what it ultimately came down to was the player solving many puzzles and exploring the island in the hope of being able to read a book. To find wisdom, and some answers that we don't necessarily even know what the full question is at the outset. No one had to die, but you were brought into a strange world where you wanted to know something. I should think that would resonate with you, Leuk Ai.'

Leuk Ai stared impassively at the old man. Outside, the streets were starting to come alive with the sound of children playing and people coming home from work.

'If they hadn't suppressed it, you might have grown up with the final story of Xieng Mieng I did. They say that when he arrived in Hell, Xieng Mieng was rightfully as terrified as anyone at first, and subjected to a great many pains and tortures by those who were supposed to inflict them, and some who weren't. But in all of that time, he never forgot who he was and what he stood for, and it was not too long before he escaped Hell to the land of the living once more. Some say he talked his way out of it with his famed trickery, others say his jailers released him for becoming too much of annoyance with his practical jokes. Others still say he gave the other souls in Hell too much hope. Perhaps it was all of the above.'

'And Hell just let him go?'

'Well, some say he was pursued by a giant Nyak named Yamanoi across time and space and every corner of the Multiverse for centuries, but he was usually one step ahead of the fiend. But one day, he WAS caught. Yamanoi in his fury screamed at Xieng Mieng that there would be no more tricks, no more bargains, no more reincarnations, regenerations, clones, robots, substitutes or distractions. This would be his very last life and he should make peace with the cosmos.'

'What happened?'

Well, the version I like most is that Xieng Mieng whispered one thing to Yamanoi, who screamed in fury, then bit his head off, which rolled off into a secret corner of the Multiverse where it is yet to be found to this day.'

'That's it? What did he whisper?'

'It's a mystery. I think the Xieng Mieng Society has often tried to guess, but I think the beauty is there is no definitive answer. May we step into the back yard? I like the fresh air.'

'It is your privilege.'

Ajahn Bounma's backyard was very ordinary to Leuk Ai, who tried to respect the teacher's sentimentality for it, even though he could have done so much more with the space.

'I hope one day you'll understand the full power our stories can have, Leuk Ai, the arrival of the Laopocalypse notwithstanding. There were so many people who didn't understand the significance of our epic, *Phra Lak Phra Lam,* our version of the *Ramakien*, which those with roots in India called the Ramayana. So many people in the United States and Europe ignored it, but you should remember how powerful it was to tell a story of a people uniting to rescue the great and wise beauty who'd been kidnapped by greedy, lust-filled, war-loving giants from across the sea. What they were willing to sacrifice for even just one person.'

'That's certainly one way of retelling it. Do you believe it?' Leuk Ai asked.

'Does it matter?'

Ajahn Bounma took in the January air, looking at the sky, listening for the noisome waves of the Pacific that had been a part of his life for so long. He reached into the box and gave Leuk Ai a badly deteriorated canister containing squarish strips of a primitive plastic. Leauk Ai could not identify it.

'It's not much, I know. Like the headless winged statue of Samothrace, I think it embodies a deeper lesson in this shape than even in its original form, my old friend. But long ago, they told stories on film, and one such story involved a criminal mastermind named Dr Mabuse, and over the course of many films they told different capers of his. But these frames come one in which the frustrated detective deduces that Dr Mabuse is behind a rash of crimes in the city. Which should have been impossible because Dr Mabuse was locked away in an insane asylum, with no contact with the outside world. When the detective goes to confront the doctor, he discovers that the doctor has been dead in his cell for a while now.'

'But how did he commit the crimes then?' Leuk Ai asked curiously.

'He hypnotized his psychiatrist and gave him his mindset and worldview, and in turn, the psychiatrist hypnotized others in the same way, and in effect, Dr Mabuse became immortal and would forever be outside of the reach of the detective and his colleagues.'

'How decadent but unlikely, Ajahn. You know that the Council frowns on such stories.'

'They frown on so much. Every Phayakee who has led them, as well. I never understood. Did you know in some nations of old, they loathed time travel stories or any stories of the future that suggested a society that flourished without the present government? So short-sighted. But it's so important to be able to imagine a future we see ourselves in, Leuk Ai. I hope the rest of the Xieng Mieng Society might one day convince them of that.'

'Are you sure you want to spend your time with me like this? You have many other things we could surely talk about,' Leuk Ai said as they began to return inside.

'Indulge me. There are but two things I will show you. Take this black shard. It is the last remnant of the prop from an ancient science fiction film. They called it a monolith. Just a simple, giant black rectangle from outer space. When it appeared on Earth in prehistoric times among monkeys, not unlike those that used to live in our jungles, it supposedly jump-started the use of tools and thought that ultimately led to life in outer space. There were different explanations given, but of them all, I prefer the simpler idea that radical transformation was possible through the very act of just looking at an object, even a rectangle, one that was not capable of being created by a natural process such as the flow of a river, the growth of a branch. Such a powerful idea. Oh, don't look so bored, Leuk Ai. It's unbecoming.'

'As you insist, Ajahn. It is no burden to humour you.'

'You've been patient, more than I would have expected, but I am delighted. Please, look at this final thing. It makes me laugh the most. In this timeline, it is the last copy of a silly science fiction story that we secretly sent back in time. In an age when we still had the technology. It's not even 5,000 words, arranged to be printed in an anthology on solar technology and the environment in a Southeast Asia you'd barely recognize. To most of the world, for centuries, it was read with little regard, but there were a few people who took it to heart and laboured in secret to bring this modern society of ours to pass. All that is good . . .'

'And all that is evil.'

'Such an abstract notion. But here we are. Did you know there was once a theory in physics that the very act of witnessing an object changed the object, especially depending on the intention of the viewer?'

'I don't understand.'

'That doesn't have to be the start of a true crime. Remember that.'

The mong chimed at 5.55 p.m. A few firecrackers and shouting began down the street, and doubtless across the country. The two looked at each other with kind smiles as the Laopocalypse finally arrived. Maybe.

'It doesn't feel like the end of the Multiverse,' Leuk Ai said with a hint of disappointment.

'You said that the last time, but only Americans thought such a moment would come all at once, for everyone, because of their sense of equality. And even then, that was only a brief and fleeting notion. There, so much for the last hour of the fabulous Dr Wow. I suppose we have five minutes left. It is required that we begin now?'

'You know that it is now required, Ajahn. Custom dictates that you have the right to request me to assume any face that comforts you or prepares you as you wish for these next moments. Perhaps a wife, a child, a lover or favourite friend or co-worker, or a favourite character from a beloved story. My files are comprehensive for this matter and your choice will be strictly confidential.'

'As if that matters,' Ajahn Bounma chuckled. 'Too many people scandalized when their heroes chose the face of their mistresses in the old day. But no, let me keep wise until the very end. Witness me with your TRUE face.'

'But I do not have one.'

'Take a moment and consider which one you would most wish to be associated with you, Leuk Ai, as if you had a preference. That too shall be our secret between . . . ah, selected so quickly, and so fitting.'

Ajahn Bounma sighed as he looked at the window.' Poor Phayakee never really understood the full grace and joy of their title. It was not just to keep them humble, but to encourage them to fertilize and nurture the nation so that wondrous things might bloom and grow. But they've no need of a final discourse from me. The key, please.'

Leuk Ai took the ornate key from around his neck and pressed it gently into Ajahn Bounma's hand. Ajahn Bounma gave a small nod and put the key into the lock. The box opened with barely a sound as they looked at contents on the white silk cushion: an old bamboo tweezers and a single grain of sticky rice.

'You may inspect it as you wish, we have three minutes,' Leuk Ai said, offering a magnifying glass from his pocket. Ajahn Bounma shook his head.

'I'm not interested in this poetry from Phayakee. I trust you that this has my name written on here. Imagine the fields this could have become, Leuk Ai, instead now laced with one of the deadliest . . .'

'Kindest.'

'Pesticides we ever devised. So many have used these tweezers before me.' He paused ruefully. 'I consider most of them worthy peers. We are all bound for the Laopocalypse, Leuk Ai. But may your wait be a comfortable one.'

He chuckled as he placed the grain upon his tongue. 'I wonder what flavour this one is.'

A moment went by. 'Oh, my favourite,' Ajahn Bounma said with a final defiant wink and smile in his last lifetime.

The teacher's student stood alone and unwatched in the room until the sun set. What ultimately set the wise elder's final home afire that night was never clear and didn't really matter.